JONATHAN NASAW IS "A LEGITIMATE HEAVYWEIGHT CONTENDER AMONG THE MASTERS OF THE PSYCHOLOGICAL THRILLER."

—Toronto Sun

Worlwide acclaim for Jonathan Nasaw's heart-pounding suspense novels

WHEN SHE WAS BAD

"Crisply written and sprinkled with both humor and gore. . . . Ex-FBI agent Pender is especially well-drawn, an endearing character. . . . Bloody good fun."

—Dave Zeltserman, author of *Small Crimes*

TWENTY-SEVEN BONES

"Explosive."

—*San Francisco Chronicle*

"Loaded with suspense. . . . A winner."

—*Library Journal*

"A first-rate thriller."

—*The Globe and Mail* (Toronto)

"Good writing, gripping action; what more could you want?"

—*The Guardian* (London)

"Colorful . . . sharply observed . . . his best yet."

—*Kirkus Reviews*

"Nasaw . . . will once again keep his many fans spellbound."

—*The Herald* (Monterey County, CA)

"Nasaw is such a clever writer. . . . He whip[s] up plenty of suspense."

—*Publishers Weekly*

"Pender is a crafty and inventive sleuth . . . it's always fun to watch him work."

—*Booklist*

FEAR ITSELF

A Selection of the Literary Guild

"Jonathan Nasaw has managed to pare down the root of psychological suspense to its essence."

—*Rocky Mountain News* (Denver)

"Darkly entertaining . . . inspiringly perverse."

—*Herald Sun* (Melbourne, Australia)

"A thriller you don't want to set down. Crackling good dialogue . . . dandy surprises and an explosive climax."

—*Toronto Sun*

THE GIRLS HE ADORED

"A superior thriller. Nasaw tells his story skillfully and makes the killer's ever-changing personality both interesting and frightening."

—*The Washington Post*

"Compelling and intellectually stimulating. . . . A complex portrait of the multiple-personality serial killer. . . . Not easy to put down or forget."

—*The Dallas Morning News*

"A creepy and truly frightening thrill ride. . . . Intelligent, fast-moving, and never less than thoroughly engaging."

—Christopher Reich, bestselling author of *Rules of Deception*

"Wickedly compelling. . . . [Nasaw is] a fine storyteller."

—*The Oregonian*

"Nasaw creates a killer who is utterly convincing, so real he makes you want to look behind you as you are reading. Don't read this book in a dimly lit room."

—*Statesman Journal* (Salem, OR)

"A fast-paced, taut narrative. . . . Nasaw's vivid characters work with chilling efficiency."

—*The Albuquerque Tribune*

"Horrifying and compelling . . . Nasaw takes readers on a roller-coaster ride through the psyche of a killer right to a bang-up ending."

—*The Pilot* (Southern Pines, NC)

Also by Jonathan Nasaw

Twenty-Seven Bones
Fear Itself
The Girls He Adored
The World on Blood
Shadows
Shakedown Street
West of the Moon
Easy Walking

JONATHAN NASAW

WHEN SHE WAS BAD

POCKET BOOKS
New York London Toronto Sydney

Pocket Books
A Division of Simon & Schuster, Inc.
1230 Avenue of the Americas
New York, NY 10020

This book is a work of fiction. Names, characters, places, and incidents either are products of the author's imagination or are used fictitiously. Any resemblance to actual events or locales or persons, living or dead, is entirely coincidental.

First Pocket Books paperback edition December 2008

POCKET and colophon are registered trademarks of Simon & Schuster, Inc.

For information about special discounts for bulk purchases, please contact Simon & Schuster Special Sales at 1-800-456-6798 or business@simonandschuster.com.

Cover illustration and design by Mirko Pohle

Manufactured in the United States of America

10 9 8 7 6 5 4 3 2 1

ISBN-13: 978-1-4165-3417-4
ISBN-10: 1-4165-3417-2

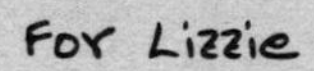

WHEN SHE WAS BAD

PROLOGUE

THREE PORTRAITS OF LILY

I

"Are you sure you're going to be all right now?"

"I'll be fine, Grandma."

"I hate to go off and leave you."

Lily rolls her eyes. "Grandma, I'm seventeen years old, I can take care of myself for two days."

"Of course you can, dear. It's just . . ." No need to complete the sentence—they both know how it ends.

"Dody, she'll be *fine,*" chimes in Lily's grandfather. "Now can we *please* get this show on the road—I want to be off the highway before dark." His night vision isn't what it used to be—but then, as he's fond of saying, what is?

In the circular driveway at the bottom of the wide marble steps waits a gleaming black Mercedes SUV loaded with enough provisions to have seen Napoleon's army safely home from Moscow. Dark-haired, dark-eyed Lily hugs her roly-poly grandmother, who smells like stale baby powder. When her grandfather stoops to give Lily a peck on the cheek, the overpowering scent of his aftershave brings tears to her eyes—apparently his sense of smell ain't what it used to be, either.

Lily waves from the top of the steps until the SUV is out of sight, then heads back inside the two-story, Mission-style Pebble Beach mansion where she's lived with her grandparents since she was almost five. To celebrate being alone, she sneaks up to her grandmother's bedroom, steals a cigarette from the pack of Dorals Grandma hides in a bureau drawer, and smokes it out on the balcony, waving it around languidly, wrist bent like some old movie actress.

But the reality of being home alone never lives up to the expectation for long. After a few puffs the cigarette tastes hot and stale, and when she stubs it out and goes back inside, the mansion is so empty and echoey that she can hear the tick-tock of the grandfather clock down in the parlor from her second-floor bedroom.

Flopping onto her bed, Lily switches on the television and clicks through the channels. MTV is showing one of its beach parties, college kids dancing on the sand, the boys in their baggy shorts and scraggly wanna-be goatees, the heavy-breasted girls in skimpy bikinis that barely cover their nipples. Lily is both disturbed and fascinated by the overt sexuality. Scaredy cat, she chides herself—don't you even *want* a normal life someday?

Just to see what it would feel like, she strips

down to her bra and panties, tries on a few moves in front of the floor-length mirror mounted on the closet door. Oh yeah, she thinks happily, blushing like a pomegranate at sunset, I could do this.

But after only a few seconds of modest abandon, an image from Lily's past fills her mind. Strong, sharp-scented male hands, large enough to palm her head like a softball, pry her jaws apart; an impossibly swollen, purple-headed penis forces itself into her mouth, choking her; a flashbulb explodes into white glare.

She reels away from the mirror, fighting for breath as if she were still that baby, and sits on the edge of the bed, head between her knees, breathing iiiin and ouuut, niiice and caaalm. A commercial for acne cream is playing; she feels around for the remote and blindly switches off the television, then guides herself through an exercise she's learned from her psychiatrist, Dr. Irene Cogan. *That* was then, *this*—she raises her head, glances around the familiar bedroom—is now. *That* was a memory, *this* is the reality. You're *not* that helpless baby anymore—no one can touch you without your consent.

And gradually the panic subsides. Lily turns on the bedroom light, slips on a bathrobe and a pair of slippers, and is halfway down the wide, curving staircase when the phone starts ringing. She charges back up the stairs, throws herself across the bed, fumbles the receiver off the hook just before the downstairs answering machine kicks in. "Hello?"

"Is this the home of . . . Lyman and Dorothy DeVries?"

"Who's calling, please?" Lily is well versed in telephone safety.

"This is Sergeant Mapes, California Highway Patrol."

Everything's gone quiet, like just before an earthquake. "Yes, this is the DeVries residence."

"Who am I speaking to?"

"This is Lily. Lily DeVries—I'm their granddaughter. Is something wrong?"

"Is there an adult around I can speak to?"

"Yes—me." It isn't the first time Lily has been mistaken for a child over the phone. "Has something happened to them?"

"There's been an accident. A bad one." A pause. "A *very* bad one." Another pause, as if he wanted Lily to ask him a question. She couldn't think of one, though—all she could think of was how tired she had suddenly become. "I'm sorry to have to be the one to break the news, Miss DeVries. From what we've been able to ascertain, your grandfather seems to have lost control of the vehicle on Highway One, a few miles south of Big Sur. It went through the guardrail, over the cliff, and landed on the rocks sixty feet below. Both bodies were still in the car. If it's any comfort, they were almost certainly killed outright."

Lily had to put the receiver under her pillow to muffle the squeaky, unintelligible sounds coming out of it. Too tired, she thought, rolling onto her stomach and closing her eyes—I'm too tired to deal with this.

2

Lilah comes awake. Her mind is blank at first—no recollection of having gone to sleep, no memories from the preceding day.

This is how it's always been for Lilah, living as she does in a more or less permanent present. No immediate past, no long-term future, just an ongoing *now,* the by-product not of meditation, but of an imperious, bonobo-like sexuality that informs Lilah's every thought and action from the moment she wakes up to the moment she retreats back into the darkness of her mind.

The first thing she does upon awakening is ground herself by rubbing the pad of her right thumb against the pads of the first two fingers of her right hand, as though she were trying to roll a little dough into a tiny ball. She hears a buzzing sound, feels around under the pillow, finds the telephone handset, and replaces it in the cradle. Immediately, it begins to ring; she lifts the receiver and slams it down again, then unplugs the phone from the jack in the wall, strips off her nightgown, and pads naked into the bathroom.

After a steaming hot shower with the spray set on needle-fine, Lilah rubs herself dry with fluffy towels until her creamy skin is pink and tingly from head to toe. She shaves her legs, paints her finger- and toenails, trims her dark pubic hair to the shape of a heart while waiting for her nails to dry, anoints her body with moisturizing lotion, and finishes off with a dusting of lilac-scented body talc.

As often happens, when Lilah returns from the bathroom she can't find a thing to wear. The drawers and closets are filled with T-shirts, jeans, sweaters, and oversize sweatshirts, but nothing suitable for the Saturday evening Lilah has in mind. It's almost as if somebody keeps throwing her good stuff out and replacing it with more modest wear.

Eventually she finds her streetwalker outfit—thong, hot pants, midriff-bearing tube top, and of course her red fuck-me pumps with the three-inch stiletto heels—crumpled into a hatbox in the far corner of the closet. It occurs to her she may have stashed it there herself a few days or weeks ago—if so, the event is lost in the cement sea of her memory.

After dressing, Lilah steps out onto the fan-shaped bedroom balcony, with its low curved parapet and potted cacti in terra-cotta urns. Below her, the wooded hills of Pebble Beach fall steeply toward a dark slice of ocean, barely visible through the trees. It's a cold summer night on the central coast. Cutting wind, no stars. She shivers, glances down at her body. Through the formfitting top, she can see her wide round aureolae have gone all pebbly and her nipples are making little thimble-shaped bumps against the Lycra. Gonna freeze them titties off, girl, she warns herself, turning back into the bedroom and closing the French doors behind her.

Lilah rummages through the walk-in closet until she finds a long Mexican sweater she can belt around her for warmth, or open when it comes time to flash the goodies. Leaving the previously pin-neat bedroom strewn with discarded clothes and towels, she clatters down the wide stone staircase carrying her beaded handbag.

The huge kitchen is immaculate. From the stand-alone, double-doored freezer Lilah selects a so-called gourmet TV dinner at random, nukes it, scarfs it down at the kitchen table while watching a Mexican game show on the maid's little countertop TV. Lilah doesn't speak much Spanish, but she loves the overheated atmosphere of the Mexican shows, the garish colors, the exaggerated sexuality, the blowsy women with their wobbly Charo boobs overflowing spangled halter tops, the smolderingly handsome Latin boy toys in tight trousers with the crotches stuffed to bulging and pirate shirts open halfway to the navel.

The telephone directory is on the counter under the wall phone. Lilah opens it to the yellow pages, calls a taxi, then waits for it out on the veranda, which is tiled and stepped like the balcony, but with even larger succulents in even larger terra-cotta urns.

Twenty minutes later, a yellow cab pulls into the circular driveway. The driver hurries around to open the rear door as Lilah descends the wide marble steps. She knows without looking that he's giving her the once-over, so she lets the sweater fall open as she brushes past him and slides into the backseat.

The horny bastard doesn't know where to look first. When he closes the door behind her, Lilah notices a gold wedding band on his hairy ring finger.

He may fuck his wife tonight, she tells herself, but he'll be thinking about me.

"Where to?" he inquires, when he's behind the wheel again.

"Just take me to Seaside—I'll tell you where to drop me when we get there."

"Seaside?" He does a double take into the mirror—that's a mostly black town, definitely the wrong side of the tracks.

"Yeah, Seaside—you got a problem with that?"

"Not me." He drops the flag to start the meter; the tires crunch gravel as the cab circles the driveway, then turns onto Paso Condor Way. Lilah catches the driver's eyes glancing at her in the rearview mirror. With a sly grin she tugs her tube top out and down, reaching underneath to heft her boobs, as if adjusting the cups of the bra she isn't wearing. The taxi veers dangerously across the winding road.

Seaside is booming on Saturday night. Drunks and music overflow from the clubs and bars out onto the sidewalks. Lilah's taxi cruises slowly up the street, bringing the hos sashaying to the edge of the curb; they turn away in disgust at the sight of the tarted-up white girl in the backseat.

But Lilah knows better than to stake out a position on an occupied block—she waits in the warm cab until she sees a sistah in an outfit similar to hers, only vinyl, climbing into the front seat of a beige Camry. Even if it's only for a hummer, the girl won't be back for at least fifteen minutes, which is usually long enough for Lilah to attract a john. (One will be plenty—Lilah's only here for the sheer gutter thrill of it; afterward she intends to head for an upscale pickup joint in Carmel to find herself a one-night stand.)

"Lemme out here."

"Here?"

"Yeah, here—is there a fucking echo or something?"

Lilah tips the cabbie better than he deserves out of the clutch of bills in her little beaded handbag. There's a dire wind whipping down the sidewalk; she pulls her sweater tighter and flattens herself against a mural of a blues band painted in black silhouette on the wall of a beer joint.

The strains of "Sweet Home Chicago" waft out through double doors with small, diamond-shaped windows. Lilah is seriously thinking about heading inside to check out the band when a big old Harley comes belching up the street and pulls over to the curb directly in front of her. Chopped and stretched, black leather seat studded with rivets, fringed leather saddlebags.

Lilah clomps across the sidewalk for a closer look at the chopper. "Nice bike," she calls over the pulsing beat of the engine. "How about a ride?"

The driver flips up the face-plate of his helmet. White guy, bearded, good-looking. "I got a lifelong rule—I don't pay for pussy."

"That's okay, I don't sell it," says Lilah.

He looks her up and down. "Could have fooled me."

"I just did. How about that ride?"

He twists around, opens a saddlebag, hands Lilah one of those Nazi-looking helmets, the kind that always reminds her of the head of a circumcised penis. Lilah pulls it on, tightens the strap, grabs the guy's shoulder for support, and throws a leg over the long, narrow leather seat. Feeling the thrumming of the engine between her legs, she presses herself up against the back of his black leather jacket. "What're you waiting for?" she yells. "Let's get this fucking show on the fucking road."

3

Lilith is born (not literally, of course, though there is certainly enough blood and pain for a birthing) a few days later in a reeking tent just outside Sturgis, South Dakota. The sound in her ears is an undifferentiated roar as she comes awake; at first she sees the world in poorly defined patches of light and shade, as newborn infants are said to do.

For a moment she hovers between two worlds, two states of being. But as the second world comes into focus, the roar resolving itself into component parts (rough male voices, the rumble of motorcycle engines) and the light and shade taking on color and form (a bobbing black shadow becomes a man lying on top of her; that dark, distant sky turns into the ceiling of a huge khaki tent), her memory of the world from which she has been summoned recedes like the last dream before waking.

All this in the time it takes to draw a breath, then the realization dawns: gang bang. Good old-fashioned, one-percenter-style gang bang, and she's the guest of honor. In addition to the biker on top of her, there are a dozen or so others standing around in a circle cheering him on; some have their cocks out, idly jerking off while they wait their turns. Everything smells of leather and sweat and grease and come.

She hears screaming—her own. A backhand swipe across the face; she tastes her own blood, thick and coppery at the back of her throat. The ogre atop her is humping away doggedly. Her eyes travel up from his grimacing face to his olive-green GI helmet, which bears the motto, hand-lettered in white ink: *Yea, though I walk through the valley of the shadow of death, I shall fear no evil, for I am the meanest motherfucker in the valley.*

We'll see about that, thinks Lilith. Then she bites his nose off. Which is harder than it sounds. A nose is all gristle and cartilage—you have to grab ahold, and shake your head, and worry at it like a dog worrying at a bone.

But when she's finished, the floor of the tent is as slippery with his blood as it is with hers. She climbs awkwardly to her feet, spits out a fleshy glob, and glances contemptuously around the circle of ogres. "Okay, boys," she calls cheerfully. "Who's next?"

Part One

The Institute

CHAPTER ONE

1

There was a dark place inside Lyssy, where he was never to go. He pictured it as a room, though it had neither floor, ceiling, nor walls, and sometimes, especially when he was alone at night, Lyssy imagined he could hear a voice inside the room, muttering quietly to itself in the darkness.

But Lyssy knew better than to discuss the dark place with his doctor, or indeed with anyone at the Reed-Chase Institute, the private psychiatric care facility in Oregon where he had been confined for almost as long as he could remember.

"No, really, I can do it myself," he protested as the nurse knelt in front of him to help him on with his prosthetic right leg. But he didn't protest too hard—this was the nurse he secretly thought of as Miss Stockings, because that's what she wore instead of the panty hose favored by the other nurses. And when she knelt, her white uniform skirt rode up with a faint whispering noise, offering Lyssy a glimpse of the shiny-smooth dark bands at the top of the stockings, a few inches of creamy gartered thighs, and even a peek at I-See-London-I-See-France.

"I just need to make sure," she said. "If you get a pressure sore and can't walk, it's my heinie on the line."

"Heinie?" Lyssy giggled.

"Oh, grow up."

Wounded pause, then: "I'm trying, Nurse. I'm trying as hard as I can." When he'd first arrived at the Institute, Lyssy had been basically a child in a man's body, with almost no memory, and the affect and intellectual functioning of a three-year-old.

Miss Stockings colored. "I'm sorry, Lyssy, I didn't mean it like that."

"No problem." He flashed her the boyish grin that had made him a staff favorite, not just here in the locked ward, but all over the Institute. Especially with the females: Lyssy's delicate, heart-shaped face, with its long-lashed brown eyes flecked with gold and its lips curved like a Cupid's bow, still retained its youthful prettiness; a lock of nut-brown hair drooped across his unlined forehead.

Just as he'd finished tucking the tails of his forest-green corduroy shirt into his neatly pressed chinos, the door to the room slid open with a whoosh, admitting a massive young man with dark curly hair and a bodybuilder's physique. He was dressed in the uniform worn by all the psych techs at the Institute: white duck trousers and a white polo shirt with the letters RCI encased in a diamond on the left breast. "There a Ulysses Maxwell in here?" he called cheerfully.

"That would be me." Big, double-chinned Wally Smets was Lyssy's favorite orderly—when Wally escorted Lyssy, somehow he made it seem as if they were just two buddies out for a stroll.

"Let's go, li'l bro—there's somebody wants to have a chat with you."

"Really? Who?"

"Just be on your best behavior—that's all I can tell you."

"Best foot forward," replied Lyssy. That was one of his and Dr. Al's jokes. The reason it was a joke was because Lyssy only *had* one foot, Dr. Al had explained—humor was one of many things Lyssy'd had to learn from scratch.

The Institute was comprised of three two-story buildings of weathered brick that formed a U around a central arboretum; on the fourth side, a spike-topped brick wall overgrown with glistening ivy separated the hospital grounds from the director's residence.

From Lyssy's room on 2-West, the maximum security ward, Wally escorted Lyssy down the long corridor to the elevator lobby, all but dwarfing his five-foot, six-inch charge, and entered his security code into a keypad. When the elevator arrived, he peered inside before allowing Lyssy to enter; exiting, he reversed the procedure.

Another long corridor led to the two adjoining conference rooms on 1-South, which also housed the reception lobby, the cafeteria, and the administrative offices. Wally ushered Lyssy into the smaller room, which had apparently been pressed into service as a storage area. Lyssy limped over to a stack of molded plastic chairs—he found it aesthetically pleasing, the way the chairs fit together, nested seat upon seat, arms upon arms. Just for the fun of it, he asked Wally to help him up to the topmost chair. Lyssy stiffened his elbows and the psych tech lifted him as easily as if he were a child, then steadied the swaying stack.

"King of the world," Lyssy exclaimed delightedly. But when he started waving his arms about, pretending the chairs were about to topple over, Wally glanced nervously at the long smoky mirror set into the side of the wall between the two conference rooms.

"Down you go," he said, swinging Lyssy from his perch by the armpits.

"No fair," whined the thirty-one-year-old Lyssy, sticking out his lower lip in a grotesque, if unintended, parody of a toddler's pout. "I never get to have any fun."

2

Okay boys, who's next?

Ten days had passed since Lilith had spat out what was left of her attacker's nose and issued her challenge to the circle of ogres in that reeking tent outside Sturgis, South Dakota. Nor would there have been any shortage of takers if a bosomy, leather-clad, middle-aged redhead carrying a double-barreled shotgun hadn't stepped through the tent flap just then and announced that the party was over.

"Hey, c'mon, Mama Rose," a squat, troll-faced biker had whined, as two of his buddies helped their mutilated colleague to his feet. "We bought her fair and square." And so they had, from the biker who'd originally picked "Lilah" up in Seaside—to his surprise, three days of her constant sexual demands had been about as much as he could stand.

"I got rock salt in one barrel and triple-ought buckshot in the other," the biker mama had replied calmly, cocking both hammers of the twelve-gauge side-by-side. "Fucking thing is, I'm not sure which is which." Then, turning to Lilith: "Get your clothes on, honey."

"Carson? How 'bout it, man?" Troll-face turned to a tall, lean man with a Viva Zapata mustache, a fringed buckskin jacket, and a leather cowboy hat, standing quietly in the shadows, leaning against a tent post. "You gonna let the cunt get away with that?"

Mama Rose had swung the shotgun around and trained both barrels on the speaker. "You best not be referring to me, Li'l T.," she said.

"I meant the girl," he'd replied quickly, without taking his eyes off Carson. "She bit Merv's fucking nose off, man."

Carson, who was obviously the alpha male of the

pack, had narrowed his eyes; a hint of a smile lifted the toothpick in the corner of his mouth. "Good thing he don't wear glasses."

The Sturgis run had lasted another three days, during which the childless Mama Rose took the dazed, penniless amnesiac under her wing. She bought Lilith clothes to replace the tattered hooker outfit, taught her how to ride a motorcycle, loaned her a .22 pistol and taught her how to shoot it, and when it had become apparent that the girl had nowhere else to go, brought her back to Shasta County after the run.

To Lilith, saddle-sore after riding pillion for close to a thousand miles, the isolated, pink-sided ranch house on a scrubby hillside north of Redding had been a veritable paradise. For the next few days she'd done little but eat, sleep, take hot tubs, and sunbathe.

Then the biker known as Swervin' Mervin had shown up at the front door in a surgical mask, demanding revenge on the girl who'd de-nosed him. Annoyed, but curious to see how it would all play out, as if Lilith were a fascinating new pet or toy, Carson invited him in, then called Lilith down from the attic dormer where she'd been napping.

"Man oh man, you just don't know when to quit, do you?" Lilith had remarked dispassionately, upon seeing him. Then she'd produced Mama Rose's Lady Beretta from behind her back and shot him in the face before he could rise from his chair.

They'd buried Swervin' Mervin in the woods below the house that night. A Coleman lantern cast giant shadows between the pines. Mama Rose had recited the Twenty-third Psalm while Carson chunked dirt upon the uncovered corpse. When she got to the part about *Yea, though I walk through the valley of the shadow of death,* Lilith broke into a triumphant grin.

"Who's the meanest motherfucker in the valley now?" she'd asked the dead man, shining the lantern down onto his rude grave and laughing when she saw that his eyes were crossed comically above the bloodstained surgical mask, as if he were trying to sneak a peek at the neat little bullet hole that had blossomed between them.

3

I never get to have any fun. . . .

On the other side of the surveillance mirror, Ruth Trotman shot Alan Corder a meaningful glance. A tough-minded, hawk-nosed forensic psychiatrist, originally from Great Britain and now working out of the Oregon Attorney General's office, she was all too aware of what "having fun" used to entail for Ulysses Christopher Maxwell.

Corder, the Institute's director, had wavy ginger hair combed straight back from a broad-cheeked, pleasant face; his characteristically placid expression often caused others to underestimate his resolve. Hastily he reached under the conference table and pushed a button: the green floor-to-ceiling curtains swept silently across the one-way glass. His mistake, he realized, was having expected Trotman to see Ulysses through his eyes: the Lyssy he had grown to love almost as a surrogate son (not surprisingly, as he had in effect raised him from a three-year-old) was a gentle, sweet-natured naif to whom violence of any kind was utterly abhorrent.

No more screwups, Corder told himself firmly—Lyssy's future was on the line here. "If you don't mind, I'd, ah, like to give you a little background before we bring Ulysses in."

"I think I have all the background I need right here," said Trotman, untying the string of the two-inch-thick manila folder in her lap and removing at random a badly photostatted coroner's report. "Paula Ann Wisniewski. She was victim number twelve, I believe. He disemboweled her. Which made her one of the lucky ones—some of the others took years to die." She slipped the document back into the folder, selected another at random. "And this would be—"

"I've *seen* the goddamn—" Corder caught himself, lowered his voice. "I've seen all that, Ruth. But what you have to understand is that for the time period during which those crimes were committed, we have an unimpeachable diagnosis of dissociative identity disorder from Irene Cogan, whom you have to agree is tops in the field and had, shall we say, unprecedented access to the patient."

Trotman looked as though she'd just bitten down on a rotten pistachio. "As far as I'm concerned, *Dr.* Corder, there's no such thing as an 'unimpeachable' diagnosis of dissociative identity disorder. And if by unprecedented access, you're referring to the fact that he kidnapped and tortured Dr. Cogan, attempted to rape her, and was preparing to kill her when she was rescued, I must say I consider your choice of terminology somewhat flippant, if not outright offensive."

"I apologize. That wasn't my intention. I was just trying to get you to see that for all intents and purposes, the man who committed those acts—terrible as they are," he added hurriedly, "that man *no longer exists.*"

"Either that, or he's sitting on the other side of that mirror having a jolly great laugh at our expense."

"But—"

"My job, Dr. Corder, is to determine whether Mr. Maxwell is competent to understand the charges against him, and to assist in his own defense. A judge and jury will sort out the rest."

"But how can he assist in his own defense if he doesn't remember a single, solitary—"

"Spare me, oh spare me. If amnesia were a bar to trial, every criminal in the world would suffer an immediate loss of memory." Trotman leaned forward, resting her forearms on the desk. "You have to understand, the pressure is on the attorney general from every direction. The media, the governor, Maxwell's surviving victims and the families of the ones who didn't, district attorneys and federal prosecutors all across the nation—they're all clamoring to know why he hasn't been brought to trial yet. Now are you going to let me do my job, or must I go back to the AG and tell him you refused to permit a court-ordered examination?"

"No, of course not." Corder reached under the desk, pressed another button. "Walter, we're, ah, ready for Ulysses now."

4

In the days that followed Mervin's death, Lilith's conscience never troubled her—she had no more conscience than a cat, and a good deal less curiosity. In a way, it was as if she came alive only when threatened; in the absence of danger she was content to spend her time soaking in the hot tub or basking like a lizard on the sun-warmed patio behind the pink house.

Then one morning Mama Rose announced at breakfast that she had to go into town to take care of some errands, and all but insisted that Lilith come along. Wearing an oversize leather bomber jacket, the girl rode pillion on Mama Rose's baby-blue Sportster with her cheek pressed against the other woman's broad back, the wind in her hair, and the scent of greasy leather in her nostrils.

But instead of traveling into Redding or Mt. Shasta, which was usually what was meant by going into town, Mama Rose drove Lilith to a generic-looking motel coffee shop in Weed—padded vinyl banquettes, Formica tables, travel posters depicting a matador, the Matterhorn, and the Eiffel tower. There were only three other customers: a middle-aged couple at the counter, and a guy with a gray ponytail who slipped out as soon as Lilith and Mama Rose arrived.

Lilith asked for a latte, though how she knew she preferred lattes when she didn't know her last name or where she came from was another of the questions she had steadfastly declined to ask herself. Mama Rose ordered an espresso, installed Lilith in a booth over by the plate-glass window, then excused herself to visit the ladies' room.

Mama Rose still hadn't returned by the time the coffees arrived. Lilith, wearing a T-shirt and low-cut jeans under the borrowed bomber jacket, was thinking about popping into the ladies' room to check on her friend when the middle-aged couple approached her booth.

"Mind if we join you?" the man asked her. Big, bald, and homely as a manatee, he wore a garish Hawaiian Sunset hula shirt, rumpled plaid Bermuda shorts, black ankle socks, and shapeless, gunboat-size beige Hush Puppies.

"I'm Dr. Cogan, this is Mr. Pender," said the woman, a slender, forty-something strawberry blond wearing a russet blazer over a crisp white blouse and matching skirt.

"Sorry, I'm with a—" A friend, Lilith was about to say, when she heard the unmistakable rumble of a Harley engine; she turned toward the window just in time to see the blue Sportster fishtailing out of the motel parking lot. "What the fuck's going on here?"

The man sat down next to her, blocking her in. Judging by his looks, he might have been a retired professional wrestler—a heavy, not a hero—or a circus strongman gone to fat. The woman sat facing her and reached across the table to pat Lilith's hand, saying, "Don't be alarmed, dear—we're here to help you."

Lilith jerked her hand away violently. "I'm not *alarmed,"* she said, surreptitiously palming a sharp-tined fork—it was either that or the butter knife. "Just tell me what the fuck's going on."

"You don't recognize either of us, then?" asked the woman. Her reddish-blond hair was cut in a rather severe helmet shape; she had mild blue eyes and a long, somewhat rabbity nose.

"Maybe I do and maybe I don't." Under the table, Lilith's hand tightened around the fork handle; she visualized herself jabbing the tines into the man's eye, then climbing over the table and running like hell for the door. "What're you, on TV or something?"

"With this face?" The man grinned as he picked up Mama Rose's untouched espresso; the little cup all but disappeared in his hand. "Waste not, want not," he said, then glanced casually under the table, toward the fork clutched in Lilith's fist. "Mind if I borrow that for a sec?"

Their eyes locked—one of those *she knew that he knew that she knew* moments—then he gently prized the fork from her clenched hand and used it to stir a packet of sugar into the brown sludge in his cup, as if that, and not disarming Lilith, had been his purpose in taking it all along. "Never could get the hang of those dinky little doll spoons," he added apologetically—but he never did return the fork.

Dr. Cogan, meanwhile, had taken an envelope full of photographs from a brown leather Coach bag the size of a Pony Express saddlebag. She slid one of the pictures across the tabletop. In the snapshot, Lilith was standing at the top of wide, terraced steps, shading her eyes against the sun. The two-story, Mission-style villa in the background was a mansion by almost any standard.

"That's your house behind you," said Dr. Cogan, enunciating every syllable with a fussy precision and taking extra care with the sibilants, as though at some point in her life she'd conquered a speech impediment. "And this one was taken behind your family's vacation home near Puerto Vallarta last winter." Another snapshot of Lilith and Dr. Cogan in bathing suits; in the background, a sprawling adobe.

"And here's your grandmother and grandfather." Old couple standing next to a gleaming black SUV, the man erect and lantern-jawed, the woman plump and apple-cheeked, her shoulders hunched a little, as if she were afraid the SUV was going to explode any second now.

"Why don't I remember any of this?" asked Lilith. "Did I get hit on the head or something?"

"I wish it were that simple," said Dr. Cogan. "Are you familiar with a psychiatric condition known as dissociative identity disorder?"

"I . . . I think so. It's like multiple personalities, right?"

"That's the old term for it, yes—we call it DID now." The doctor turned to the man. "Pen, could you give us a few minutes?"

"You bet." He slid out of the booth, taking Mama Rose's espresso and Lilith's fork with him, picked up a newspaper from a neighboring booth, and shambled over to a table for one, halfway between the women and the front door.

"Who's he?" Lilith asked Dr. Cogan.

"An old friend. He helped coordinate the search."

"What search?"

"The search for you." Dr. Cogan fished around in her bag again, emerged from the depths with a pearl-gray tape recorder the size of a pack of playing cards. "Here, I have something I'd like you to listen to." She pressed Play.

"My name is Lily DeVries," said a childlike female voice. "And whoever you are who's hearing this, so is yours. What Dr. Irene has to tell you may sound a little weird at first, but you really need to hear her out, okay? For both our sakes."

Looking up to meet Dr. Cogan's eyes, Lilith experienced a sense of déjà vu so intense it was almost dizzying. It dawned on her that all the questions she'd failed to ask over the last ten days were about to be answered. She wished she still had Mama Rose's Beretta; for that matter, she wished she still had the damn fork. "Go ahead," she said. "Let's get this over with."

5

"Ulysses, this is Dr. Trotman," said Dr. Al.

"Pleased to meet you." Lyssy limped across the conference room with his right hand outstretched, palm down to hide the burn scars. Wally waited by the door.

Dr. Trotman brushed his hand with her fingertips. "How do you do, Mr. Maxwell."

That meant *how are you?* But not really—it was all part of what Dr. Al called phatic communication, which was one more thing Lyssy had had to learn from scratch, though without complete success: his mind still tended toward the literal.

"Okay, I guess. Except sometimes I get phantom pains in my leg." A shy Lyssy grin. "You know, the one that isn't there?"

"Do you remember how you lost that leg?" asked Trotman.

Puzzled, Lyssy turned to Corder. "Is that a joke?"

"What? Oh—no, it's an idiomatic expression. She doesn't mean did you *lose* it, she means do you remember how your leg came to be amputated?"

"No, ma'am—that happened before."

"Before what?"

"Before I can remember."

"What about your hands?"

He looked down at the small, dreadfully scarred appendages hanging at his sides as though he'd never seen them before. The flesh had melted away from the inner surfaces of the fingers, leaving the hourglass shape of the bones distinguishable beneath the shiny scar tissue; livid white patches of unlined, grafted skin stretched tautly across both palms. Ultimately, though, the plastic surgeons had done their job well: those deformed hands not only functioned, but were as inexorable as claws or talons once they'd grabbed hold of something—it was letting go that they found difficult. "Also before."

"Aren't you curious?"

"No, ma'am."

"Why not?"

"Because I know what happened."

"But you just said you didn't know."

"No, I didn't."

"Are you playing games with me, Mr. Maxwell?"

Lyssy gave Dr. Al a helpless glance, as if to say, I'm doing my best here. Dr. Al nodded encouragingly. Lyssy turned back to Trotman. "You asked me if I *remembered,*" he explained earnestly. "I don't *remember* much of anything that happened before I came here. But Dr. Al *told* me some of it. When I was sixteen, I guess I tried to put a fire out with my bare hands. Not the smartest move, hunh?"

Trotman turned to Corder and gave him a raised-eyebrow *What are you still doing here?* glance. He nodded. "We'll be next door if you need us." Wally followed him into the adjoining conference room.

"Have a seat, Mr. Maxwell," said the psychiatrist. Two molded plastic chairs, identical to the ones stacked in the smaller room, faced each other at a forty-five-degree angle at the end of the conference table, the top of which was made of some black, unreflective space-age polymer, like the obelisk in *2001: A Space Odyssey.* Lyssy took the end chair; Dr. Trotman tucked the back of her skirt under her as she lowered herself into the other one. "I'm just going to ask you a few questions, if you don't mind."

"Not at all."

"Let's begin with your name."

"Begin what?" Dr. Al would have smiled patiently at that; Dr. Trotman glanced up sharply from the notebook in her lap. "Sorry," said Lyssy, mock-chastened. "My name is Lyssy."

"Full name?"

"Ulysses Christopher Maxwell."

"Do you know what day it is?"

"Monday."

"Date, month, year?"

He got that right, too, adding shyly, "My birthday's on Wednesday—I'll be thirty-two."

"Happy birthday in advance. Can you tell me where we are right now?"

"1-South—the conference room." She waited. "Oh, you mean the hospital? It's the Reed-Chase Institute."

OX3, the psychiatrist noted on the pad—oriented times three. "Do you know *why* you're here?"

Dial down the grin, ratchet up the earnest factor—it was very important to Lyssy that she understand. "When I was little, my parents abused me real bad—I mean, badly. And there are some people, I'm one of them, who when they're little and bad things happen to them, their mind tries to protect itself by splitting up into all these different identities. And the different identities, they all think they're separate people, and the real person doesn't have any control over them. Sometimes he doesn't even know what they're doing."

"I see."

"And in my case, some of those alters were really psychologically disturbed because of what had happened, the abuse and all, and so they went on to abuse other people. Dr. Al says that happens a lot, that abuse gets passed along. And, and, and they—Well, they're gone, now, the others—there's just me. But lots of people, they don't believe in such a thing as multiple personalities—they think *I'm* a bad person, and that if I get out, I'd do bad things. But I wouldn't, I couldn't—I don't even like to think about bad things."

"I see," she said again, then jotted down another note and looked up. "Do you ever hear voices, Mr. Maxwell?"

"Sure, all the time," he blurted cheerfully, and felt an immediate change in the atmosphere, as if the room had grown colder.

"What do they say, these voices?"

He furrowed his brow, bit his lower lip—he wanted to get this one exactly right. "The last one, it said . . . right, right: 'What do they say, these voices?' "

Trotman looked as though she might be suppressing a grin. "What I meant was, do you ever hear voices other than your own inside your head, or voices outside your head that no one else can hear?"

Absolutely not, said a voice in Lyssy's head.

"Absolutely not," said Lyssy.

6

Lily DeVries was four years old when her parents were arrested for sexually abusing her, Dr. Cogan explained to Lilith. Really awful stuff that had begun when she was still an infant.

A strange, volatile child, Lily had been removed from her parents' custody and placed with her grandparents. Withdrawn and depressed one moment, outgoing and flirtatious the next, now as winsome and girlish as Shirley Temple, now a tree-climbing tomboy or an autist devoid of affect, and plagued at intervals by fugue states and bouts of severe amnesia, she had already been misdiagnosed twice, once as bipolar and once as schizophrenic, by the time her grandparents brought her to Dr. Cogan.

A psychiatrist specializing in dissociative disorders, Dr. Cogan had no trouble diagnosing a near textbook case of dissociative identity (formerly multiple personality) disorder. In the face of the abuse she'd suffered, Lily's psyche had splintered off into several alternate identities—alters, for short.

Over the next twelve years, Dr. Cogan continued, she had worked with Lily to help her face her traumatic past and reintegrate her psyche. They'd made some progress—extraordinary progress, given that DID was generally considered to be a treatment-resistant disorder. Sure, there were backward steps—puberty, for instance, had hit Lily like a ton of bricks, causing a new identity to split off, a sex-obsessed alter who called herself Lilah.

But most of her childhood alters had ceased to manifest by the time Lily graduated from the local charter high school that had supervised her homeschooling, and as she approached her eighteenth birthday, even Lilah's appearances had grown fewer and further between.

All that had changed two weeks ago when Lily's grandfather drove his SUV—and his wife—over a cliff on Highway 1. Unable to deal with the catastrophic turn of events, Lily had run away from home. "And from that point on," Dr. Cogan concluded, "you certainly know more about what's been happening to her than I do."

"Because I'm her," said Lilith flatly.

"Because you're her."

"And I'm rich."

"By most standards."

"I have a big house in Pebble Beach."

Dr. Cogan nodded.

"Any wheels?"

"A Lexus, as I recall."

Lilith mulled it all over for a good three or four seconds, then: "Cool—let's go."

"I'm afraid it's not that easy," said Dr. Cogan.

"Why the fuck not? I could use a little bling in my life—I've been living like a fucking pauper."

"For one thing, you're underage. For another, you're still suffering from a serious psychiatric—"

"Oh, horseshit," Lilith broke in. "I'm fine—I just forget stuff, that's all."

"A serious psychiatric disorder," Dr. Cogan insisted softly as she went spelunking through the depths of her purse again and emerged with a slick-looking full-color brochure. "Here, I'd like you to take a look at this." She slid the brochure across the table to Lilith, who held it up dubiously between her thumb and forefinger, as if she'd just seen it fished out of a slime-covered pond.

"The Reed-Chase Institute," she read aloud from the cover, then slid the brochure back to the doctor. "That wouldn't happen to be an insane asylum, would it? You know, as in nuthouse? Funny farm? Snake pit?"

Cogan's thin lips tightened. "It's a *hospital.* One of the finest psychiatric hospitals in the country. And most important of all, it's the *only* facility in the country with any kind of a track record when it comes to dissociative identity disorder. Dr. Corder, the director, treats the DID patients personally, and he does seem to be coming up with some surprising results."

"Results," echoed Lilith doubtfully. "As in, cure?"

"In some cases, yes."

"Then answer me this. Say, just for the sake of argument, the DID gets cured."

"Yes?"

"What happens to me?—what happens to Lilith?" But the look on the doctor's face was all the answer she needed. "Yeah, that's what I figured." She stood up, muttering something about having to use the ladies' room.

"I think I'll join you." Cogan gathered up the tape recorder, the photographs, and the brochure, and slung her purse over her shoulder.

"I figured that, too," said Lilith. She already knew from Mama Rose's furtive exit that there had to be a back way out, and had decided she could easily overpower the older woman once the two were alone. It was Pender she was worried about. But he made no move to follow—just smiled up at them as they passed his table, then turned back to his newspaper.

Short corridor, cinder-block walls. Restroom doors on the left, a door marked Office on the right, and at the end of the hallway, a heavy-looking door with a push bar and a warning: Emergency Exit Only.

Lilith opened the ladies' room door, peeked in. Toilet in the corner, sink against the wall. One customer at a time. "After you," she said, backing away.

"No, you first," Dr. Cogan said firmly.

Lilith closed the door behind her, sat on the toilet long enough to warm it, flushed, washed her hands, splashed cold water on her face. Lily, my ass, she thought, staring at her reflection in the dingy mirror over the sink, then dried her hands with a coarse brown paper towel, opened the door, and stepped out into the corridor, where Dr. Cogan had stationed herself between Lilith and the exit.

"Your turn," said Lilith.

"Funny thing, I don't seem to—"

Lilith charged, drove her lowered shoulder into the doctor's midsection, knocking her backward and sending her purse flying. The girl hit the breaker bar with both hands, crashed through to daylight, and ran straight into what felt like a wall of meat.

"Going somewhere?" said the man called Pender, wrapping his arms around her and, in one impossibly smooth, tango-like move, grabbing her wrists, spinning her around, and forcing her arms behind her back. Lilith kicked backward at his shins; he wrenched her wrists upward, just high enough for the pain to immobilize her.

Squirming, almost weeping with frustration, she swore at him like a biker's bitch as Dr. Cogan came stumbling out into the glare with her jacket twisted sideways and her blouse hiked out from her skirt. "Nice catch," she told Pender grimly, fumbling around in her purse and taking out a hypodermic syringe.

"Just a—whoa there, easy honey—just a hunch. As Quasimodo once said." Pender had of course circled the building as soon as they'd arrived, and mentally noted all the potential exits.

Lilith watched in horror as the doctor held the syringe up to the sky and tapped it a few times with a tapered, reddish-orange fingernail. "What's that for?"

"Just something to calm you down."

She was behind Lilith now, pushing up the sleeve of Lilith's T-shirt and swabbing her tricep with an antiseptic towelette. A pinch, a needle prick. The sky darkened and the macadam opened beneath Lilith. She felt herself falling, falling, through bottomless space like Alice through the rabbit hole, until the darkness closed in overhead and swallowed her up.

7

The room that housed Ulysses Maxwell seemed unremarkable at first glance. Pale blue walls; dark blue carpet; white acoustic ceiling; single bed with a cheerful yellow comforter, open-shelved dresser, bookcase and TV/VCR hutch of blond wood; and in the corner a computer station and a low-backed, ergonomic desk chair—it all looked normal enough to Lyssy, who had little basis for comparison.

But there were no sharp edges anywhere. The walls met each other in smoothly rounded curves, the closet and adjoining bathroom were doorless alcoves, the furniture was all rounded at the corners, and with the exception of the desk chair it was all bolted to the floor. The only lights were set behind opaque panels in the ceiling and the panes in the sealed window overlooking the arboretum were made of two sheets of unbreakable glass sandwiching a layer of fine steel mesh.

What really gave the game away, though, was the smooth-faced, Starship *Enterprise*–looking door. Made of padded reinforced steel, it opened with a pneumatic whoosh, sliding sideways into the wall when a valid security code had been entered into a keypad, then closed and locked automatically as soon as the doorway had been cleared.

Still wearing his chinos and green corduroy shirt—he had half a dozen similar shirts, all in solid colors—Lyssy was at his computer playing chess when he heard the door slide open behind him. "Be right with you," he said without turning around, then placed the cursor on his queen, clicked and held down the left button on the mouse, slid the queen up to KB-3, released the button, and sat back grinning as the word *CHECKMATE!* flashed across the screen, accompanied by an explosion of pixeled tickertape and a tinny fanfare.

"Better luck next time," Lyssy said cheerfully as he logged off and swiveled his chair around. "Oh, hi, Dr. Al. Long time no see." Humor: less than an hour had passed since the meeting with Dr. Trotman. "How about a game?"

"I'm not sure my, ah, ego can stand another butt-whipping this morning," said Corder, who'd taught Lyssy how to play chess only a year ago. With an IQ that tested nearly off the charts, the pupil had quickly outstripped the teacher; it had been a little over six months since the psychiatrist had earned better than a draw against his patient.

"Another?" By now, Lyssy was almost preternaturally alert to his doctor's every nuance, gesture, and mannerism; for him, as for a one-master dog, it was a survival skill.

"In a manner of speaking." Corder sat down heavily on the edge of Lyssy's bed. With his gingery hair and his round-lensed tortoise-shell eyeglasses, he reminded Lyssy of an orange cat named Garfield in a picture book Dr. Al had given him when he was a child—or, more accurately, when his mental age was still that of a child. "How do you feel the meeting with Dr. Trotman went?"

"I don't think she likes me much."

"Yes, well, I'm sure it's nothing personal. Did she tell you by any chance *why* she wanted to meet with you?"

"She didn't have to," said Lyssy. "I've been around here long enough to know when somebody's doing a psychiatric evaluation."

"Right with Eversharp," said Corder. "Dr. Trotman has been asked by the court to give an opinion as to whether you're competent to stand trial for some of the, ah, the things that happened before you came here."

"Oh, crum," said Lyssy—swearing was not one of the skills he'd learned from his beloved psychiatrist/father figure.

"Come on over here." Corder beckoned to Lyssy with a plump forefinger. Lyssy limped across the room and sat down next to him; the doctor draped his arm companionably around his patient's shoulders. "I've been walking a narrow tightrope lately, Lyss, as far as how much to tell you about all the legal machinations going on behind the scenes. On the one hand, I didn't want to worry you prematurely; on the other hand, I don't want you to be blindsided, either."

The arm tightened around Lyssy's shoulders. He shrugged out from under it, crossed over to the small window, and put his nose against the glass so he could make out the arboretum through the steel mesh.

Not surprisingly, this little pocket park with its bright ground flowers and dramatic contrasts of light and shade had become Lyssy's favorite place in his admittedly circumscribed world. Here he had practiced walking hour after hour, rain or shine—he'd have worn his stump raw if they'd have let him—until by now he knew every flower, bird, and squirrel, every meander of the gravel path, every sharp-scented, rough-barked pine, every board of the Japanese footbridge, and every stone in the cement-banked brook as well as he knew his own room. "How long do I have?" he asked eventually.

"Hard to say," replied Corder. "I spoke to O'Hare this morning." F. Frank O'Hare, slick, expensive, and media-savvy, was Lyssy's defense attorney. "He says they'll probably issue an arrest warrant in Umpqua County as soon as Dr. Trotman turns in her report. *If* she finds you competent to stand trial, of course, but nobody realistically sees her going any other way.

"Once that happens, some officers will arrive here to take you into custody and drive you down to Umpqua City. You'll be held in the county jail before and during the trial. O'Hare says they'll probably be housing you in a private cell, so that's, ah, something, anyway."

"If you're trying to cheer me up, Dr. Al, that's just not going to cut it."

"Now don't give up hope yet," said Corder, partly to alleviate his own sense of guilt—on some level he must have known that he'd only been fattening the calf for slaughter these last few years. "O'Hare and his team are preparing a vigorous psychiatric defense—he thinks you stand an excellent chance of avoiding the death penalty."

"At least in Oregon." Lyssy understood perfectly well that if he didn't get the death penalty here, they'd ship him down to California to try him for however many murders he was supposed to have committed there.

"If you'd like, I could give you some medication to help you deal with any anxiety you might be experiencing." Corder glanced at his watch. "I'm sorry, Lyss, I have a new patient to meet. It's almost lunchtime—do you want me to get you a psych tech to escort you down to the dining hall?"

"I'm not very hungry," said Lyssy through clenched teeth.

"I understand. Look, Lyssy, it's okay to be upset. This is a lousy rotten deal you're getting, it's okay to be upset about it."

But it wasn't, thought Lyssy. Not for him. Because the more upset he got, the louder the muttering in the dark place. By now it was already loud enough that he could almost make out the words—and whoever it was in there, he didn't sound happy.

CHAPTER TWO

1

"Basically, you had this couple living way the hell and gone on a ridgetop in Oregon," explained retired FBI Special Agent E. L. Pender, sitting in the copilot seat of the air ambulance transporting himself, Dr. Cogan, and her sedated patient from Redding to Portland. The pilot, recognizing Pender from the book tour he'd taken to promote his ghostwritten autobiography a few years ago, had invited him up to the cockpit for a chat; as happened more often than not, the conversation had turned to the most notorious case of Pender's career. "Maxwell, he was so crazy he thought he was ten different people, and his foster mother/lover/accomplice, *she* was so crazy she made *him* look sane.

"Only in her case she had a pretty good excuse. The bad news was, about half the skin on her body had been burned off—the worse news was, it was the front half. A real horror show—not much face left to speak of, and no more hair than yours truly."

Pender lifted his brown Basque beret and rubbed a hand the size of an oven mitt across the barren expanse of his scalp by way of illustration. "Originally she was his elementary school teacher. Fourth, fifth grade, something like that. They say she was a gorgeous young strawberry blond—the kind of teacher every boy student gets a crush on and every girl student wants to grow up to be like. Then one day Maxwell shows up at school with both eyes swollen shut from a beating, and the whole story comes out. Turns out his parents were members of this twisted satanic cult whose leader was a flat-out pederast; they'd been abusing the kid since he was like, three, sexually, ritually, physically, you name it. Cowards to the end, the parents kill themselves—technically, it was a homicide/suicide—and the teacher gets custody of little Ulysses. But then for some equally twisted reasons of her own—probably because she'd been abused as a child—her idea of parenting included having sex with the kid on a regular basis."

"Oh, man." The pilot—fit, tanned, with Ray-Ban sunglasses and close-cropped hair graying at the temples—winced.

"It gets worse. The sex continued until Maxwell was around sixteen, then she told him it was all over, that part of the relationship, and that she was going to marry the high school shop teacher. He went ballistic, snuck into the bedroom while she and her fiancé were doing the nasty, stabbed him about fifty times with an icepick, and set the bedroom on fire. Burned the shit out of his hands, left her looking like something out of *The House of Wax*.

"But she told the police that her fiancé was trying to rape her, and that the fire got started accidentally. Then when she got out of the hospital, she sprang him from the juvie farm and he moved in with her. Only from then on, around once a year or so she sent the lad out hunting, with orders to come back with a strawberry blond. That was about the only criteria—it had to be a woman and she had to have strawberry blond hair. To make wigs for the old horror."

"Jesus."

"I'd been searching for Maxwell for close to ten years before he finally slipped up and ran a stop sign down in Monterey with a dead strawberry blond in the passenger seat. I was about ninety percent sure he was the one who'd killed all those other women, but just to be sure, I talked the sheriff into putting me into a cell with him for an undercover interview. Bad mistake." Pender raised his beret again to show the pilot the livid, trident-shaped scar across his scalp. "By the time I woke up in the hospital he'd already busted out, killed three deputy sheriffs, a highway patrolman, and at least two civilians. . . .

"When I finally caught up to Maxwell, there were a dozen strawberry blond wigs in a glass case in his basement, plus two half-starved survivors who looked like concentration camp victims." Plus Dr. Cogan, of course, but as always, Pender chose to protect her anonymity.

"He drew down on me, I put one round

through his shoulder, a second through his knee, and between you, me, and the lamppost, I gave some serious goddamn consideration to putting a third round right through there"—touching a forefinger the size of a ballpark frank to where his third eye would have been, if he'd been a Hindu deity—"and saving everybody a shitload of trouble. As it was, he narrowly missed bleeding to death before we could get him to a hospital—they had to amputate what was left of his leg."

But as Pender started to explain how the old woman had died in a fall shortly after the shootout, he realized the pilot was no longer really listening—just nodding politely at intervals as he checked gauges and flipped switches, preparing the plane for descent.

Oh shit, oh dear, thought Pender, his cheeks burning with embarrassment. How bored he used to get, pretending to listen politely in cop bars as some over-the-hill agent blathered on about his adventures back in the day. Pender had sworn more than once that he'd eat his 9mm SIG Sauer P226 before he'd let that happen to him.

The pilot pushed gently forward on the steering yoke, sending the plane nosing downward into the roiling cloud cover. "We'll be touchin' down in Portland in just a few minutes," he told Pender in a standard issue, *Right Stuff* drawl. "Would you mind headin' on back and makin' sure everybody's buckled in?"

Pender nodded briskly—he decided he'd probably done enough talking for one fat old man, for one morning.

2

Irene Cogan had suffered two brutal blows in her lifetime. Six years earlier, stunned by the unexpected death of her husband, she had more or less shut down emotionally, while her kidnapping and subsequent ordeal at the scarred hands of the serial killer Ulysses Maxwell three years later seemed to have had precisely the opposite effect.

With death imminent, Irene had promised herself that if she did by some miracle survive, she would spend less time working and more time smelling the roses. Unlike most such promises, that one had been kept—the second part, anyway. Her recovery from post-traumatic stress disorder hadn't exactly been a picnic—three years after her kidnapping she still suffered from the occasional PTSD flashback—but in general she had come through it with a renewed sense of possibilities, stronger where she was weak, less brittle where she was strong, a good deal kinder to herself, and an inveterate smeller of roses.

"You're just in time," she greeted Pender upon his return to the cabin, which resembled a long, narrow hospital room. Lily lay strapped into the adjustable bed, fully clothed, tossing restlessly in her sleep. "I think she's starting to come out of it."

"Which *she* would that be?" asked Pender.

"Hard to say. Stress, trauma, periods of unconsciousness as opposed to natural sleep all tend to trigger alter switches. But as to which alter comes out the other side, that's a crap shoot. Or I suppose I should say a game of roulette—you know, round and round she goes, and where she stops . . . "

". . . nobody knows," Lily said sleepily, opening her eyes. "Oh, hi, Dr. Irene. Boy, am I glad to see *you.* I just had the strangest dream. I dreamed I was home alone, and the phone rang, and it was this policeman, and he, he said . . . " Her dark eyes widened as she took in her surroundings; she sat up, looking around dazedly. "Am I still dreaming?"

"Not at all." Irene took Lily's hand in one of hers and patted it with her other hand to help Lily ground herself. "We're in an airplane—it's like a flying ambulance. You've had a rather severe dissociative episode—I'm afraid I had to sedate you."

"Was it Lilah?"

"No, a new alter—she called herself Lilith. She was quite a character—something like a biker moll in training."

"Speaking of flying." Pender stepped to the foot of the bed. "Pilot says everybody needs to buckle up—we'll be landing in just a few minutes."

Seeing Pender made Lily feel a little like smiling in spite of . . . well, in spite of everything. "Hello, Uncle Pen."

"Hi, doll." He and the doctor helped her up and led her over to one of three swiveling chairs bolted to the starboard wall; Pender buckled her seat belt for her as the jet began a sharp leftward bank.

Lily rubbed her palms against the soft upholstery, continuing the grounding process. So many questions crowded her mind: how much time had passed? What had this "Lilith" been up to with *her* body? Any harm done—to herself or others? And where were Grandma and Grandpa, how come they had sent Dr. Irene and Uncle Pen instead of—

Suddenly she moaned.

"What is it, dear—are you all right?" asked Irene, lowering herself into the chair to Lily's left. "Do you need anything? A glass of water or something?"

Lily turned her head. Her eyes swam with tears, blurring and brightening the silvery glare filtering in through the oval windows. "The phone call from the policeman—that wasn't something I dreamed, was it, Dr. Irene?"

"I'm afraid not."

"How—how long has it been?" The plane straightened out again; Lily felt the pressure of the descent in her ears.

"Not quite three weeks."

"Did I miss the funeral?"

Thud—the cabin trembled briefly as the landing gear let down. "The memorial service, yes, I'm afraid so. But your uncle Rollie said to tell you that he's saving the ashes until you get home so the two of you can scatter them in the bay."

Ashes, thought Lily. Ashes, ashes, all fall down. "Dr. Irene?"

"Yes?"

"When we get home, can I stay at your house for a while? I don't think I could handle being alone in the hacienda."

Thwwwwt—it was as if all the air had been

sucked out of the cabin, replaced by a shivery silence. The white-striped black tarmac rushed by on either side of the plane. Then, as the wheels hit the tarmac at the shallowest of angles, rebounded into the air, and skipped along the runway for a few dozen yards like a stone skimming across a pond, the last piece of the puzzle fell into place.

"We're not *going* home, are we?" she called, over the whine of the braking engines.

"I'm—No, no we're not." I'm afraid not, Irene had started to say, before it occurred to her how frequently she'd used the word *afraid* in the last few minutes.

Now why is that? she asked herself, as the plane taxied toward the terminal. It couldn't possibly have anything to do with the fact that in about twenty minutes she'd be in the same building as Ulysses Maxwell, could it?

Well, yes, actually it could. But there was nothing to be afraid *of,* the psychiatrist reminded herself, unconsciously rubbing her forefinger over the burn scar on the back of her hand where the alter known as Max had held a cigarette lighter to her flesh. Because he can't hurt you anymore, she told herself firmly. He can't hurt you ever again.

3

Fighting panic during the last leg of the journey to the Reed-Chase Institute—*Is this really happening? Oh*

God, is this really happening?—afterward Lily would remember the ride only in disconnected flashes. The anonymous-looking white van that met them at the Portland airport; Uncle Pen in his ridiculous hula shirt standing at the curb waving good-bye; the subaqueous light through the van's dark-tinted windows; a girdered bridge over a shining river; a rolling, landscaped parkway; Dr. Irene reminding her to breathe, dear, don't forget to breathe.

As soon as she left the van, her perception tunneled. She took in the suburban-looking sidewalk beneath her feet, the cement walkway bordered with bright petunias and ranunculuses, and the sliding glass doors with the RCI diamond, but as if in a nightmare, she would not, could not raise her eyes to the stern-fronted, two-story brick building, and would later recall it only as a brooding presence looming before her.

To ease the apprehension of patients and allay the misgivings of the family members responsible for committing them, the reception area at Reed-Chase was designed to look more like a hotel lobby than a hospital waiting room. Instead of linoleum, a plush gray wall-to-wall carpet; instead of the usual rows of hard-backed chairs, upholstered furniture in separate groupings, each with its own floor or table lamp; tall rubber plants in urns or tubs furthered the resemblance to an old-fashioned hotel lobby.

"Irene, so good to see you." A plump, shirt-sleeved man bustled across the lobby and hugged Dr. Cogan warmly. "And you must be Lily," he added, holding out a pudgy pink hand that was well-scrubbed even by Lily's demanding standards. "Hi, I'm Dr. Corder."

Lily shook hands reluctantly, then she and Dr. Cogan followed Corder through another set of sliding glass doors behind and to the right of the reception desk, and down a short corridor to a high-ceilinged office with walnut bookshelves and arched windows covered with dark valanced curtains.

Corder ushered the women into chairs drawn up in front of his imposing desk, then walked around behind the desk and sat down in a high-backed leather chair. "Welcome to the Institute. How was your flight?"

"Very comfortable," replied Dr. Cogan. "From now on, I'm going to fly by ambulance."

Corder chuckled. "How about you, Lily?"

"Well, for once I didn't get airsick." She wasn't sure why that was funny, but both doctors chuckled. "Is that your family?" Nodding toward a triptych picture frame on the desk: blond woman on the left, blond teenage girl on the right, and in the center a snapshot of a younger, thinner Corder in a green smock, his surgical mask dangling from his neck as he cradled a newborn baby in his arms.

"My wife, Cheryl; my daughter, Alison; I, ah, don't know who that cute devil in the middle is."

Suddenly it was all too much for Lily—the picture of the helpless baby in its father's arms had sent the old sadness stealing over her. Where other people had childhoods, happier or unhappier by degree, Lily had a great dark hole inside her from which her childhood had been violently torn. And as if that weren't bad enough, now her grandparents were both dead and she was being institutionalized. Ashes, ashes, she thought. All . . . fall . . .

"Lily, no!" Dr. Cogan leapt from her chair as the girl buried her face in her hands; she grabbed Lily's wrists and forced them apart. "Stay with us, honey, you need to stay with us."

Corder had jumped to his feet. "Alter switch?"

Cogan nodded; Lily struggled halfheartedly to free her hands.

"No, let her," said Corder softly.

But it was too late. Still herself, Lily glanced up, embarrassed, as the psychiatrists sat down again. "Sorry about that."

"Don't be," said Corder. "Before we're done, you and I, I'm going to want to meet all your alters. I have something very important to teach them."

"What's that?" Lily wanted to know; so did Irene Cogan.

"That they're not welcome here—that their, ah, time is up."

"I don't think they're going to like that," said Lily, almost inaudibly.

"Makes no never mind what they like or don't like," said Corder folksily. "Around here we're much more concerned with reinforcing the original personality—that's *you,* young lady."

"I know that," said Lily; the doctors chuckled pleasantly, pointlessly again, as though she'd been cracking jokes left and right.

"The way we do that is by making you as happy

and comfortable as possible. Gourmet cuisine or comfort food, as you prefer—I warn you, you may put on a few pounds; I certainly have." He patted his belly. "Walks in the arboretum, swimming in the lap pool, movies in our own little theater—basically anything that will help you avoid stress, since stress is the number-one trigger for alter switches."

"No kidding," said Lily, to another round of forced chuckles.

"That's the spirit," said Corder. "Now, if you're both ready, I'd like to show you around. And if *you* don't mind, Irene, there's someone I'd like Lily to meet. Someone who's, ah, been through what she's been through, and come out the other side."

It took Irene another few seconds to realize what Corder had in mind; when it dawned on her, she felt a sudden chill, followed by a churning in her lower bowel, as if she'd just polished off a plateful of bad mussels.

4

No matter how badly Lyssy's day was going, he always felt better in the arboretum. His senses started coming alive the moment he passed through the entrance arch, two red-lacquered vertical timbers supporting a slanting, overlapping red lintel beam, which together, according to Dr. Corder, formed an oriental character symbolizing tranquillity. Lyssy drank in the dappled light, the satisfying crunch of the blue-gray pea gravel underfoot, the dry biting scent of the evergreens, the harsh chatter of the jays.

Sitting with Dr. Al on a marble bench at the end of a short allée of pine trees were an older woman with helmet-shaped, reddish-blond hair, and a dark-haired girl in jeans and an oversize leather bomber jacket, huddled with her knees together and her elbows pressed against her sides, as if she were waiting for a bus in the cold. Lyssy's heart went out to her—he would, he thought, have recognized her as a new patient even if Wally the psych tech hadn't already clued him in in the elevator on their way down.

Dr. Al performed the introductions. Lyssy stuck out his hand, palm down to hide the scars, shook hands with each woman in turn, and asked them how they were. They both said they were fine; the girl asked him how he was in return.

"Just fine," he replied, glancing over to Dr. Al to see how he was doing, phatically speaking.

Dr. Al gave him a circled-thumb-and-forefinger okay sign and an encouraging nod. "Lyssy knows the arboretum like the back of his hand," he told Lily. "Perhaps he'd, ah, be willing to show you around."

"My pleasure," said Lyssy, crooking his arm the way he'd seen men do it in old movies. But Lily made no effort to take it, leaving him standing there with one elbow awkwardly akimbo for a few seconds, before he turned and limped away up the gravel path. After a frightened-doe backward glance toward Dr. Cogan, who gave *her* an encouraging nod, Lily followed Lyssy. Wally started after them, but Corder caught his arm.

"Let's give them a little time to get to know each other, Walter," he said.

"It's not so bad here, really," Lyssy explained, when Lily had caught up to him. "Everybody on the staff is nice—the mean ones don't last long. And the patients on 1-East aren't even very crazy. Dr. Al calls them the Desperate Housewives—some of them come here more for a rest than anything else. If they have enough money, of course.

"Then there's the ODDs and CODs—those are teenagers with oppositional defiant disorder or conduct disorder. Dr. Al says their parents send 'em here either as a voluntary alternative to military school or an involuntary alternative to reform school. They're mostly on 2-East, where the game room is. He treats 'em with behavior mod—he says the smart ones usually figure it out pretty quick."

He was interrupted by maniacal laughter from somewhere overhead. They looked up, saw a bird with a round red cap clinging vertically to the trunk of the oak. "That's an acorn woodpecker," Lyssy explained. "The other day I saw one of 'em fly into a wire—"

Lily flinched.

"No, no, it didn't hurt itself," he added quickly. "Just clipped it with a wing, caught itself in midair, then it was all like—" He puffed out his chest, darted his head around stiffly—a dead-on imitation of an embarrassed woodpecker: *" 'I meant to do that, really I did.' "*

"That's pretty good," said Lily, smiling tentatively.

"Want to hear my imitation of Dr. Al?"

"Sure."

He glanced around to make sure the other three were out of earshot, then drew his chin back against his chest to double it. *" 'Perhaps, ah, Lyssy would be willing to, ah, show you around.' "*

Lily's smile faded as a tall, unshaven man shuffled toward them wearing a seersucker bathrobe over pajamas and slippers. Instinctively she dropped back and ducked behind Lyssy. "Don't sweat it," he whispered, proud at how she'd sought his protection. "That's Colonel Lamp. He's a schizo. Completely harmless—they keep him medicated to the gills. Here, watch this." As he passed the old fellow, Lyssy snapped off a salute.

Stiffly, the colonel drew himself up to his full height to return the salute, but missed his forehead by a few inches, hitting himself in the side of the jaw instead. "Carry on," he said thickly, spittle flying.

"Boo-yah," replied Lyssy.

The path looped and forked and curled in on itself so many times that after walking for a few minutes, they were only twenty or thirty yards from the entrance, as the crow flies. By then Lyssy's limp had grown more pronounced—he had to use the railing to help him across the wooden footbridge, red-lacquered like the entranceway, that arched steeply over a little streamlet with cement banks bordered by flower beds.

On the far side of the bridge, terraced steps led

up to a cozy-looking little domed gazebo with flowering vines climbing the trellised sides. They sat next to each other with a good eighteen inches of marble bench separating them. Try as she might to convince herself that it would okay to ask him about his limp, she just couldn't bring herself to do it. They sat in silence, listening to the maniacal laughter of the woodpeckers. "Have you seen your room yet?" he asked eventually.

"Just for a second. It's on the second floor of the front building? Kind of peach colored, with an adjoining bathroom?"

"That's just the observation suite," Lyssy told her. "It's only temporary, until they decide how close of an eye they need to keep on you. A word to the wise, though: there's a reason they call it the *observation* suite."

But the warning did not fully register—nor would it, until the following morning. "Can I ask you a personal question?" Lily asked him after another uncomfortable pause.

Lyssy's heart sank. Here it comes, he thought. For a few minutes there, he'd allowed himself to hope that she hadn't recognized him, that she didn't know anything about his murderous past. "Go ahead," he said, bracing himself.

"Is it true you used to have DID, and Dr. Corder cured you?"

"Oh, that," said Lyssy, almost giddy with relief. "Yeah, sure—I haven't had an alter switch in like, two years or something. No fugue states, no blackouts. Sometimes, though. . . . " But he caught himself just in time. No sense scaring her, when Dr. Al would have wanted him to be as encouraging as possible. Besides, out here in the sweet air of a summer afternoon, it was easy to believe he'd only imagined the dark place and the muttering voice.

And even if he hadn't, divulging the existence of either would have been risky—if the girl passed his misgivings on to Dr. Al, it would mean an end to Lyssy's hard-earned privileges. No more trips to the game room to hang out with the ODDs and CODs, no more meals in the dining hall, and worst of all, no more visits to the director's residence to visit Alison and Mrs. Corder—Lyssy would be spending his remaining time at the Institute in a locked room on the locked ward.

"Well, you know, sometimes, it seems like it's almost too good to be true," he finished awkwardly.

"Yeah, tell me about it," said the girl. Then those dark round eyes narrowed. "But if you're better, how come you're still here?"

"Actually, I'm due to leave pretty soon," said Lyssy, truthfully enough.

"And you're cured? You're really, *really* cured?"

"A, ah, paragon of mental health," replied Lyssy, once again mimicking Dr. Al.

5

Alan Corder had long maintained that the standard setup for a modern psychiatric evaluation—two people sitting on opposite sides of a desk; one asks questions or administers tests while the other responds—left much to be desired.

Once she'd recovered from her initial shock at finding herself face-to-face with the man who still figured in her nightmares, Irene had to agree. Walking with Lyssy in the pleasant pocket forest after she and Corder had caught up to their patients at the gazebo, observing him as he interacted with the enriched sensory environment, she found that the disarming awkwardness of his body language, his mercurial attention span, his childish delight in the magical appearance of a hummingbird, as well as his eagerness to share that delight with his companions, all spoke volumes—volumes that would never even have been opened in the usual office setting.

What she didn't see was equally as important. As a multiple, Maxwell had almost always exhibited an upward, rightward eyeball roll when changing alters, and the new alter had frequently exhibited grounding behavior afterward, rubbing a thigh as if to verify that he (or in the case of one alter, she) was in fact in the body.

But Irene observed none of this behavior during their walk. When she made eye contact with Lyssy, even when she caught him unawares, there was no sign of Max or Kinch, the Maxwell alters she'd learned to fear—with good reason.

"I have to admit, I'm impressed," she conceded to Corder when they were alone in his office, sitting in matching leather armchairs in front of the fireplace. "How long since an alter has surfaced?"

"Just under two years," replied Corder.

"You're sure about that?"

"I can show you the optical exams if you'd like." Variations in optical functioning were among the most reliable indicators for a personality switch: a 1989 study had confirmed that DID subjects had close to five times more such changes than control subjects who'd been asked to feign the disorder.

"I'll take your word for it," said Irene, smoothing the travel wrinkles from her skirt. "What about the possibility of co-consciousness?" That was a state of being, uncommon but not unknown, where one alter was able to directly and simultaneously experience the thoughts, feelings, and actions of another. (Researchers still weren't exactly sure how the mind managed the feat, but one thing they all agreed on was that the human brain seemed to have evolved with redundancy as one of its basic design principles: there was more than enough gray matter in there to operate two personalities simultaneously.)

"There'd have been some indication—confusion, mini-fugue states, contradictory responses." Corder grinned suddenly, then slapped the arm of his chair. "I'm afraid you're going to have to face it sooner or later, Irene: I *can* treat DID successfully."

"But you're not going to tell me how, are you?"

"No, I'm not." Corder grabbed a poker from the brass stand by the fireplace and prodded at the neatly stacked logs—a bit of fidgeting that would have been less revealing if there'd actually been a fire going at the time. "And for good reason. I'm sorry to have to be so mysterious about this, but the last thing I want to do is get caught up in a debate about my methodology until I have my ducks in a row and I'm ready to publish."

"At least give me a hint—I'm feeling badly enough about leaving Lily, as it is." The decision to have Lily committed to Reed-Chase had been made by her new guardian, her uncle Rollie, who'd learned about Corder's success with multiples from various DID websites. Irene's feelings had been hurt, of course—her first inclination had been to wash her hands of the whole damn case. She and Lily had grown too close over the last dozen years anyway, she'd told herself—it would probably be a relief to have all that weight off her shoulders.

But that was sour grapes, and she knew it. And in the end, she couldn't leave Lily to be hunted down and dragged off to an asylum by strangers. So she'd enlisted Ed Pender in the cause. Pender in turn had brought in a skip tracer from Santa Cruz who'd tracked Lily to Shasta County; the rest of the story had played itself out in the coffee shop in Weed.

"All right, one hint," said Corder, begrudgingly. "But you have to promise not to tell *anybody anything* until I publish."

"I swear on my DSM." A little professional humor: the *Diagnostic and Statistical Manual of Mental Disorders* was sometimes referred to as the clinical psychiatrist's Bible.

"Okay, here it is: screw integration."

That brought Irene up short. The standard approach to treating multiples was to integrate the alter identities with the original personality to the greatest achievable extent. And the alternative to that would be . . . ?

"Good lord, Al—you're not talking about somehow eliminating the alters instead of integrating them, are you?"

Corder's response consisted of a wink so smug and feline Irene could practically see canary feathers floating behind him as he led her up to Lily's provisional quarters on 2-South. The security precautions were impressive as always—he had to punch codes into keypads to gain entrance to the glassed-in elevator lobby, again to summon the elevator, and a third time to gain access to the observation suite, a largish room decorated in shades of peach, apricot, and burnt umber. Lily lay on a comfortable-looking single bed—not a hospital bed—with her head turned resolutely toward the wall.

"Good seeing you again, Irene," said Corder, framed in the doorway. "I'll leave you two alone to talk—when you're done, just press that intercom button over there. And Lily, you have a good night, don't be shy about asking the nurses for anything you need." He stepped backward as the door slid closed again.

"What a lovely room," said Irene, approaching the bed. "And look, you have your own television!" As if that were something entirely new and marvelous. Attagirl, Irene told herself, perching on the edge of the bed. Could you *possibly* be any more fatuous?

"What do you care?" Lily's elation at learning that Corder might be able to cure her DID had been short-lived, disappearing as soon as the door to her room had closed and locked behind her. "If you cared, you wouldn't go away and leave me here."

"Please don't make this any harder than it is already." Irene reached out to pat the girl's shoulder. She was sorely tempted to blurt out the unspeakable truth—that bringing Lily here hadn't been her idea—but didn't want to take a chance on upsetting the girl even more, or on selfishly undermining Lily's relationship with her new doctor.

Lily stiffened at the touch, then wrenched herself around almost violently, turning a tear-streaked face toward Irene. "I miss them, Dr. Irene—Grandma and Grandpa, I miss them so much. And I'm so scared. Please don't leave me here. Something terrible is going to happen, I know it is."

"Ssh, ssh, it's okay, I won't let anything bad happen to you," Irene crooned soothingly, taking the girl into her arms and hugging her tightly—something she'd never have been able to do before her ordeal with Maxwell. Awkwardly, one-handed, she fumbled around in her enormous purse for her card case and a pen, scribbled her home and cell numbers on the back of one of her business cards, and handed it to Lily. "Here, take this," she said. "I'm no farther than the telephone. You can call me anytime you like, even if it's just to talk, and if you really need me, just say the word and I'll come running."

A tear plopped onto the card; carefully, so as not to smear the ink, Lily brushed it away with her sleeve. "Is that a promise?" she said, slipping the card into the tight back pocket of her jeans.

"Cross my heart," said the psychiatrist. They

hugged for a few seconds, then Irene pressed the intercom button. Lily flinched when the door slid open, then lay back and turned her face to the wall; when she turned around again, she was alone.

Welcome to the snake pit, Lily told herself. She knew why they used to call mental hospitals snake pits: because—no lie!—doctors once thought the best way to cure people of certain disorders was to hang them upside down over a pit filled with poisonous snakes!

Of course, there were no snakes here at the Reed-Chase Institute—or if there were, they were very expensive, exclusive snakes, she thought wryly.

But no amount of pampering could pad the shock of finding yourself living out the single worst fear of your life. Ever since she could remember, Lily had been terrified of being locked up in an asylum—and now here she was. Talk about the other shoe dropping, she thought. In a way, it was like that old cliché about careful what you wish for because you might get it, only with a new twist. Be careful what you're afraid of, is what they *should* say, Lily decided. Be careful what you're afraid of, because someday it might get *you.*

6

As much as he disliked the responsibilities that came with being the director of an institution the size of Reed-Chase—the administrative details that threatened to swamp him on a daily basis, the weight of all the people, staff and patients alike, whose welfare depended on his decisions—Al Corder had to admit that you couldn't beat the commute.

It was close to six o'clock when he left Irene Cogan and Lily to say their good-byes. Only minutes later he unlocked and ducked through the arch-topped door set into the ivy-covered brick wall bordering the northern end of the arboretum, strolled across the lawn, passed the disused swing-and-slide set, and let himself in through the back entrance of the eighty-year-old, half-timbered, Tudor-style fieldstone manor that came with the director's job. End of commute.

"Home is the hunter, home from the hills," he called.

"Hi, I'm in the kitchen."

As he passed through the dining room, Corder noticed the table was set for two. "The princess does not deign to dine with the commoners this evening?"

Cheryl Corder was at the stove, wooden spoon in one hand, kettle lid in the other, her dark blond hair limp from the steam. "The princess," she replied over her shoulder, "is a little down in the dumps."

"Boy trouble?" Corder gave her a peck on the back of the neck, then peered over her shoulder into the kettle and inhaled greedily.

"What else?" She replaced the lid, set the spoon down carefully on a folded paper towel.

"Should I have a fatherly chat with her?"

"I suppose you might as well give it a shot—Lord knows she won't confide in me."

Knock, knock. "Allie? Allie, it's Dad."

"Yeah, I guessed from your voice."

She can't help it, Corder reminded himself, she's an adolescent. "May I come in?"

"If you promise not to act like a psychiatrist."

"Word," said Corder; it sounded lame even to him, so he hastily added, "On it, you have my word on it."

His quintessentially fifteen-year-old daughter lay facedown on the bed, her right hand under her cheek, her left hand dangling just above the carpet. She was wearing a pair of skintight, below-the-navel jeans and a cutoff top. She edged her legs away from the side of the bed to give him room to perch—a major concession.

"Speaking not as a psychiatrist but as a father—you want me to beat him up?"

He was rewarded with a giggle. "Oh, Daddy, he's a football player."

"I was on the track team—I could pop him one, then run away quick."

As Alison rolled over and sat up, it struck Corder once again that somehow, almost overnight, his little girl had metamorphosed into, for want of a better word, a hottie.

"How come boys are such a-holes, Daddy?"

"Hormones, sweetie—at that age, they're a raging stew of hormones. Speaking of which, your mother is cooking up a heavenly beef bourguignonne—if there's beef bourguignonne in heaven. I'm, ah, thinking about cracking a real nice-looking '98 Napa cabernet to go with it."

She cocked her head like a curious jay. "Aaaand . . . ?"

"Your mother and I were talking the other night about whether you were old enough—or I should say, mature enough—for us to start initiating you into the proper enjoyment of the, ah, fruits of the vine. So I was thinking, maybe I'd set out an extra glass tonight—if you're feeling well enough to join us for dinner, that is."

She nodded, slowly, responsibly, maturely. "Sure, okay."

"Good, good—I'll set a place, we'll call you when dinner's ready." He patted her ankle and stood up, thinking that he'd surely kept his promise not to act like a psychiatrist. Making a unilateral decision—yes, he and Cheryl had talked about letting Allie have a glass of wine at the dinner table, but they hadn't exactly reached a conclusion—not to mention bribing an underage kid with alcohol: that was about as unpsychiatrist-like as it gets.

But Cheryl let him off the hook with a raised eyebrow, while Alison was the picture of condescending adolescent maturity all through the meal, chatting politely with her parents just as if they weren't hopelessly retarded. The only down note came when Corder told them about Ulysses Maxwell's visitor that morning.

"What do you think's going to happen to him?"

asked Alison. Her father had first brought Lyssy over for Sunday dinner—along with one of his attendants, whom they made a pretext of treating as just another guest—when Alison was thirteen. The two had hit it off famously, not least because at that point Lyssy was more or less a boy of thirteen in a thirty-year-old body. Since then, he'd been invited to the director's residence for dinner every few months or so—always with an attendant in tow, of course.

"Life without parole, at best. At worst, lethal injection."

"But that's not fair! Lyssy's so gentle—he wouldn't hurt a fly—you know he wouldn't."

"That's true—but in a way, that's also a function of his former disorder."

"The DID, you mean?"

Corder nodded. "When a child's psyche dissociates—that just means it breaks apart—it splits off, not into lots of other complex personalities, but into its own component parts. Each of the alter identities represents a particular, ah, *aspect* of the original personality—so far we've identified sixteen classes of alters"—administrators, analgesics, autistics, children, cross-genders, demons/spirits, handicapped, hosts, imposters, internal self helpers, MTPs or memory trace personalities, persecutors, promiscuous, protectors, substance abusers, suicidals—"that work together to help the child deal with traumas he or she has no other way to deal with.

"And many of these alter identities embody or express the character traits that the original identity finds disturbing. Sexuality, anger, feelings of aggression, and so on. In Lyssy's case, all the anger he felt at having been abused, along with the desire to strike out, to avenge himself, all those feelings that if expressed would only have resulted in even more abuse, were, ah, segregated into alter identities.

"So while it's true that Lyssy, as Lyssy, the original personality, couldn't hurt a fly—or protect himself from one, for that matter—his psyche manifested at least two alters, Max and Kinch, who gloried in violence."

"But they don't exist anymore, right? Because you helped him get rid of them."

"Well, yes. Unfortunately, though, no jury has ever bought DID as a defense in a criminal case."

"But couldn't you convince them?"

"I'm going to try, sweetheart."

"You better." Alison sipped thoughtfully at her wine, trying not to pull a sour face, then looked up brightly. "I just remembered—doesn't Lyssy have a birthday coming up this month?"

Corder nodded glumly. "On Wednesday."

"Are we going to have a party for him again?"

"I don't know—it's a stressful time for Lyssy, and—"

"Please? You know how much he loves coming over—and if what you said is true, it could be the last birthday party he ever gets to have."

"That's true enough." Corder glanced over to his wife. "What do you say, hon?"

She shook her head dubiously. "Wednesday's a bear for me. I'm getting my hair done in the morning, my book club meets in the afternoon, I'm not sure how I'd—"

"Please, Mom? I'll bake the cake."

"That I have to see," said Cheryl Corder—and so the family's fate was decided.

7

For three years, Irene Cogan had been nursing an unlikely crush on the man who'd risked his own life to save her from Ulysses Maxwell's hellhole. Or perhaps not so unlikely, despite his unprepossessing (well, okay, downright homely) appearance—she didn't need her Stanford degrees to understand how a damsel in distress might develop an affinity for the knight in shining armor who'd ridden to her rescue, or to recognize the resemblance between Pender and both her father *and* her late husband—big, easygoing men in whose strong arms a gal couldn't help feeling safe and protected.

At the time, though, Irene had been too traumatized by Maxwell to trust her feelings for Pender, never mind *acting* on them, and any remaining chance of a relationship developing between them seemed to have dissolved entirely when instead of moving out to California following his retirement from the FBI, as he'd once thought of doing, Pender had accepted a law enforcement job on the island of St. Luke, a U.S. protectorate in the eastern Caribbean.

Irene told herself it was just as well, that it would never have worked out for the two of them anyway.

Then a few months ago Pender had called Irene out of the blue to tell her his plans had changed, that things hadn't panned out for him on St. Luke, and that he was thinking about moving to the central coast after all.

So much for *just as well.* Irene had helped Pender find a cottage to rent only a few blocks from her place in Pacific Grove, and he'd quickly been assimilated into her circle of friends and acquaintances. He'd grown particularly close to the DeVries family—Lily had taken to calling him Uncle Pen, and he'd become golfing buddies with both her real uncle, Rollie DeVries, and her grandfather Lyman.

But when it came to reciprocating Irene's romantic feelings, nothing had changed—their relationship was platonic, and in dire peril of remaining so. Then, a little over a month ago, Irene and Pender had each been contacted by *The People's Posse,* a Portland-based basic cable show on the order of *America's Most Wanted,* and asked to appear on an upcoming episode featuring the Maxwell case.

The offer—an all-expense-paid trip to Portland and a modest emolument—wasn't all that tempting until the two compared notes and discovered they were scheduled to be interviewed on consecutive days. To Irene it had seemed like a perfect opportunity to take one last shot at upgrading the relationship. She'd suggested to Pender that they make a joint vacation out of it; when he agreed, she booked them adjoining rooms at an upscale hotel advertising romantic midweek getaways.

She'd nearly lost her nerve a dozen times since

then. As late as the previous Saturday she'd been on the verge of calling the whole thing off; instead the business with Lily had brought them to Portland a full day ahead of schedule.

Luckily there'd been no problem checking into their hotel a day early, Pender told Irene when he picked her up at the Institute in the white Toyota he'd rented at the airport. "Not only that, I talked to Marti Reynolds at TPP, they're going to move our interviews up a day apiece—mine's tomorrow now, yours is Wednesday."

"And the airline tickets?"

"I cancelled the round-trip reservations, got us seats for the last flight to San Jose on Wednesday evening—we can take the shuttle home from there."

Irene shook her head in admiration. "Pender, if I'd ever had a secretary that good—well, I'd still have a secretary."

"I always knew I had to be good at *something,"* he said—receiving compliments, even left-handed ones, was never his strength. "How'd it go with Lily?"

Irene shrugged. "It went."

"Want to talk about it?"

"Hey, that's *my* line," she told him.

The hotel proved to be a standard chain affair—nothing particularly romantic about it. But the adjoining rooms were large and comfortable, with enormous beds and a handsome view of the Willamette. Upon arriving, Irene took a long hot shower to wash off the hospital vibes. She could feel her nerve starting to fail her again—she'd never seduced a man before, and wasn't sure she'd be able to manage it.

Fortunately, the restaurant Irene had selected with the help of the hotel concierge was both romantic enough for her purposes and informal enough to accommodate Pender's tragic wardrobe, which tonight consisted of a madras sport jacket, a boldly striped sport shirt, and rumpled polyester slacks; the only items that didn't clash were his brown Basque beret and his beige Hush Puppies.

Irene herself wore a green frock that showed off her best feature, her long slender legs. Emboldened by an unaccustomed intake of alcohol—she'd polished off most of a carafe of house red while Pender stuck to his Jim Beam on the rocks—she contrived to rest her hand on his more than once during the meal. And in the backseat of the cab on the way back to their hotel she edged closer and closer to him, until their thighs were touching—any closer and she'd have been in his lap.

But still he seemed clueless. In the elevator on the way up to their adjoining rooms he kept plenty of space between them. When they reached his door and she turned her face up to his for a good-night kiss, closing her eyes expectantly, all she got for her brazenness was a platonic peck on the cheek.

So what's a gal to do? Persuading herself she was drunker than she actually was, Irene took another shower, changed into a slinky, nearly transparent black negligee, and knocked on the door that communicated between her room and Pender's.

"Pen?"

"Yeah?"

"Can I come in for a sec?"

The door opened. Pender, wearing a too-small hotel bathrobe—one size fits *almost* all—looked down at Irene, standing in the doorway with her arms at her sides. "Oh, shit, oh dear," he said.

Irene wanted to sink through the floor—or failing that, die on the spot. Instead, feeling stunned and foolish, she began backing away, her arms crossed over her chest. Pender, realizing the enormity of his gaffe, took her by the wrist and drew her back into his room. "I'm sorry," he said, "I didn't mean it like that."

"No, it's my fault," she heard herself say. "I shouldn't have just . . . I mean, I had no right to. . . . "

"Ssshh," he murmured, wrapping his arms around Irene and pulling her tightly against him. "It's not your fault—there's no way you could have known."

"Known what?" she said, in a tiny voice.

"Long story," Pender replied gently.

After six months, either the pain was beginning to subside or he was growing inured to it, Pender explained to Irene a few minutes later. The two were sitting side by side on the edge of his bed; he'd fetched her the monogrammed hotel bathrobe from her room, filled an ice bucket, and fixed them each a glass of Jim Beam on the rocks. Rare now were the body blows, he told her, the attacks of grief so visceral the sobbing literally doubled him over.

The trouble was, said Pender, he wasn't so sure he *wanted* the pain to subside. Except for his memories and a few trinkets, it was all he had left of his second wife, who'd died from pancreatic cancer only a few months after their wedding. So perhaps it had been a mistake to leave the tropical paradise where the two had met, wed, and lived happily ever after—if three months qualifies as ever after.

But at the time, the reminders had been too plentiful and too painful to bear. Every Caribbean sunset broke Pender's heart all over again, and with booze duty-free on the island and a bar on virtually every corner, it didn't take him long to realize that you can't drown your sorrows in alcohol, you can only pickle them. So he'd opted for the geographical solution instead, resigning his post as St. Luke's chief of detectives and moving nearly four thousand miles west to the golfing mecca of the Monterey peninsula to take another stab at retirement—and at lowering his handicap, which after twenty years on the links still hovered around the drinking age.

Not that there was any shortage of either booze or bars on the peninsula, he told Irene. But at least there nobody felt sorry for him—largely because he'd told no one of his loss. "So you can see, it's nothing personal," he concluded. "You're an attractive, intelligent woman, Irene—*with* legs to die for, don't think I haven't noticed. And I'm flattered as hell you'd even consider . . . well, you know. But it's too soon—I'm just not ready yet."

Irene raised her head—she'd spent the last few minutes studying the carpet—and cocked it to the side, looking up into Pender's pained eyes. "*Yet* being the operative word?" she asked him.

"Oh, definitely," said Pender.

She smiled. "Well that's going to be a little awkward, isn't it? Waiting for *yet,* I mean."

Pender thought it over. "Tell you what. When the time is right, *I'll* show up at *your* door in a slinky negligee," he said, just as Irene raised her glass to her lips.

And so what was to have been an evening of romance dissolved into a spit take. But afterward, alone in her room, when her mind insisted on exploring her moment of humiliation the way a tongue explores a broken tooth, up popped the image of Pender knocking on her door in a see-through negligee, carrying a box of candy and a floral bouquet, and she found herself smiling instead of weeping.

Pender too, had a well-developed sense of the ridiculous. Smooth move, Ex-Lax, he told himself, when he was alone in his room again. Turning down that elegant trim at your age—good God, man, you must have lost your mind.

8

"Anything else before I go?" inquired the chunky, bespectacled night nurse. She had already brought Lyssy a glass of water, given him his sleeping pill, helped him take off his leg and change into his pajamas, and tucked the covers around him.

"Yeah, could you move my crutches closer to the bed? In case I have to go to the bathroom?" Lyssy, who'd been trying to postpone the inevitable, began to sense the nurse's growing impatience. The problem was, he wasn't just afraid of the dark, he was afraid of anybody *knowing* he was afraid.

"There you go. Anything else?" She waited by the door, her finger poised at the keypad, ready to punch in the security code.

"I guess not."

"Good night, then."

"Good night."

The heavy door slid open, then closed again behind the nurse, locking automatically. The ceiling panels dimmed gradually; soon the only illumination in the room was a faint trapezoid the color of moonlight, cast onto the carpet by the recessed night-light in the bathroom.

What a roller coaster of a day, thought Lyssy, slipping one hand under his pajama bottoms and closing it around his penis, which was already satisfactorily heavy with anticipation.

To make it hard, he thought about the girl he'd met this afternoon, then plugged her image into his standard masturbatory template, which always involved a rescue. Tonight he would save Lily from a fire—another night it might be Miss Stockings whom he saved from a flood, or the pretty black nutritionist who had to be rescued from one of Lyssy's neighbors on the locked ward. And after the fire (because for Lyssy the idea of even taking the initiative in a sexual encounter, much less resorting to coercion or violence, was a brake-screeching turnoff), Lily became the grateful aggressor. *I know what you want,* she whispered as she began to undress herself at the foot of the bed, *I know what you need. . . .*

Another feature common to Lyssy's sexual fantasies was that the actual sex tended to be indistinct, breast-oriented, and R-rated—he rarely got as far as the nitty-gritty before reaching orgasm.

Tonight, though, strange things started happening. Lyssy had stroked himself into a sort of trance state, picturing the girl turning her back to him while she slipped off her bomber jacket. But when she turned around to face him again, she was no longer Lily—instead, she had turned into Dr. Al's wife.

Nothing too unusual there. Though she was in her midforties and starting to spread a little in the waist and rear, Cheryl Corder was still nice and bosomy up front, and had a sort of Martha Stewart ice-queen thing going: frosted hair, knowing eyes that crinkled at the corners, and a wry, crooked smile.

Nor was there anything unusual about the way the fantasy played out at first. Stripped down to her panties, Mrs. Corder sashayed around the bed until she was standing directly in front of Lyssy, then cupped her breasts in both hands for him to nuzzle, kiss, tongue, and suckle.

Most nights, that would have been enough to bring the furiously masturbating Lyssy to orgasm. If not, he'd picture her climbing onto his lap and lowering herself onto him—that would generally do the trick. But tonight, instead of waiting passively, he grabbed the woman roughly by the hair and threw her facedown onto the bed—not his own narrow twin, but a big double bed with satin sheets.

Frightened now, whimpering, *No, please,* she tried to crawl away. Unable to stop himself—it was as if someone else had hijacked his fantasy—Lyssy threw himself on top of her, jerked her panties down roughly. His cock was huge, red-knobbed, and throbbing, a real two-hander. *You like it rough, don't you,* he said as he spread her cheeks and thrust himself into her hard. She screamed; the more she screamed, the better he liked it. Humping, driving, crushing her down, feeling the dark tightness enveloping him as one scarred hand gripped her hair for control while the other snaked under her to play with her fat, white, heavy-hanging breasts.

Gone was any semblance of control over his own fantasy—Lyssy wasn't even surprised, when he turned his head, to see Dr. Al and young Alison tied to chairs at the foot of the bed, both naked, bound and gagged, forced to watch. *Don't worry, your turn's coming,* he hissed to Alison in a voice that was no more his own than was the fantasy. *And you'll get yours too,* he confided to Dr. Al.

And as he began to come, a succession of disconnected images flashed before Lyssy's eyes—a knife being drawn across a throat, blood spattering a wall, a lolling head, a slumping body. . . .

Lyssy opened his eyes, found himself back in his own bed, frightened and ashamed, his hands sticky with semen. With a moan of horror he threw back the covers and hopped into the bathroom, where he scrubbed his hands with soap and hot water, roughly, obsessively, until the scar tissue stretched across the palms was red and raw.

And though in the forefront of his mind he was repeating the same phrase over and over, like a mantra, as he scrubbed—*it's not my fault, it wasn't me; it's not my fault, it wasn't me*—in the back of his mind Lyssy was pretty sure he could hear dry laughter emanating from the dark place where he was never to go.

CHAPTER THREE

1

Lily awoke to the sound of an over-hearty female voice bidding her good morning through a speaker in the wall near the head of the bed. For a few seconds that seemed to last an eternity, she felt lost and frightened, totally disoriented. Then it all came flooding back: the airplane, her grandparents, and—oh God—the Institute!

A moment later the room's only door slid open, then closed behind a massively built young woman in white duck trousers and a tight-sleeved white polo shirt with the RCI logo over the left breast. Her light brown hair was cut in a mullet: shaved sidewalls, buzzed on top, hanging straight down to her powerful shoulders in back. PATRICIA BENOIT, PSYCH. TECH., read the plastic name badge pinned to her shirt.

"Hi, I'm Patty. Dr. Corder wants me to stick with

you this morning, kinda show you the ropes, get you orientated, how's that sound?"

"I have to pee."

"You might want to try out the shower, too." Patty wrinkled her nose. "Getting a little gamy, if you catch my drift. I'll be at the nurses' station—buzz me when you're ready." At the doorway, Patty angled her body to block Lily's view of the keypad before punching in the code.

Although she was wearing a modest cotton-flannel nightgown from the suitcase full of clothes and personal effects Dr. Cogan had packed and brought along for her (the nurse who'd helped her unpack last night had confiscated her tweezers and nail file), Lily waited until the door had closed again before pulling the covers back and climbing out of bed. In the bathroom, she wiped off the toilet seat with a neatly folded square of toilet tissue before sitting down, and patted herself dry afterward with another neatly folded square, keeping her nightgown rucked up onto her lap the whole time. Lily hated exposing herself—even at home, she preferred to lock the bedroom door before disrobing, and the bathroom door as well, whether for a quick pee or a long bath.

Here, though, there was no bathroom door to lock, or shower-stall door, or even a shower curtain—the recessed shower head set high and flush in the curved wall angled away from the open stall doorway, and a six-inch-high tiled ledge in the bottom of the doorway kept the water from flooding the bathroom.

After brushing her teeth, Lily reluctantly pulled her nightgown over her head and looked around the bathroom for a place to hang it. There being no hooks or towel racks, she folded the nightie and placed it on top of the towels and washcloths stacked on a high rounded shelf. Naked, she peered tentatively into the shower stall. There were no temperature controls, no faucets, no taps, but the moment she stepped inside, warm water cascaded from the single jet eighteen inches above her head. Electric eye, she guessed; a little experimenting proved her right.

Boy, they thought of everything, Lily told herself as she soaped up and lathered her luxurious dark mane—shampoo, body wash, conditioner in tiny motel-size plastic bottles were arrayed on a recessed shelf under the jet. You couldn't drown yourself, scald yourself, hang yourself, cut yourself, or even tweeze yourself. Not enough in the little bottles to poison yourself, either. Maybe you could choke or something if you tried to swallow one, but they probably even—

Then suddenly Lily remembered what Lyssy had mentioned yesterday—there's a reason they call it the *observation* suite—and all at once, she *knew* she was being watched. Panic seized her; she squatted on her heels with her legs together and her knees drawn up, crossing her arms over her breasts and hugging herself miserably. The shower turned itself off; she was below the electric eye. Cold and shivering, rocking on her heels, Lily uncrossed her arms and buried her face in her hands.

2

Lilah emerges from her blackout to find herself crouched naked in a shower stall, rubbing her right thumb against the pads of the first two fingers. Awakening abruptly in unfamiliar surroundings is nothing new for Lilah—her life has always been a disconnected series of sudden appearances.

So she rises—and jumps back against the wall of the stall with a startled laugh as the water comes on. Electric eye—cool. Fragrant soap, water not as hot as she likes it, spray not as needle-fine, but there doesn't seem to be any way to control it. She lathers and rinses luxuriously, sensuously, with special attention to the erogenous zones, idly masturbating for the sheer sensation of it, no intention of going for an orgasm.

The water shuts off when she steps out of the oddly doorless stall. Wherever she is, she tells herself—if it's a hotel, it's one of those modern ones—at least the towels are clean, thick, and plentiful. She wraps a bath towel around her torso, makes a turban of a second, and is drying herself with a third when she hears a knock. "Be right out!"

But as Lilah tightens the towel under her armpits and steps out of the bathroom—another oddity, there's no bathroom door—the room door slides open to admit a powerful-looking woman in a white polo shirt, white duck trousers, and a mullet haircut. Lilah, who is nearsighted but too vain to wear eyeglasses, squints at the plastic tag on the woman's breast. She can just make out the name—Patricia Benoit—but the letters below it are a blur.

Probably a maid, thinks Lilah. And if it's true what they say—the butcher they are, the sweeter the tongue—she probably gives some heavenly head. "Is that Ben-*oyt* or Ben-*wa?*" She lets a giggle escape.

"Ben-oyt—but you can call me Patty. What's so funny?"

"I was thinking about ben-wa balls. You ever heard of them? They're these like, sex toys, you stick 'em inside your—"

"Oh, right, right." Patty colors. "I've heard of them, I just didn't know that's what they were called."

"Ever use 'em?" asks Lilah, slyly, as she brushes past the much larger woman; her damp feet leave tidy little Robinson Crusoe footprints on the carpet as she crosses the room to examine the clothes folded and stacked in the waist-high blond dresser, which has recessed shelves instead of drawers.

Patty lets the question drop. She's worked with DID patients before, and some of them—not Lyssy, of course—she's suspected of feigning the disorder either knowingly or unknowingly. It was fun for them to impersonate different characters, they received lots of attention, and it was also a nifty way to deflect responsibility for their actions. Or at least, it was nifty until Dr. Corder got hold of them.

But this Lily DeVries is for real—after watching the alter switch in the shower on the security monitor at the nurses' station, Patty has no doubt of that. Not even Jody Foster, whom Patty idolizes, is that good an actress. Lily hasn't just changed her affect or adopted a set of mannerisms, like the fakers do—the very way she inhabits her body is strikingly different.

This alter, the towel-clad, gutter-mouthed tramp swearing quietly over the selection of clothes available to her, seems entirely comfortable with her physicality. She carries her shoulders low; her walk is liquid and balanced, her hips loose and swaying, and when she unwraps her long brown-black hair and hunkers down on her heels to examine the clothes on the bottom shelf, she reminds Patty of one of Gauguin's tantalizingly unself-conscious Polynesian girls.

Having been fully briefed by Dr. Corder this morning, and having reviewed the so-called "map" of alters drawn up by Lily's former psychiatrist, Patty now has a reasonably good idea who this one is. Name: Lilah; alter class: promiscuous; age: actual; self-image: actual; affect: sexually provocative.

"Are you here to make up the room?" asks Lilah, still hunkered down on her heels.

"No, I *was* here to escort you down to the dining hall," says Patty, with an emphasis on the past tense.

Escort, Lilah thinks. This must be one hell of a ritzy place. "Want to help me work up an appetite?" She rises, letting the towel fall. Stark naked, she holds her hands out at her side, as if to say, *here I am, and I'm all yours if you want me.*

"That is *so* not happening, young lady." Patty looks down at the carpet; she'd have turned down the offer even if she hadn't known about the hidden security cameras. Taking sexual advantage of one of her charges, even one as extraordinarily desirable and apparently willing as Lilah, is simply unthinkable for Patty.

Nevertheless, she has the feeling that this latest acquisition, the searing image of the naked girl offering herself, has just acceded to the permanent collection in her private museum of erotic images; she also has the feeling that this was precisely Lilah's intention. "I'll be right back," she tells her charge.

Alone again, Lilah selects a sweatshirt and a pair of panties and jeans at random—while the place may be ritzy, judging from the selection of clothes it's also informal—but just as she finishes changing into them, the door slides open again and Patty announces a change in plans.

"Time to begin your therapy," she says, tossing Lilah a green hospital gown as the door slides closed behind her. "Take those off, put this on."

Therapy? thinks Lilah. Then she reads the fine print—PSYCH. TECH.—on Patty's name tag and suddenly fear floods her system. A desperate plan begins to take shape. "Could I have a little privacy to get dressed, please?"

"Now it's *privacy* you want?" Patty turns away and punches her security code into the keypad. As the door begins to slide open, Lilah dashes across the room, jukes right, then left, and ducks under Patty's flailing arm. She races down a long green corridor toward a door with a breaker bar and a sign reading Emergency Exit Only, unable to shake the eerie sensation that she's done this before—and not so long ago, either.

Heads turn as Lilah passes the nurses' station;

the faces are white and blank as night-blooming flowers. She hits the breaker bar, crashes through the door, and bolts barefoot down a flight of stairs.

But the door on the next landing is locked. And here's Patty lumbering down the stairs after her, red-faced and puffing, her arms mottled and meaty-looking as two legs of lamb, spread wide to block Lilah's retreat. "Come on now, oh come on," she's saying, in a voice less of anger than of schoolmarmish annoyance.

Joining Patty on the stairs is another massive, white-clad figure who fills his polo shirt like the Mighty Hulk. If this is a dream, I'd really like to wake up now, thinks Lilah. It sure feels like a dream, the way she's rooted to the landing, frozen in place as the two close in on her, looking nightmarishly similar in their white uniforms, like Tweedledee and Tweedledum in a madhouse production of *Alice in Wonderland.*

They flank her, each taking an arm, and walk her back up the stairs and down the corridor; this time the nurses all turn away busily as they pass the desk. Patty accompanies Lilah into the peach colored room while her male counterpart—his name tag reads simply, *Wally*—waits outside. "Let's try this again," says Patty, picking up the discarded hospital gown and shoving it firmly into Lilah's hands.

3

Hotel dining room. White tablecloths, tinkle of glass and clatter of tableware, muted breakfast conversations. Striking vistas of Portland through tinted plate-glass windows. From the entrance alcove, Pender scanned the premises and spotted Irene Cogan, wearing a white blouse with a Peter Pan collar, sitting alone reading the *Oregonian* and picking desultorily at a grapefruit.

He crossed the room, his head pounding with every footfall, despite the double padding of his rubber-soled Hush Puppies on a thick gray carpet patterned with the hotel chain's interlocking initials in burgundy. "Mind if I join you?"

"I like your outfit," she said, gesturing graciously toward the empty chair across from her. He was wearing a white-on-white guayabera shirttails-out over not-yet-rumpled brown slacks. "Have we been invited to a Mexican wedding?"

"Har de har har," said Pender, whose interview at the TPP offices down by the warehouse district was to begin in less than an hour and was expected to take all day. He turned to the hovering, white-jacketed waiter. "Screwdriver. Light on the oj, heavy on the Stoli. If it takes, I may consider solid food."

"Hungover?" asked Irene, after the waiter left.

"Aaaargh! As Charlie Brown used to say."

"Serves you right."

"For what?"

"For all the booze you drank last night, what else?"

"Oh, that," replied Pender, then: "Look, about last night . . . "

She held up both hands; two silver bracelets jingled as they slid down her long slender wrist. "Please, let's not talk about it, okay?"

From that high point, the conversation flagged. Irene dissected her grapefruit and skimmed the newspaper; Pender sipped at his orange-tinted Stoli and gazed out the window at the cityscape below. "I'm sure glad this didn't turn out awkward," he said after a few minutes.

"Me too," said Irene over the top of the newspaper. Then she folded it and slipped it into her gigantic Coach bag. "I keep thinking I ought to give Lily a call just to see how she's doing. I know it's inappropriate, but—"

"Why inappropriate? I mean, think of that poor kid, waking up in a strange place, not knowing anybody. And it's probably just starting to sink in about her grandparents—of course you should call her, why shouldn't you?"

Because she's no longer my patient, thought Irene. Then she reminded herself that as far as her relationship with Lily was concerned, she'd crossed that line a long time ago. "You know, I think I will," she told Pender.

"Tell her Uncle Pen says hi."

4

"Where are we going? Where are you taking me?"

No answer. Dressed in an open-backed green gown with strings in back that tie in front and paper slippers that keep threatening to slide off, Lilah shuffles down the long green corridor, flanked by a white-clad psych tech on either side. When they reach the elevator, Mullet Woman punches in the security code and steps inside first, while Hulk follows Lilah. Exiting one floor below, they reverse the process, then flank Lilah again and march her down another long green corridor, this one two-toned with a waist-high, olive-colored wainscoting, to a door marked AUTHORIZED PERSONNEL ONLY.

The door opens, revealing a large tiled room dominated by an enormous padded table in the shape of a cross; it looks more like a medieval torture device than a piece of furniture. Beside it, seated behind a gray metal desk, is a plumpish, bespectacled man in a white lab coat, his reddish-brown hair combed back in waves from a high round forehead. He gestures toward the empty wooden chair across the desk, politely asks her to take a seat. She shakes off the hands of her escorts, puts a little extra hip swivel into her walk as she crosses the room.

"Do you know who I am?" is his first question.

She draws the hospital gown tightly around her, shrugs noncommittally.

"Ever seen me before?"

"Not that I know of." A seductive smile. "You are kinda cute, though."

He's not biting. "What's your name?"

"Lilah."

"Last name?"

She frowns prettily. "Sorry—sometimes I have trouble remembering things."

"Do you know where you are?"

"Some kind of mental hospital?"

"Do you know what day it is?"

She shrugs, causing the hospital gown to fall open. His eyes flicker downward—only for a moment, but a quickening of his breath gives her a sense of power. She leans forward provocatively. "Look, whoever you are, could we talk in private for a couple minutes?"

"No, we can't." He breaks eye contact, types something onto a laptop computer on the desk, then looks up again. "Just a few more questions. You were right about this being a mental hospital—do you have any idea *why* you're here?"

Both the room and the man are too chilly for her to go around with her boobs hanging out. Lilah pulls the lapels of her hospital gown closed again. "Because your goons over there wouldn't let me leave."

"I mean why you were brought here in the first place."

"I don't know. Amnesia, maybe?" She waits for him to finish typing another note into the laptop. "Well, am I right?"

"You're experiencing some loss of memory, then?"

"Yeah, I got CRS—can't remember shit."

"Tell me the last memories you do have—before coming here, that is."

"Well there was this biker, he picked me up in Seaside, I was pretending to be a hooker—I do that sometimes, just for the fun of it. . . . "

She tells him the rest readily enough—Lilah feels no sense of shame where sexual matters are concerned. When she finishes, he closes the notebook, then does something that takes her completely by surprise: he leans earnestly across the table and stares hard into her eyes, saying, "Lily? Lily, if you're there . . . if you can hear me . . . if you're in any way conscious . . . if you have any conscious control over any of this . . . if any of this alter switching is in any way voluntary to any extent, now's the time to speak up. Believe me, nobody here is going to think less of you."

Lilah draws back, tearing her eyes from his searching gaze. "He's the crazy one, not me," she tells Mullet Woman over her shoulder.

But Mullet Woman's not looking at Lilah, she's looking over Lilah's head at the crazy doctor, who sighs, blows the air out like a man who's just made a tough decision, then nods toward the cross-shaped table.

"No way," says Lilah. "No fucking way."

Yes fucking way. Hulk and Mullet Woman each take an arm and lift her onto the table as easily as if she were a scarecrow, then force her arms away from her sides and fasten her wrists to the crosspieces with fleece-lined clamps. "Help me," she screams, kicking futilely as strong arms yank her legs out straight and clamp her ankles to the table. "Please somebody, help—"

Something is forced between her teeth, cutting her off in mid-scream. She tastes rubber. Another fleece-lined clamp swings over her forehead, clicks into place to immobilize her head. Out of the corner of her eye she glimpses the man in the white coat fiddling with the knobs of a machine about the size of a metal briefcase. Then he turns back from the machine and holds a syringe up to the light.

"You're going to be taking a little nap now," he tells Lilah, patting the inside of her elbow for a vein. "That's all, just a little nap."

She feels the needle sliding in, then a burning sensation in the crook of her arm. Please, somebody help me, she thinks. Somebody, anybody. . . .

5

Once the short-acting sedative had taken hold, Alan Corder injected his patient with an even shorter-acting neuromuscular blocker known as succinylcholine—brand name, Anectine—to prevent her from breaking any bones while her body was convulsing.

Then an oxygen mask was placed over her nose and mouth, a conducting jelly rubbed on her temples, and the electrodes attached. "Let's clear now," Corder said quietly. Patty and Wally stepped back from the table; Corder pushed the green button on the front of the MECTA device, and silently, without drama, one hundred joules of electricity—about enough current to light a 110-watt bulb—passed down the leads into the electrodes, and thence to the patient's brain, for a duration of one second.

The resulting grand mal lasted thirty endless seconds. Patty looked as though she wanted to throw herself across Lily's thrashing body to keep her from hurting herself. Corder put his hand on Patty's arm and smiled reassuringly. "She doesn't feel a thing, she won't remember a thing."

"I know, it's just . . . "

"I know."

Then it was over—nothing to do but wait.

Most laymen, and many mental health professionals, think of electroshock therapy, formally known as ECT, or electroconvulsive therapy, as barbaric and archaic—*One Flew Over the Cuckoo's Nest,* and all that. But for some psychiatrists, ECT is a valuable tool for treating major depressive and bipolar disorders: it's estimated that despite the opposition of a well-organized, patient-led anti-ECT movement, one hundred thousand patients a year receive electroshock treatments in the United States alone.

Alan Corder had first discovered the efficacy of ECT in treating dissociative identity disorder in the accidental fashion common to so many other scientific breakthroughs. Four years earlier, treating a severely depressed, medication-resistant female patient with several suicide attempts behind her, he decided to try electroshock as a last resort. The results were immediate and spectacular—the patient came out of the anesthetic feeling absolutely *chipper.*

But she was also an entirely different personality. At first Corder was afraid that what appeared to be a case of iatrogenic (therapist-induced) DID was an unwanted side effect of the electroshock. In a follow-up hypnotherapy session, however, he was able to determine that the depressive personality had been an alter all along—it wasn't depressive disorder the patient had been suffering from, but rather dissociative identity disorder. And after the electroshock, that particular alter never appeared again.

That was the breakthrough Corder had been hoping for. He didn't pretend to know exactly how or why it worked—but then, nobody knows exactly how ECT worked on those other disorders, either. So he continued to treat his patient for DID—every time another alter surfaced, it was back to the ECT table for her. And shortly after Patient One had been discharged as cured, Patient Two, Ulysses Maxwell, arrived at Reed-Chase.

In many ways, Maxwell was the perfect guinea pig for Corder. He arrived with a definitive diagnosis of DID from Irene Cogan, one of the country's leading experts in the field, and had no relatives to ask questions or raise a fuss. Nor was there much difficulty identifying Maxwell's alters—each was clearly defined and easily delineated, and one by one, as soon as they appeared, they were dispatched to the cross-shaped table in the ECT room to be shocked out of existence.

That's how it worked with the first several alters, anyway—the malevolent host alter who called himself Max proved strong enough to resist the initial treatments. But Corder, to whom alters were not people but symptoms, was pitiless, stepping up the voltage with every successive treatment, until finally, after a bilateral jolt of close to 150 joules (roughly the equivalent in foot-pound energy of a 110-pound weight being dropped on a person's head from a height of twelve inches), Max gave up the ghost—or whatever alters did when they ceased to manifest. Then there was only Lyssy.

Obviously, with such a complete remission, there was no point in treating him for DID. Corder could of course have attempted to treat Lyssy's amnesia, could have regressed him to foster recollection. But for what benefit, and at what risk? The only benefit, if one could even call it that, would have been to instill a sense of remorse in Lyssy; the risk would be inducing a recurrence of the DID.

So Corder made the decision to treat the developmental rather than the dissociative disorder, to progress Lyssy rather than regress him, and the results spoke for themselves. Over the course of the next two years, using a modified homeschooling Internet curriculum augmented with outside tutors, Corder brought Lyssy forward from kindergarten through high school, until by now he was operating at an adult level, intellectually if not emotionally or socially; it was in furtherance of Lyssy's social development that Corder had initiated the visits with his own family.

Following his success with Maxwell, Corder had treated two more DID patients with ECT, without asking permission, but with equally spectacular results, and eventually word began going around the DID community, via websites and chat rooms, that something important was going on at the Reed-Chase Institute.

But secrecy was still of paramount importance. The anti-ECT lobby was not just vocal, it was loud and growing increasingly influential—the city of Berkeley, California, for instance, had officially (and illegally, as it proved) attempted to ban electroshock therapy within city limits. And by employing ECT for a disorder other than the ones for which its use had been approved by the American Psychiatric Association, Corder knew he was risking not just his reputation, but possibly even his license.

Fortunately, neither Lyssy nor the other patients Corder had successfully treated with ECT had any idea how their cures had been accomplished that knowledge had disappeared along with the alters who had undergone the procedure.

And that was the way Corder intended to keep it until he had compiled such a demonstrable record of successes that even the most virulent ECT critics would be unable to deny the efficacy of the treatment—and even then, he expected there would be a hell of a battle when word finally did get out. . . .

Patty and Corder were alone with the patient when she regained consciousness. Thirty minutes had passed—the clamps and electrodes had been removed, the telltale goo wiped from the girl's temples, and a Band-Aid covered the puncture on the inside of her elbow.

"Lily?" Patty said softly, as the girl's eyelids fluttered open.

Corder put his hand on Patty's beefy arm to get her attention, and shook his head forcefully. "Don't want to plant any suggestions," he whispered, then tugged her back from the table and took her place in the patient's line of vision. "How are you feeling?"

"My head," she whispered, "Oh God, my head."

"We can give you something for the pain in just a second. First though, I need you to tell me your name."

A moment of panic; Lilith felt the seconds ticking by as she searched her memory—or rather, searched *for* her memory. Then it all came flooding back to her—the tent, the circle of ogres, Mama Rose and Carson, the coffee shop, the psychiatrist, the photos, the tape recorder—and somehow, though confused and disoriented, Lilith understood that her very survival depended on these sadists thinking she *was* that poor little rich girl the shrink had told her about. "Lily," she whispered, in a rough approximation of the girlish voice on the tape recorder. "Lily DeVries."

"Is it?"

It is as far as you're concerned, asshole, thought Lilith, nodding her head gingerly. But even that slight motion sent nauseating, purply-black waves of pain sloshing against the inside of her skull. "I think I'm gonna—"

"Hasten, Jason, get the basin," recited the mountain of mulleted flesh at Lilith's side as she slid a curved metal pan under Lilith's chin.

Lilith turned her head and vomited clear bile into the receptacle. "Better out than in," said the other woman, tenderly wiping the clinging strands from Lilith's chin.

Fuck you and the ox you rode in on, thought

Lilith, closing her eyes to hide the murder in her heart. Just a little closer, she thought—just bring that nose a little closer. . . .

6

Lyssy was in love. Lily had been his last thought before he fell asleep and his first upon awakening. Picturing her—those eyes, so big and dark; that rich dark hair, like midnight and cream when the light hit it just so; the soft voice; the shy smile; the promise of a luscious figure under that too-large bomber jacket—filled him with emotions he'd only read about before. He took all his meals that day in the dining hall and wore the psych techs out with repeated requests to visit all the places he might run into her—the arboretum, the library, the pool, the game room. When she wasn't at any of them, he realized why people said love hurt—and why five minutes of that hurt was preferable to a hundred years without it.

But the timing! Falling in love just as his life was beginning to crumble around him struck Lyssy as profoundly unfair. He tortured himself with wild schemes and improbable hopes, even allowing himself to consider, for the first time, the possibility of escaping from the Institute before the deputies came to take him away. Then when Dr. Al dropped off the invitation to Lyssy's own birthday party, hand-lettered and decorated by Alison with birthday icons—balloons, a cake with candles, packages tied up in ribbons and bows—he realized with a heady sense of guilt that that would be the perfect opportunity: freedom would be as close as the front door of the director's residence.

But Lyssy couldn't think of anywhere to escape *to,* even if he had been able to convince Lily to come with him—nor could he think of any reason she'd want to. Outside of Lyssy's fantasies, they scarcely knew each other. Perhaps, though, that could be changed—when Wally brought him down to the director's office for his weekly therapy session that afternoon, with his heart beating like a rabbit's from the strain of trying to sound offhand and casual, he asked Dr. Al how the new girl—what was her name, Lily?—how Lily was doing.

"Settling in," the doctor replied, not at all fooled. "I noticed you two seem to have hit it off quite nicely yesterday."

"Yes sir, we did. Matter of fact, I was hoping I could invite Lily to my birthday party tomorrow."

"Well I can't make you any promises yet," said Dr. Al. "There are quite a few variables that would have to be—Lyssy? What is it, son?"

For Lyssy's gold-flecked brown eyes were swimming with tears. Turning away, he shook his head in anguish. "I love her, Dr. Al. I know it sounds stupid, but I really really love her." And it all came pouring out—or almost all: Lyssy knew better than to mention that he'd even considered the possibility of escape.

"There's nothing for you to be ashamed of," said Corder, when Lyssy had finished. "She's a lovely young lady, and the two of you have so much in common, it would be almost unhealthy if you *weren't* attracted to her."

"But of all the times for this to happen," Lyssy moaned. "It's all so . . . so hopeless."

You can say *that* again, thought Corder. His heart went out to poor Lyssy—he decided to inform the staff that if Lily seemed amenable, they were to give the two patients a little more room and a little more privacy. Let them have their walks, get to know each other in the short time Lyssy had left.

As for the birthday party, he told himself, that would depend on how quickly Lily recovered from the morning's ECT therapy. If there were no complications and no further alter switches, he decided, he'd ask Patty to escort Lily to the party tomorrow after work. It would mean paying two, three hours at time-and-a-half to Patty as well as Wally, but that was a small enough price to make Lyssy's last birthday here as happy as possible. (It was also fully billable.)

And in the meantime, there was one other thing he could do to help relieve Lyssy's anxiety. "Grab some couch, young man," he said, pushing his chair back from the desk. "I think we're long overdue for a hypnotherapy session."

The book of things that *all* DID patients have in common would be a short one indeed: 1) they all suffered egregious abuse in childhood, really over the top stuff; 2) they all have at least one alter identity; and 3) they are all tremendously suggestible when it comes to hypnosis—which may in fact be the very quality that engenders the disorder in the first place.

For a psychiatrist, having a patient who can be slipped into a trance state so easily is the equivalent of an internist having a patient with a glass abdomen—it makes it a lot easier to see what's going on. For that reason, and to save time, early in their association Al Corder had implanted a code phrase in Lyssy's subconscious mind, one that would trigger a hypnotic trance state whenever he heard it.

From then on, all Corder had to do to put Lyssy under was whisper that trigger phrase in his ear. It even worked on the alters, which indicated to Corder something that may have been intuitively obvious, but had never been proved clinically: that the alters all share the same subconscious from which they had sprung.

After dabbing away his tears and blowing his nose with a tissue from the box on the desk, Lyssy limped over to the green leather couch across the room from the fireplace and lay on his back, his head resting on a hard leather cushion encased in a disposable paper pillow cover—a cootie protector, Lyssy called it.

"Comfy?" asked Dr. Al, taking a shiny silver dollar out of his pocket, holding it over Lyssy's head, and deftly walking it from knuckle to knuckle to distract Lyssy's attention while he leaned in close and whispered the trigger phrase into Lyssy's ear: "Lyssy is a *goooood* boy; Lyssy is a *goooood* boy."

That was all it took: Lyssy's breathing slowed,

then his eyes fluttered closed. To test him, Corder suggested to Lyssy that his right arm was growing lighter and lighter, so weightless it was floating off the chair—and it did.

The rest of the session occupied only a few minutes, which Corder used to implant the following suggestion in his eminently suggestible patient: that when he, Lyssy, grew frightened thinking about the future, about leaving the Institute, about his trial, about jail or whatever, instead of giving in to panic he would tell himself: *Whatever happens, I can handle it; I can handle whatever happens.*

"Okay, let me hear you say it."

"Whatever happens, I can handle it; I can handle whatever happens."

"Again."

"Whatever happens, I can handle it; I can handle whatever happens."

As always, extracting Lyssy from his trance state took longer than getting him into it. Corder had to explain the exit strategy—when I snap my fingers twice, you will awaken refreshed and calm—as well as reinforce the trigger phrase for the next session. But when they were done, and Lyssy was sitting on the edge of the couch, his little feet, one real, one prosthetic, swinging just short of the carpet, Corder was well pleased with his afternoon's work.

And when he asked Lyssy at the end of the session, casually, almost as an afterthought, how he was feeling now, the boy—no, the man!, Corder had to remind himself; with Lyssy it was easy to forget—flashed him a wink and a thousand-watt grin. "I dunno, Dr. Al, but somehow I feel like, whatever happens, I can handle it; I can handle whatever happens."

"That's my boy," said Corder.

7

Just after Irene had finished showering and drying her hair with a pistol-grip blower supplied by the hotel—she'd spent the afternoon browsing at Portland's famed Powell's bookstore—she heard a rap on the door between the adjoining rooms, then the verbal equivalent:

"Knock knock," called Pender.

"Who's there?" Irene said suspiciously.

"Love me."

Even more suspiciously: "Love me who?"

"Love me Pender, love me true, never let me go," he sang—the tune, of course, was Elvis Presley's "Love Me Tender."

Irene groaned as she opened the door. His outfit was sedate, for him: brown slacks, short-sleeved white pongee sport shirt, green socks, tan Hush Puppies; he had two glasses in one hand, an ice bucket in the other, and a bottle of Jim Beam under his arm. "Did you have a good day?"

"Not bad. How'd the interview go?"

"Not bad either, thanks to a trick I learned in the media workshop the publishers sent me to before my book tour."

"What's that?"

"If you don't want to answer the question the interviewers actually ask, just answer the question they *should* have asked." He handed Irene a glass of mostly ice, with a splash of Kentucky's finest. "Did you ever get hold of Lily?"

"Her room didn't answer all day." Irene took a sip, grimaced, smacked her lips gamely. "I left a couple messages for her with the switchboard."

"They're probably keeping her pretty busy," Pender suggested. "I'm sure if anything was really wrong, she'd have called you."

"I don't know—I just don't know." Irene sat down heavily on the edge of her bed—or as heavily as her hundred-and-twenty-pound frame could manage. "I can't help thinking it's a terrible mistake, leaving her there."

"It wasn't your decision," Pender reminded her. He was standing by the window, looking out over the city; the sky was steely gray, but it didn't look like rain. "Besides, I distinctly remember you telling me last night at dinner how you were so knocked out over all the progress Corder had made with Maxwell."

"I suppose I was. But the more I think about it, the less comfortable I am with it."

"With what?"

"It's a little hard to explain."

"Try me."

Another sip, another grimace. "Okay, you know how in DID the psyche splits up into various identities in response to childhood abuse?" Pender nodded. "What you have to bear in mind is that instead of being a complex bundle of personality traits, like the rest of us, these alter identities generally embody one-sided aspects of the original personality. Lily's Lilah represents sex, for instance, Maxwell's Kinch is pure rage, and so on. Concentrate of Character, we used to joke: just add water.

"That's why the traditional goal of DID treatment has been integrative. To make a whole, healthy human being, you need to *integrate* the aspects of personality embodied in the various alters with the *original* personality. But judging by what little he told me yesterday, Al Corder appears to be taking the exact *opposite* approach, banishing or discouraging or somehow destroying the alter personalities instead of integrating them."

"But isn't it a fair trade-off?" asked Pender. "You can't tell me Maxwell isn't better off without monsters like Max or Kinch crawling around in his subconscious."

"From society's point of view, yes, of course, although personally I'm not altogether convinced the Lyssy I met yesterday would survive five minutes in prison without Max or Kinch. But that's a rather extreme example. In Lily's case, I keep asking myself questions like, will Lily be able to lead the sort of life we'd all want for her *without* Lilah's sexuality? Or take this newest alter, Lilith. Until Lilith's appearance, Lily's system of alters was unusual among the multiples I've treated, in that it never manifested any sort of protective identity—even the alters that appeared when she was being actively abused as a child ranged in personality from passive to very passive to downright autistic.

"So in some ways, the appearance of a protector alter at this stage in her development represents a positive step for Lily. If I were still her doctor, I'd like to see Lilith's confidence and sense of self *integrated* into Lily's personality, not eliminated from it."

"Have you talked to her uncle about any of this?"

"Not yet. But I fully intend to when we get back. First, though, I'd really like to talk to Lily again, see how she's feeling. If she's settling in, the last thing I'd want to do is uproot her all over again." She held out her glass, which now contained only melting ice cubes. "Here, hit me again."

"You sure about that?" Pender asked her—the night before he'd had to help her back to bed (alone) after two shots.

"Right now I'm not sure of anything," said Irene.

"Welcome to the club," said Pender.

8

"Good night, Lyssy."

"Good night." The door to the blue room slid closed behind the squat, homely night nurse. No stalling, for a change—Lyssy still didn't care for the dark, but since his session with Dr. Al this afternoon he'd recovered some of his old optimism. Whatever happens, he thought, I can handle it.

He was even looking forward to the darkness, for the privacy it afforded him. With his optimism restored, he'd managed to convince himself that last night's runaway masturbatory fantasy had come about because he'd dozed off while jacking off—and as Dr. Al had often told him, none of us was responsible for our dreams. We all had depths and dark sides, Lyssy remembered him saying—you didn't have to be a multiple for that.

On with tonight's fantasy, then. Starring Lily, of course: after saving her by shooting a rabid dog that had come wandering up the dusty street of the town where they lived (an image conflated from *Old Yeller* and *To Kill a Mockingbird*), he had to help her back to her house. As soon as they were alone, she covered him with grateful kisses. Her jacket fell open—her breasts were naked beneath it. She pulled his face tightly against the round, warm, sweet-smelling softness. . . .

Lyssy. Time for you to go now, Lyssy. A dry, whispery, unbearably intimate voice, like acid eating through glass.

Startled from his fantasy, Lyssy opens his eyes and is shaken to see that the room has gone entirely black, blacker than it's ever been before. "Who's there?"

An old friend.

"You're not my friend. Now turn the night-light back on, you're scaring me, I don't like the dark."

Lyssy, Lyssy, Lyssy. The voice is pretend-sad. *Have you forgotten already?*

"Forgot what?"

How many worse things there are than darkness.

And suddenly there are flames everywhere, crackling flames, angry flames, searing, leaping, hungry flames. "No!" Lyssy cries, as the smell of roasting flesh fills his nostrils; his hands are clenched and burning. "Please—please, I'm sorry."

As abruptly as they had flared into existence, the flames are gone.

Sleep now, Lyssy.

The voice is gentler, soothing. The darkness is cool and comforting. Lyssy pulls it around himself like a blanket, like the folds in the fabric of space and time, and allows himself to drift away. . . .

A hand rubs a thigh for grounding, the eyes roll upward and to the right, and Max is back. The unaccustomed physical sensation sends a shudder through the body. *"My* dick," he whispers aloud, peeking under the covers. *"My* hand, *my* dick—and about fucking time."

For the last two and a half years, Max has confined himself to seeing through Lyssy's eyes and hearing through Lyssy's ears, but without sensation or control. This arrangement, which the psychiatrists call co-consciousness, is at best a skewed and distorted two-dimensional simulacrum of real life, like watching somebody else play a video game; at worst, it's a frustrating, helpless feeling, like riding in the passenger seat of a car that's heading toward a cliff.

But patience is the watchword, and that was something Max had had to cultivate, once he'd realized what the ECT sessions were doing to him. It wasn't just the headaches following the shock treatments, or the overall bone-deep soreness, as if his body had been tossed around in a giant Cuisinart, but rather the realization that he was gradually losing his memory, and along with it his identity (which basically speaking was all he had and all he was), that had finally convinced Max he couldn't beat Corder at his own game.

And why should he even try? he'd asked himself, after the third session. Why *fight* Lyssy for consciousness when the only way out of this madhouse for either of them was *through* Lyssy? All Max really had to do, he recognized eventually, was wait patiently while darling Lyssy earned the trust and even the love of Dr. Al and his staff, causing the security measures surrounding them to grow less stringent with every passing year.

But Lyssy has taken them as far as he can—to the very door of the director's residence, so to speak. All he can do between now and the party tomorrow night is screw it up by blurting out something incriminating.

So: to the dark place for Lyssy, and into the body for Max. He throws back the covers and hops into the bathroom on his crutches. The light goes on automatically; catching sight of his reflection in the slightly warped, unbreakable mirror over the sink, he breaks into a crooked grin. "Don't I know you from somewhere?" He cackles, then tries on his earnest, goofy Lyssy face—the one he's going to have to deploy nonstop for the next twenty-four hours or so.

"Hi there, Dr. Al, guess what time it is?" he chirps cheerfully, in Lyssy's voice, then leans closer to the mirror.

The grin fades, the eyes narrow and harden. "No, actually it's payback time, my friend," whispers Max. "With interest."

His mouth is dry as sandpaper. He fills a paper cup at the sink, glugs it down greedily. It's his first drink in two and a half years—he's forgotten how good something as simple as water can taste.

Pissing feels damn good, too. Lyssy the Sissy's been hogging all the good stuff, thinks Max, hopping back into the bedroom without washing up afterward (start with the little sins, he tells himself, work your way up).

He climbs back into bed and slides his scarred hand under the waistband of his pajama bottoms to take up where Lyssy had left off. But soon Lyssy's fantasy of rescue and passive sex is subsumed by Max's own, immeasurably darker fantasies of rage, rape, torture, and murder (which strictly speaking are not so much fantasies as memories), while Lyssy waits in the dark place, unable to escape for the same reason the dark place is so dark: because he has no body there. No eyes to see, no legs to run, and no voice with which to cry out.

CHAPTER FOUR

1

Lilith's headache is gone when she awakens the next morning. She discovers she can *think* again, and what she thinks about, with concentrated, pinpoint, laser-like intensity, is escape. Not *why* she needs to escape—for a limited consciousness like Lilith's, there are no whys. Somebody's raping you, you bite their nose off; somebody locks you up, you escape.

There is a complication, though: the need to keep Mullet Woman and the Mad Doctor from discovering her true identity, so to speak. It is imperative they continue to think of her as Lily. Because where Lilith gets a zillion volts of electricity through the brain, Lily gets her brow tenderly mopped. Where Lilith is under room arrest, Lily, eventually, will have the run of the hospital.

Unfortunately, Lilith knows very little about Lily.

She's rich, she lives in Pebble Beach, has a place in Puerto Vallarta; she has a mental disorder; her grandparents were recently killed in a car wreck—everything else will have to be improvised.

The door to her room slides open. "How're you feeling this morning?" asks Mullet Woman.

"Lots better," replies Lilith, mimicking as best she can the childish voice on Dr. Cogan's tape recorder. "A little sore, but at least my headache's gone."

"Good, good. Do you think you're up to having breakfast in the dining hall?"

"Sure," Lilith simpers. "I guess."

In Alan Corder's well-informed opinion, the better the food was in an institution, the less guilty rich people felt about committing their relatives. After a welcome in the spacious reception lobby, a turn around the arboretum followed by a meal in the dining hall had sealed many a deal for Dr. Al.

When Lilith and Patty reached the dining hall, a high-ceilinged, wood-paneled room with white tablecloths and a cafeteria-style counter, half a dozen white-clad nurses and psych techs on break or coming on or off duty were chowing down in great good humor at the largest table, laughing, gesticulating, spearing food from each other's plates. At a table for one sat a gray-haired man in wrinkled pajamas and limp seersucker bathrobe, chewing single-mindedly at a corner of toast. Somehow a pat of butter, backing paper attached, had managed to affix itself to the side of his head; as they passed him on their way to the counter, Patty reached down and plucked it away.

Food *and* free entertainment, thought Lilith—but she kept the joke to herself. Turning up her determined little nose at the precooked scrambled eggs in the chafing dish, she ordered two eggs fried sunny-side up, not dry but not runny either, and polished off a Danish and a cup of coffee while she was waiting.

By the time her eggs and Patty's flapjacks arrived, the room had emptied out until there were only two other diners present. At a corner table, sitting with a huge, curly-haired psych tech, was an oddly familiar-looking little guy in chinos and a dark blue corduroy shirt. Gorgeous, heart-shaped face, bowed cherub lips, and long-lashed, gold-flecked brown eyes. His hair too was brown—not the color people call brown because it's neither black nor blond, but a deep, rich nut-brown like Guinness ale.

Lilith was on the verge of asking Mullet Woman who he was when it occurred to her that perhaps the reason he looked familiar was that she had met him before, as Lily, at some point during the missing time between Monday morning, when Dr. Cogan gave her that needle behind the coffee shop in Weed, and Tuesday afternoon, when she'd awakened on the cross-shaped torture table with the mother of all headaches.

But while Lilith was trying to figure out a way to get the information she needed without giving herself away, the young man and his attendant rose to leave. On their way out, they stopped by the table where Lilith and Patty sat. The two psych techs exchanged hi's; the two patients locked eyes for a few milliseconds of the shortest, most intense staring contest in the history of the universe. Then the boyish-looking young man broke into a crooked grin. "Hi, 'member me? I'm Lyssy," he chirped. "I showed you around the arboretum the other day."

"Of course—how are you, Lyssy?"

"Pretty good. Hey, me and Wally, we're on our way to the arboretum. Do you guys wanna come? Is that okay with you, Patty?"

The attendants swapped meaningful glances; at the staff meeting that morning, Dr. Corder had instructed the psych techs to give Lyssy and Lily as much privacy as the dictates of security allowed. "I think we can arrange that," said Patty, through a mouthful of flapjacks. "Meet you at the gate in half an hour."

2

Irene Cogan opened her eyes to steely daylight. Across the room, dirty dishes were piled high on a room-service cart; there was an empty bottle of Jim Beam on the dresser. She groaned and sat up, pressing her palms tightly against the sides of her throbbing head as if she'd just glued the pieces of her skull back together and was waiting for the Elmer's to dry.

Looking down, she realized she had fallen

asleep in her sweatshirt and sweatpants, but didn't remember changing into them. From the adjoining room came a bubbling snort. Irene turned stiffly, rotating her torso along with her head so the pain wouldn't flare up, and discovered that the connecting door was wide open. Ohmigod! she thought, What *happened* last night? Then she saw the clock on the bedside table—8:15 A.M. Another heartfelt ohmigod!—she was supposed to be at the TV studio at 9:00.

On the toilet, in the shower, brushing her teeth, changing into the russet jacket and skirt outfit she'd worn Monday, making up her face, the question continued to bounce around in her head: What *happened* last night? Pender was no help—he was still sound asleep when Irene closed and locked the door between their rooms. And though she tried to pay attention to the cab driver as he explained why he was taking *this* bridge and not *that* bridge or some *other* bridge—apparently bridges were very important in Portland—the half of her brain that wasn't writing mind-screenplays about the upcoming interview was desperately trying to recall what had happened after that second glass of Jim Beam.

TPP Productions was housed in a converted warehouse close to the river. A production assistant met her at the reception desk and hustled her back to makeup, where a gum-chewing, big-haired cosmetician in her twenties admired her fair complexion, then all but obliterated it under pancake so she wouldn't fade into Casper the Friendly Ghost under the TV lights.

From makeup, Irene was led to a soundstage in the corner of the hangar-like building. The set was bare-bones: a lone wooden stool, a black curtain hanging in folds to provide a textured backdrop. Technicians crowded around, fussily posing and reposing her, turning the chair a few degrees to one side, then the other, holding light meters to her face, clipping a tiny lapel mike to her jacket and cautioning her not to touch it, darting forward to mop the sweat already beading up on her forehead—and cutting through the chaos, the voice of a pimply young man with a headset and clipboard ordering her to just relax and be herself.

Easy for *you* to say, thought Irene.

3

It's hard to imagine two personalities less alike than the pair who shared Ulysses Maxwell's mind. Where Lyssy was sunny and outgoing, as friendly and disingenuous as a puppy dog, Max was brooding and saturnine, with a sardonic wit and the compassion of a starving alley cat—if they hadn't occupied the same body, he'd have strangled the cheerful little bastard years ago.

In the good old days, in fact, Lyssy was only permitted consciousness when great pain or long periods of boredom had to be endured. The rest of the time the original personality was confined to the dark place, while in the external world his alter identities, under Max's direction, functioned together as a sort of strawberry blond processing plant. At one end was the charming Christopher, whose job it was to seduce them; waiting at the other end was Kinch the Knife.

But the other alters were gone now. Some had faded from existence while the body lay bleeding out on the floor of the barn at Scorned Ridge after being shot by Pender, while others had failed to return from their ECT sessions. Of that once-feared gang, only Max and Lyssy remained. In a way, thought Max, it was a lot like the end of the Arthurian legend, when the king and his page were all that were left of the mighty Round Table.

Only in his case, the king wasn't going to die—not if he was successfully able to masquerade as the page. And thus far Max had made it through his first meal in two and half years—his first crap in two and a half years, for that matter—without any of the staff noticing anything amiss. The cockteaser of a nurse Lyssy had dubbed Miss Stockings, the huge, dumb-as-a-sack-of-onions psych tech named Wally, even the sharp-eyed Patty Benoit—like most people, they saw whom they expected to see.

Not Max, though. The instant he and the girl in the dining hall had locked eyes that morning, he'd realized that she had to have undergone an alter switch since Lyssy had shown her around the arboretum Monday—otherwise there'd have been at least a glimmer of recognition on her part. And if it hadn't been for a challenging look in this new alter's eyes, something steely and questing and determined behind her momentary confusion, he'd have busted her on it then and there, maybe picked up some brownie points with the staff.

Instead, he'd bailed her out by prompting her with his name. And in just a few minutes, he told himself as the two of them set off down the sun-dappled path between the pines, followed at a respectable distance by their escorts, he'd find out whether fate had brought him a potential ally, or merely a momentary distraction.

Until they achieved a little more separation from the trailing psych techs, though, Max confined himself to vintage Lyssy-babble. "It's pretty here in the morning, hunh? Everything's so fresh and new. Of course, it's always pretty, even when it's raining. That's the neat thing about the arboretum, how it's different at different times of the day. My favorite is around sunset, when the sky and everything lights up like the pictures in this Maxfield Parrish book my art therapy tutor gave me. The violet hour, she called it. Only it's not always easy getting an escort that time of day, so. . . ."

They reached a point where the gravel path, bordered on the right by a seven-foot hedge, looped tightly around on itself like a paper clip. Max glanced over his shoulder—the escorts had dropped back out of sight. "Wanna play a trick on them?"

"Sure, I guess."

He took the girl's hand—how warm and alive it felt, like a small soft animal—and ducked lopsidedly through a gap in the hedge, good leg first, bad leg dragging. They rejoined the path on the other side.

Still clutching one of her hands in one of his, Max held the forefinger of his free hand to his lips as the psych techs strolled by on the other side of the hedge, uniforms flashing white through the dark green leaves, then tugged the girl back through the hedge as the psych techs disappeared around a sharp bend.

"They think *they're* behind *us,* but now *we're* behind *them,*" he whispered, his glance sliding downward to the swell of her breasts under a brown T-shirt the same color as her hair.

"Hey! Anybody ever tell you it was rude to stare?"

"I wasn't . . . I mean, I didn't mean to . . . " stammered Max, as Lyssy; if he could have forced a blush, he would have.

"Just messing with you," said the girl. "You like?"

"What's . . . what's not to like?"

"You want?" Taking his hand in both of hers, she pressed his scarred palm between her breasts, against her heart, which was thumping a mile a minute. Gone was the little girl whisper; the alter's true voice was low-pitched, with a husky, thrilling catch in it.

Staring directly into her eyes now, he cupped his palm under her right breast, stroked the stiffening nipple with his thumb. "I wouldn't throw you out of bed for eating potato chips," he whispered, using his own voice, the one that sounded like acid eating through glass, for the first time that day.

"Okay then," she said. "But there's something

you have to do for me first." Her breath was moist and sweet, her eyes so dark there was no border between pupil and iris.

"What's that?"

"Get me out of this fucking loony bin."

4

For three hours, Irene perched uncomfortably on a hard stool under hot lights, talking about things she'd just as soon have forgotten. She was disappointed to learn that Sandy Wells, the show's host, would not be present—she'd pictured him sitting across from her wearing one of his trademark leather jackets, his eyes narrowed like a gunslinger's and his bulldog jaw out-thrust, with not a hair of his gray, razor-cut head out of place.

Instead, questions and prompts were tossed at her, flat-voiced, by one of Wells's flunkies, Marti Reynolds, from a canvas-backed director's chair. Minutes into the taping, Irene realized that she and Ms. Reynolds had conflicting agendas. Irene would have preferred to discuss her kidnapping and subsequent ordeal from a psychiatrist's point of view—it was fascinating stuff, as far as she was concerned: a close, extended, and unprecedented look at dissociative identity disorder, with a side trip into psychopathy—and to remain emotionally detached while doing so.

But what Wells, Reynolds, and presumably the

television audience, wanted to hear about was how it felt to be kidnapped, held hostage during an extended killing spree, and threatened with rape and murder—in short, what was it like being a victim? Within that context, of course, Irene was expected to present herself in a courageous light—Wells and his audience liked their victims spunky—although a few reluctant tears wouldn't have been unwelcome.

In the end, the only thing that made the interview tolerable for Irene was the advice Pender had given her: if you don't like a question, ignore it—answer the question that should have been asked instead. So when Reynolds wanted to know how Irene had felt when she came within a whisker of being murdered by the homocidal alter known as Kinch, she responded with, "Kinch? Oh, Kinch was a real piece of work. Pure id, pure rage. All the anger Lyssy felt at his years of abuse, but was unable to express for fear of retaliation, seemed to have been concentrated in the persona of Kinch. When the alter known as Max killed, it was for necessity, convenience, or sheer enjoyment; when Kinch killed, it was because he couldn't do otherwise. He was more of a weapon than a viable personality. *Kinch,* I've been told, means blade in Gaelic, and in a very real way, Kinch was little more than the continuation of the knife in his hand."

They broke for lunch at noon—Irene was invited to fill a plate from the backstage buffet known for some reason as the crafts table. After eating, she took her cell phone outside and tried calling Lily again. The room phone rang and rang, then kicked back to the switchboard. Irene left yet another message, then asked to speak to the director, reached his secretary instead, and left a message with her.

By this time her disaster-movie screenwriter—you don't have to be a multiple to have one—was hard at work coming up with various explanations for the communications failure. Lily had switched alters; escaped; turned catatonic or autistic; was trying to reach Irene but being held incommunicado to prevent her from revealing Corder's methods; and so on.

Then Irene's scenarist turned to her other current project. What *Happened* Last Night? was the working title. Please don't let me have made a fool of myself again, she thought as she selected Pender's cell number in her own phone's address-book file, then pushed Call.

"Hello?"

"Pen?"

"Oh, hi, Irene. How's the interview going?"

"Not bad—as long as I don't pay any attention to the questions, of course."

Pender laughed. "As my sister Ida would have said, 'Truer words were never.' " Then: "Any particular reason you called, Irene?"

"Nothing important. I was just wondering . . . ?"

"Unh-hunh?"

"About last night . . . ?"

"Unh-hunh?"

"Did, did I . . . ? did we . . . ? I mean, did anything . . . ?"

"Whoa, whoa, whoa, hold it right there," Pender

interrupted her. "We're two consenting adults, you don't have *anything* to apologize for. I admit, I thought it was a bad idea when you invited the maid and the room service kid to take off their clothes and join us, but I have to confess, I really enjoyed it."

A few seconds ticked by. Irene's sandwich turned to mucilage in her mouth. Then the light dawned. "Damn it, Pender, you really had me going there for a minute."

Pender chuckled. "You passed out about halfway through *Abbott and Costello Meet Frankenstein* and three-quarters through your fourth shot of Jim Beam. Your last words, as I recall, were something like, 'This stuff kinda grows on you.' "

Irene shook her head ruefully. "You're a bad influence, Pen."

"And proud of it. Have fun this afternoon."

"You too," replied Irene. She pressed the End Call button, then returned to the address-book screen and tried to reach Lily one more time.

5

The girl was waiting with Patty Benoit at the same table as before, her back to the roomful of loonies and staff and her creamy dark hair all tumbled down over her shoulders.

As Max limped toward them carrying his lunch tray, his features arranged into Lyssy's chuckle-headed grin, suddenly it struck him, with a sense of irony about as subtle as a bowling ball, that he had no idea whether this was Lily, the simpering original personality, or Lilith, the alter he'd met a few hours ago. And when she looked up and met his eyes, he realized—here came that bowling ball again—that *she* must be wondering the same thing about *him.*

"We probably should have worked out a password," he whispered, a good deal more casually than he felt, as soon as they were alone—Patty had joined Wally at a nearby table to give them their privacy.

Whoosh. The tension left her body like air rushing out of a punctured balloon. "I was just thinking the same thing."

"Did you hear? Corder gave the okay for you to come to my party tonight."

"I heard. The bad news is, Mullet Woman there is coming with me."

"You think you can handle her?"

"If I could handle Swervin' Mervin, I can handle her. But we won't have much time for pin the tail on the donkey. According to Patty, we're only gonna be there two hours, tops, and the way I figure, we're gonna need most of that for a head start." Lilith glanced over to the psych techs' table to see how closely they were being watched, then took a big, two-handed bite out of her juicy-rare cheeseburger. "What's the matter? You look disappointed," she said with her mouth full.

"I've been looking forward to my payback for years," he replied. "There is no conceivable way I'm going to rush it, head start or no head start."

Lilith looked him in the eye—not the easiest

thing to do. "Maybe you ought to rethink your priorities."

"Revenge *is* the priority," Max whispered, leaning across the table—they were sitting catty-corner from each other—and dabbing a spot of ketchup from the corner of her mouth with his own napkin.

At the neighboring table, the burly psych techs exchanged knowing glances. "Don't they make a cute couple?" said Wally.

Patty grinned. "Multiples in love," she said. "Imagine the possibilities."

6

The message-waiting button on the in-room telephone was blinking when Lilith returned to the observation suite after lunch to wait out the last few hours of her captivity—the less contact with the staff, she and Max had agreed, the slimmer the chances of their respective masquerades being uncovered.

Lilith picked up the handset, pressed the lighted button, and was informed by the switchboard operator that Dr. Cogan had called her again—twice. Lilith thanked her. Yeah, I'll get right back to her, she thought. When hell needs a Zamboni.

She hung up the phone and lay down, looking up at the ceiling. The acoustic tiles were white and textured like the surface of the moon—Lilith discovered that if she held her breath and let her eyes drift out of focus, it felt as if, instead of lying on her back looking up, she was skimming low over that desolate moonscape, looking down at a land of barren white rocks and sharp black shadows. . . .

Four o'clock. Another hour to kill. Max's skin was beginning to crawl. He sat up, looked around the little blue room for something to occupy his mind. Lyssy's books, most of them Christmas or birthday presents from Dr. Al, were chronologically arrayed on a recessed shelf, ranging left to right from the Suesses and Sendaks suitable for the three-year-old mentality with which Lyssy had arrived, through the Robert Louis Stevensons and Harry Potters of his so-called childhood, to the required high school reading—*Catcher in the Rye, To Kill a Mockingbird,* and the rest of that aging canon.

But there was nothing Max might have chosen for himself. No Stephen King, no Thomas Harris, no true crime or graphic novels—in short, nothing to engage the interest of your average American adolescent, not to mention a thirty-one—no, thirty-*two*-year-old sociopathic alter.

Ditto for the pitiful collection of PG-rated videos Lyssy had accrued over the last few years. *Charlotte's Web, Old Yeller, The Princess Bride, Time Bandits.* Max tried watching television for a little while, but sitting there staring at the screen was too much like being in co-consciousness. He limped over to the window. From here, he could see a sliver of the tiled roof of the director's residence peeking through the arboretum pines.

His thoughts drifted back to the last time he and Lyssy had been over there. It had been, what, six, eight weeks ago? The girl, Alison, had taken Lyssy up to her room, ordered his attendant to wait outside. She and Lyssy sat together on her little bed while she gushed on and on about her new boyfriend, some lummox from the football team. From her point of view Lyssy might as well have been one of the cute little stuffed animals propped up against the headboard, but life-size, with a marvelous ability to nod on cue.

Things would be different tonight, though, Max promised himself. His hand found its way into his trouser pocket and he began fondling himself through the fabric, thinking about how soon all that sweet pink virginal softness would be his. And if revenge was indeed the priority, it would be doubly—no, triply sweet. Because the suffering he'd be inflicting directly on Corder, the fear, the pain, even the man's death, would be chump change compared to the sheer delight of drinking in Dr. Al's helplessness and humiliation as he watched his wife and daughter being raped and tortured. That, as they say in the credit card commercials, was going to be priceless.

And it would be only the beginning. Though their plan called for Lilith and Max to lie low with her biker friends until the heat died down, afterward there would be plenty of opportunity to settle old scores, and plenty of old scores to settle. Pender, for instance, the fat old G-man who'd gunned him down three years ago, costing him his leg and very nearly his life—Max would definitely be looking *him* up.

Then there was Dr. Irene Cogan, who'd almost become the last of the strawberry blonds to go through the processing plant. But Max, after breaking out of the Monterey County Jail, hadn't kidnapped her and brought her up to Scorned Ridge for her hair, but rather for her professional services. He'd been having trouble controlling the other alters—that's how he'd been captured in the first place—and figured that with the help of a good psychiatrist, he could tighten his hegemony over the system.

And like everyone he'd ever trusted, she'd turned on him. Taken his confidences and ground them into the dirt. Talk about a breach of professional ethics—just thinking about her had his free hand tightening around the hilt of an imaginary knife.

But grasping even an imaginary knife was a mistake—suddenly, in his mind's eye, Max pictured Kinch sitting up in the darkness like a corpse rising from an open coffin, and his half-hearted erection wilted like a week-old stalk of celery. . . .

A telephone rang. From the twilight land halfway between dreaming and waking, Lilith reached out and fumbled the receiver off the hook. "H'lo?" she murmured, cotton-mouthed from sleep.

"Lily?" A not-unfamiliar female voice jarred Lilith into full consciousness.

Oh fuck, she thought. "Dr. Cogan?"

"Yes, I— Wait a minute, who is this?"

Double fuck—Lilith realized suddenly that she'd used her own voice. She faked a cough, tried again. "Sorry, I must have had something stuck in my throat."

She waited for a response, heard only a puzzled silence, hastened to fill it. "Listen, Dr. Cogan, I really want to tell you about everything that's been happening, but now's not a good time, 'cause . . . " She glanced at the clock-radio bolted to the nightstand: 5:15 P.M.—she'd slept the afternoon away. " 'Cause I'm just getting ready for dinner. Maybe I could call you back later tonight. How's that? Or come to think of it, tomorrow morning'd be even better. I'll call you back first thing tomorrow morning, I promise."

Lilith hung up without waiting for a reply. The phone began ringing again; when it stopped, she took the receiver off the hook and went into the bathroom to splash cold water on her face.

7

After showering, Max dried and powdered his stump. He loathed the sight of it—the way the surgeon had drawn a flap of skin underneath the femur and reattached it to the back of the thigh with a sort of tucked-in curl made it look a little like a shrimp's head.

His newest prosthetic leg was handsome, though, with a locking knee-joint and a contoured pink calf instead of a stark titanium rod. It was held on by suction, too—no more cumbersome harness. And once he was dressed (Lyssy's favorite outfit, comfortable chinos and a dove-gray corduroy shirt, gray socks, black sneakers) there was no way anybody could tell him apart from a two-legged man—at least as long as he was standing still.

Just after five o'clock, Wally arrived. He'd changed from his hospital whites into baggy shorts and a green bowling shirt worn unbuttoned over a ribbed wife-beater undershirt. Sandals, no socks—the *Big Lebowski* look. "Happy birthday, dude," he said, producing a small gift-wrapped box from behind his back. "That's from the whole staff—we all chipped in."

Max tore it open greedily—it was an MP3 player, with earphones and software. "Wow," he Lyssy'd. "Wow, thanks, this is—I don't know what to say."

"We thought it would come in handy in— Well, you know."

In jail, thought Max. Yeah, I know.

Patty and Lilith were waiting for them at the arboretum gate. Patty too had changed out of her whites, into a denim shirt and wide-bottomed jeans with the seat worn shiny. Lilith was wearing the tight hip-hugger jeans she'd arrived in, and a dark-brown, V-neck, cashmere sweater that showed both her figure and her glossy brown hair to best advantage.

Patty gave Lyssy a hug and wished him happy

birthday. Lilith kept her eyes trained on the ground as she wished him the same. Little girl voice, diffident posture—but was it a disguise, or had the alter switched back to her original personality since lunch? Once again, Max realized that he had no way of knowing for sure.

"We never did work out that password, did we?" he whispered out of the side of his mouth, as he and the girl walked on ahead together, trailed at a distance of ten yards or so by their escorts.

"What password?" said the girl. "Who are you, anyway?"

8

Irene had finally managed to contact Lily from the taxicab, she told Pender when she returned to the hotel. Only it wasn't Lily, she went on to explain, it couldn't have been. "She called me Dr. Cogan. She's never called me Dr. Cogan—not once in all these years. It's been Dr. Irene this, Dr. Irene that from the time she was four."

"Dr. Cogan is probably what Corder calls you," suggested Pender, who was wearing his horseblanket-plaid slacks and a periwinkle polo shirt. "Maybe she picked it up from him."

"And the way she rushed through the call, like she couldn't get rid of me fast enough? I'm telling you, it was Lilith, it had to have been. And the only reason she'd be trying to trick me into thinking she's

Lily is if she had something up her sleeve—something like, say, escaping?"

"Well gosh, Irene, in that case maybe we ought to get her moved to some kind of maximum-security facility where— Oh, wait a minute, I just remembered—she's already *in* one."

She blew him a juicy raspberry. "Not funny, Pender."

"M'dear, you spent half of last night talking my ear off about how hard a time you were having letting go of Lily, but how you knew it was the right thing for both of you. You sure this isn't just more of the same?"

"I don't know, maybe you're right, Pen. Only. . . ." Sitting on the edge of the bed, scarcely aware of what she was doing, Irene had unwrapped a complimentary pillow mint and popped it into her mouth before she remembered she couldn't stand the taste of peppermint. Genteelly, she spat it out into a tissue, and tossed the tissue into the wastebasket.

"Only what?" prompted Pender.

"If I were Al Corder, I'd want to be told."

"Call him, then."

"I tried, but he must have left for the day—all I got was his voice mail. They won't give me his home number either—it's unlisted."

Pender's cetaceous brow creased in thought. "I could be missing something here, but if Corder's already left for the day, maybe he's not the person you need to talk to. Our flight's at ten-thirty, right?"

"Yes, but we're supposed to be at the airport no later than nine thirty. Oh, and I got us an extension on the checkout time, but we still have to be out of our rooms by six-thirty at the latest or we'll get charged for an extra night."

"Which gives us a couple hours to kill. We might as well stop by the hospital after dinner, see if we can wangle a visit with Lily. If not, maybe we could talk to whoever's in charge, give 'em a heads-up. At the very least, it'll be one less thing for you to worry about. How's that for a plan?"

"How about *before* dinner," Irene suggested.

"Fair enough," said Pender. "Can I have your other mint?"

CHAPTER FIVE

1

Al Corder changed into khaki slacks and a soft old blue-and-brown-checked flannel shirt, worn tails-out to cover his paunch, then he transferred the contents of his pockets—wallet, coins, fifty bucks in a $-shaped money clip, a hospital pager, and a Swiss Army knife—from the suit pants to either the khakis or the top of the bureau. As he tossed the suit into the dry-cleaning pile in the closet, Cheryl emerged from the bathroom in her slip and began rummaging through her bureau.

"You done in the bathroom?" he asked her, patting her plump rear as he brushed past her.

"Yeah, go ahead."

But he quickly doubled back, stooped in a Groucho Marx crouch, to ogle the white breasts dangling fatly beneath the thin fabric of her slip as she bent over to search the bottom drawer of her bureau. "Why, I haven't seen a pair of melons like that since they closed the farmers' market." He waggled his eyebrows and tapped the ash from an imaginary cigar.

"Steady there," said Cheryl, but she allowed her husband a quick fondle before changing into a dark blue skirt and a white cotton blouse with a moderate neckline—over the last year or so, she'd caught Lyssy staring at her chest with more than passing interest. She crossed the hall and rapped at Alison's door. "You almost ready, honey?"

Alison opened the door wearing below-the-navel jeans and a skintight sleeveless top that barely reached the bottom of her rib cage. "Oh, Allie, you're not wearing that, are you?"

The girl looked down at herself. "Well, yeah, Mom—I appear to be," she observed drily.

"At least put on a sweater."

"I'm not cold."

"It's not *your* temperature I'm worried about," her mother retorted.

While mother and daughter fought their age-old battle, father ran an electric razor over his five-o'clock shadow, then splashed on some Old Spice aftershave, which he preferred to the designer brands his wife and daughter continued to give him every Father's Day. Cheryl and Alison were still arguing in the hallway when he left the bedroom. "Holy cow, is that what you're wearing?" he asked Alison guilelessly.

"I'm not a baby anymore!" she shouted. "Why don't the two of you just grow up!"

2

It took Max a few seconds to recover from his near-coronary over Lilith's ostensible failure to recognize him.

"Just messin' with your head," she told him with a wink and a grin.

"If you *ever* do that again, I swear I'll—"

But the psych techs had caught up to them. "Let's get moving, Lyssy," said Wally. "You don't want to be late to your own party."

The sky was Portland pewter, with a fitful summer breeze rustling through the pines as the patients and their escorts hiked through the arboretum. Wally unlocked the gate; the little procession ducked through the arch-topped door set into the spike-topped brick wall.

Everything felt different on the other side. The openness, the wide lawn, the heavenly smell of new-mown grass, the rusting swing set, the clothes drying on the line—a delighted Max spread his arms and turned in a clumsy circle, like a Bizarro-World version of Julie Andrews in *The Sound of Music.* "Wa-ow," he said—the two-syllable *wow* was the cornerstone of his Christopher Walken impression.

"Wow what?" said Lilith.

Max glanced around to be sure the psych techs weren't watching. "No walls," he whispered. "No fuckin' walls."

Silver cardboard letters spelling out Happy Birthday dangled crazily from a string across the top of the front doorway of the director's residence; it was the director himself who answered the bell. "The gals are in the kitchen preparing the, ah, birthday repast," Alan Corder announced as he ushered the four of them inside. Lilith said she wanted to help, so Patty accompanied her into the kitchen. Soon, Max mouthed to Lilith as they parted; she nodded curtly and turned away.

But just how soon, not even Max could have predicted. The menfolk had just repaired to the living room, which was decorated with helium balloons and crepe-paper party streamers. Corder was still at the sideboard fixing their drinks—orange soda on the rocks for Wally and "Lyssy"; a weak Scotch and soda for himself—when Patty and Lilith passed the living room on their way upstairs.

"Everything all right?" called Corder.

"Lily's feeling a little queasy," replied Patty. "Mrs. Corder said for us to use the guest bathroom."

Five, ten minutes later—Max was on the sofa sipping his soda; Corder and Wally were in the matching green leather recliners that flanked the fireplace—Lilith returned alone. "Patty had to take a dump. She said for me to wait for her down here," she announced as she plopped onto the sofa next to Max, breathing hard.

Damn, he thought, be a little more careful with your language, would you? *Take a dump* was pure Lilith, not like Lily at all. But Wally and Corder didn't seem to notice anything amiss—they were too busy talking shop. Without mentioning names, Wally seemed to be complaining about one of the other psych techs, who was not, in Wally's opinion, pulling his fair share of the load. As Corder promised to look into it, Lilith slipped something into the crack between the sofa cushions. Max shifted position to cover the motion with his thigh as he reached down and felt—

A knife. A steak knife with a sharp serrated blade a good four inches in length. Obviously Lilith had purloined it from a cabinet drawer while she was in the kitchen earlier. But as his fingers closed around the handle, Max sensed Kinch stirring in the darkness. Quickly Max slid the knife point-first into the front pocket of his chinos, and the stirring subsided.

And now the ball was in his court. "Hey, Wally?"

"Yeah, Lyss?"

"I think maybe I have to go to the little boy's room." Infantile, sure—but *very* Lyssy.

"You can use the one off the kitchen," said Corder.

So far, so good. Max led the way; Wally followed close behind. "Hi, Lyssy, happy birthday, don't peek," called Alison as they passed through the kitchen. She was wearing one of her trampy Britney Spears outfits under an oversize letter sweater; she and her mother closed ranks in front of the kitchen table in order to hide the slightly lopsided birthday cake they were decorating.

A dark hallway led from the kitchen to the back door, with a pantry on the right and the bathroom door on the left. Max glanced behind him, past Wally, to make sure they were both well out of sight of the women in the kitchen, then grasped the doorknob and rattled it, as though the door were stuck or locked.

"Here, let me," said Wally. Max stepped aside, slipping his hand into his pocket and palming the knife. Wally opened the door easily. "There you go," he said, turning back to Max.

"And there *you* go," said Max, as a gash like a second mouth sprouted under Wally's chin, a ghastly, ear-to-ear grin spurting blood at both ends. Wally's hands flew to his throat; blood welled through his clutching fingers as he dropped to his knees, staring up at Max with one of the saddest, most surprised expressions Max had ever seen—and he'd seen quite a few in his day.

It was over in seconds. When he stooped to wipe the blade clean on Wally's shorts, Max caught a glimpse of the wristwatch on the corpse's outflung arm, and discovered to his surprise that it wasn't even quarter to six. Less than fifteen minutes had elapsed since they first entered the house, and yet the most difficult and potentially dangerous aspect of tonight's business had already been successfully negotiated.

Which meant he might be able to enjoy the next part, the *real* fun part, in relative leisure. "Hey, Wal," he said aloud, as Lyssy. "You know what, I think this is going to be the best birthday party ever!"

3

Pender parked the rent-a-car at the curb. The front doors of the Institute were open, but the grand lobby was largely deserted, and a security guard with Elvis sideburns now sat behind the reception desk. "Evening," he said.

"Good evening," said Irene; Pender nodded.

"Can I help you?"

"Yes, I need to . . . Well, to . . . " To what? Irene found herself wishing she'd thought this out a little more carefully on the way over. "Is Dr. Corder available, by any chance? I know it's—"

The guard tapped a few strokes on a keyboard hidden beneath the high counter. "Sorry, he signed out an hour ago," he said unhelpfully; *your move,* read his expression.

"All right, well, here's the thing," said Irene, then paused, momentarily appalled. Here's the thing? She thought: how very glib! She soldiered on. "My name is Irene Cogan. *Dr.* Irene Cogan. I'm a psychiatrist."

"Unh-hunh?" the guard grunted, with a rising inflection, as if to say, go on, this ought to be good.

"One of my patients—my former patients—is a patient here now," she went on, trying not to sound quite so much like a potential customer herself. "Her name is Lily DeVries—is there any chance I might be able to see her?"

He consulted the computer again, shook his head. "Sorry, I don't seem to find you on the list."

"It'd only be for a second. I just want to—"

He cut her off. "Sorry. My orders are that all visitors have to be approved in advance by the patient's doctor."

"I understand," said Irene. "But here's the . . . " Whoops, she thought, and tried again. "Here's the situation: I have some important information about Lily that her doctor needs to know."

"And her doctor is . . . ?"

"Dr. Corder is handling her case personally."

"Then you should probably call him in the morning, because there's nothing I can do for you tonight."

"Oh, sure there is," said Pender pleasantly but firmly; they were the first words he'd spoken since they'd entered.

"And you are?"

"E. L. Pender, Special Agent Emeritus, Federal Bureau of Investigation." He was, of course, counting on the guard having no idea what *emeritus* meant. "And what you can do for us," he continued, without raising his voice, "and for yourself, assuming you'd like to keep your current position, or ever hold another job in the security industry, is get on the horn to whoever's in charge of this facility at the present moment, and get him or her down here asap—that's alpha sierra alpha papa, as in immediately, toot sweet, and pronto, do you copy?"

"Sure, whyn't you say so in the first place?" grumbled the guard, turning his back to the visitors and picking up the telephone.

"Very impressive," whispered Irene.

Pender winked. "Well, you know what Harry Truman said when he gave the order to drop the bomb on Hiroshima: 'Sometimes you just have to get their attention.' "

9

Strained small talk in the living room:

"Are you enjoying your stay so far, Lily?"

"Yes, very much, thank you, Dr. Corder."

"Everybody treating you all right?"

"Oh yeah, everybody couldn't be nicer."

"Good, good." Thoughtful nod. "Can I get you something to drink?"

"Do you have any Dubonnet?"

"I was thinking more in terms of something, ah, nonalcoholic."

"That's okay, never mind."

Corder checked his watch. "Maybe I'd better go see what's keeping everyone," he said, but before he could push himself up from the deep recliner, his wife came stumbling through the archway, with a blood-spattered Ulysses Maxwell shuffling in lockstep behind her, holding a knife to her throat with one hand, half-dragging young Alison by her long blond hair with the other.

"Lyssy, what are you doing? Have you lost your mind?"

An amused glance, a barking laugh. "I'm afraid Lyssy is no longer with us, Dr. Al."

"Who—who are you?" Corder managed to choke the words out.

"What's the matter, don't you recognize me, Doc?" he said, slinging Alison to the floor.

"Oh, God," Corder moaned. "God, no."

The familiar-looking stranger chuckled. "I'm afraid He's no longer with us, either."

5

Martín Cohen was a short, tidy-looking, brown-skinned Hispanic in dark slacks, a short-sleeved white shirt, and a powder-blue bowtie. He looked awfully young to Irene—scarcely old enough to be one of her students.

"Sorry for the delay—I was just getting ready to make my rounds," he said in a pleasantly textured Mexican accent as he ushered Irene and Pender over to a three-armchair grouping in the lobby and turned up the dimmer switch on a tall floor lamp with an upside-down frosted-glass shade. "I'm Dr. Cohen. Senior resident. Please, have a seat."

"I'm Irene Cogan, this is Agent Pender. We won't take up much of your time, I promise," said Irene; she and Pender sat across a low round table from each other, flanking Cohen.

"I appreciate it. I gather this is about your former patient, Miss DeVries?"

"You're familiar with the case?"

"I'm familiar with all our cases," he said, glancing pointedly at his wristwatch. "Please, go on."

"Here's the situation. I've been trying to contact Lily by phone for two days—unsuccessfully. But I finally spoke to her about . . . " She glanced at her own watch. ". . . a little over an hour ago, and I had a very strong impression that it wasn't Lily I was speaking with, it was one of her alter personalities."

"I see," said Cohen; to Irene it sounded more like so what?

She understood his point of view. A patient's erstwhile doctor shows up after hours insisting that her erstwhile patient has been displaying symptoms of the disorder for which she'd been admitted in the first place—not exactly earth-shattering news.

But Irene persevered, making the same points she'd made earlier to Pender, and eventually, to his credit, Cohen caught on. Curtly, he excused himself to make a phone call, leaving Irene and Pender waiting in the lobby. When he returned a few minutes later, it was to Pender that he addressed himself. "I understand you're with the FBI?"

"For almost thirty years," said Pender ambiguously.

"Okay, sure, well, the reason I ask, we may have a small problem here." He told them about the birthday party at the director's residence. "There's probably no reason to worry—Walter and Patricia are very experienced psych techs, nobody's going to pull a fast one on them. Only when I call over there, there's no answer, nobody's picking up the phone, and Dr. Corder, he's not answering his pager. I'll keep trying, but I was wondering, just to err on the side of caution, if you wouldn't mind maybe going over there, make sure everything's okay?"

"Of course." Pender's turn to glance at *his* watch. "How far is it?"

"Right around the corner," said Cohen.

"I know where it is," added Irene. "C'mon, I'll show you."

6

Max wasn't just being a wise guy when he'd made his earlier crack about God no longer being around. Even in co-consciousness, he had always enjoyed attending the nondenominational services held in the little chapel next to the dining hall every Sunday morning—after all, nothing supports the contention that the Creator has indeed abandoned His creation quite so powerfully as a sparsely attended service in a madhouse.

But if additional proof had been required, the tableau of a helpless girl sobbing at her father's feet while Max held a knife to her mother's throat would surely have supplied it, he thought, as Lilith raced around the house locking doors, drawing blinds, ripping the telephones from their sockets.

She returned carrying a length of clothesline from the laundry room, with a hunting knife in a sheath stuck in the waistband of her low-rider jeans—unfortunately, she reported, there were no firearms to be found. Max switched hostages, tossing the mother to the floor, then dragging the girl to her feet and holding the steak knife to *her* throat while Lilith tied the parents together back-to-back with coil upon coil of polyester clothesline.

"My Swiss Army knife's in my front pocket," Corder whispered to his wife as Lilith and Maxwell conferred across the room. His plan, such as it was, was four-fold. One, get the little knife out—it wasn't much of a weapon, but it was all he had. Two, get Max close enough to drop a little bomb in his ear. Three: take advantage of subsequent confusion by inserting knife into Maxwell. And four: repeat step three as necessary.

"Hey, you two—no talking," ordered Max, quickly slipping the steak knife back into his pocket—Kinch was stirring again in the darkness. "I don't want to have to gag you—I'd much rather hear you moan while I do your little girl—but I will if I have to."

Do your little girl—hearing the words, Alison went limp. Max lowered her sagging body to the carpet. "You a virgin, honey?" he asked pleasantly.

Alison moaned; Cheryl slumped backward against her husband.

"Please, Max, you're making a terrible mistake," said Corder, desperately trying to buy time; in the guise of collapsing against him, Cheryl had worked her hand into his pocket. "Even if you escape, how long before they, ah, they recapture you? And what kind of a life will you have out there on the run?"

As he spoke, he and Cheryl inched their bodies around so that he was facing Max; shielded by his back, Cheryl had withdrawn the knife from his pocket, opened the longer blade (not an easy trick one-handed), and was trying to saw through the coils of rope one at a time without being too obvious about it. Not that Max or Lilith were paying much attention to them. Max was kneeling beside the apparently unconscious Alison, trying to bring her around by fanning her with a magazine from the coffee table, while Lilith snatched up a pillow from the sofa and slipped it under the younger girl's head.

Cheryl kept sawing, Corder kept talking. He felt the last coils slackening; any second now, he'd be able to free his hands. "Enough to make it worth your while spending the rest of your life in some maximum security prison? Because that's what's going to happen. All these years, I've been the only one standing between you and the penitentiary—possibly even a death sentence. But if you lay a finger on my daughter, I won't protect you anymore. Do you understand me?"

Max glanced toward them; his eyes widened in alarm. "God-*damn*-it!" he shouted, taking out the steak knife again and limping across the room. He looked over Corder's shoulder, saw the knife in Cheryl's hand, the cut coils. "Naughty, naughty," he said.

Their faces were only inches apart; though his hands weren't free yet, Corder realized he had to make his move now. "Lyssy is a *goood* boy," he said, firmly but soothingly, then repeated the code phrase: "Lyssy is a *goood* boy."

Whoa shit, thought Max—he hadn't seen *that* coming. Kinch roared in his ears; his consciousness seemed to be flowing downward, toward the knife in his hand. There's going to be hell to pay, he told himself as he rushed toward darkness. Absolute hell.

Wssh-wssh, wssh-wssh . . .

A soft, whisking sound. Lyssy glanced down and

discovered he was making the noise himself, brushing the back of his hand against the thigh of his chinos. Grounding behavior, he thought—one of the alters has been paying a visit. Uh-oh—don't let Dr. Al find out.

He looked around, found himself sitting on the bottom of the front stairs at the director's residence. No idea how he'd gotten here, or how much time had passed since . . . since when? He vaguely remembered a voice like dried corn husks whispering in his ear, then flames, then cool, cool darkness—but all that had to have been a dream, it just had to.

Lyssy took inventory. His right shoulder was so sore he could scarcely lift his arm, and his clothes were spattered with ketchup or food coloring or something.

Suddenly the silence in the room was broken by a beeping noise coming from the Corder's living room. A hospital pager—he would have recognized the sound anywhere. But before he could get up, he heard footsteps behind him. He turned, saw his beautiful new friend Lily coming down the stairs wearing a brown sweater and tight-fitting jeans, holding one hand behind her back as if to hide something.

By now, Lyssy had concluded only that this had to have been the birthday party he'd been waiting for. But he was utterly clueless as to how long he'd been out of it, which alter had surfaced and done what to whom, or why his clothes were all stained and spattered. In any event, the usual imperative was in play: fake it as long as you can, hope nobody noticed anything out of what passed for the ordinary around here. "Oh, hi," he said. "Been upstairs, hunh?"

She came closer, peered deeply into Lyssy's eyes as though she were looking for something—or someone. "You're fucking with my head, right? To get even for before, in the arboretum."

"If you say so," said Lyssy with a weak chuckle.

Her dark eyes narrowed, then widened again in recognition. "Lyssy?"

"Who else?"

"Oh, swell." In the living room, the beeping started up again. The girl sheathed the hunting knife she was holding behind her back, took a key ring from her pocket. Dr. Al's key ring—something else Lyssy would have recognized anywhere. "C'mon, let's get outta here."

"I—I can't. I'm not supposed to leave the premises."

"Fine by me," said the girl contemptuously. "Stay here and rot, see if I care."

7

This is ridiculous, Irene decided as the car pulled up in front of the director's residence after a journey of fifty, maybe seventy-five yards from the hospital around the corner. It was such a pleasant midsummer evening, after all, with the smell of new-mown grass in the air. Al Corder's going to open the door,

Irene told herself, look at us like *what the hell?* and there we'll be, standing on the doorstep with egg on our faces.

But the house was dead quiet and the curtains and blinds drawn upstairs and down. No response when Irene rang the bell, though she and Pender could hear the pretentious, two-toned chimes resounding through the house—*Bing-bong, bing-bong.* "They're not answering," she said, unnecessarily.

"See if it's locked."

The knob turned easily in her hand, the sturdy, handsomely brass-bound oak door swung open under the Happy Birthday banner. "Age before beauty," said Pender, shouldering past Irene with a humorless smile. "Wait here, okay? Just til we know what's what."

She understood he was trying to protect her, but even knowing there was something in her personality that both appreciated and elicited that behavior from him, she resented it, and hurried after him.

But he'd only gone as far as the arched, crepe paper-festooned entrance to the Corder's living room. "Oh, dear God," she said, looking away quickly—but not quickly enough to prevent the sight from burning itself into her memory. For Al and Cheryl Corder were propped up back-to-back beneath the cheerful birthday bunting and bobbing balloons, bound with coils of rope, their clothes and bodies slashed and shredded, minced flesh and shockingly white bone visible through tatters of bloody cloth, and their faces unrecognizable, so gashed and gouged the features had been all but obliterated. And so much blood—the furniture, the walls, the fireplace, the inside of the curtains, the once-beige carpet, now a Jackson Pollock in crimson and black; even some of the crepe-paper streamers were spattered with gore. *Kinch,* she mouthed—she'd intended to say it aloud, but no sound emerged.

Pender heard the noise first: an insistent, rhythmic thumping somewhere overhead. He touched a forefinger to his lips, then pointed to the ceiling. When she realized that something or someone was still up there, still inside the house, Irene was torn between a powerful urge to flee and an equally powerful, almost physical need to stick close to Pender.

But it was no contest, really, not with Maxwell back in her world. The first few months after her kidnapping Irene had kept all the shades drawn in her home, even on the second floor, because she couldn't pass an outside window without imagining his grinning face popping up like a jack-in-the-box. Mirrors were no good either—for a while there, she couldn't even sit at her vanity for fear she'd see him in the mirror, over her shoulder—and dark rooms were totally unacceptable: her PG&E bill had nearly doubled by the time autumn rolled around. And all that despite knowing Maxwell was locked up in a maximum security facility and couldn't possibly get at her.

So what *was* the prognosis for PTSD patients who find themselves back in a war zone? Irene asked herself as she hurried after Pender, who had already started up the stairs, moving quietly on his rubber-soled Hush Puppies.

She caught up to him on the second floor landing and followed him so closely down the dusky hallway that she could smell his aftershave. The thumping emanated from behind a closed door with a sign reading *My* Room, *My* Mess, *My* Business. Pender gestured for Irene to step away. With his back against the wall to the side of the doorway, he reached around, turned the knob, and threw the door open.

Inside, the thumping grew more frenzied. Pender peered around the doorjamb, saw a girl's bedroom with posters of the U.S. Women's World Cup soccer team on the pale pink walls and stuffed animals crowding the bedspread. On the floor next to the bed a teenage girl lay on her back, her wrists and ankles bound with adhesive tape. Another strip of tape covered her mouth completely—her taut bare midriff jerked spasmodically as she fought to draw breath through nostrils bubbling with snot. A few more minutes and she'd almost certainly have suffocated, Pender thought with a shudder as he knelt beside the girl. What a nightmarish way to go.

Irene had followed him into the room. *Call nine-one-one,* he mouthed to her over his shoulder. She fished her cell phone out of her purse, took it out into the hall, and closed the door behind her—she didn't want Alison to have to listen to her telling the police about the bodies downstairs.

"It's okay, honey, you're safe now," Pender crooned soothingly to the girl as he scooped her up in his arms and set her down gently on the bed. "Nobody's going to hurt you. Bet you'd like to get *this* damn thing off toot sweet, though."

Alison nodded. Pender gave her a big clownish wink, pinched her earlobe hard with one hand to distract her, then yanked the tape free with his other hand while she was still in mid-yelp. "Here, blow," he said, handing her his handkerchief. When she was done blowing, she gave it back to him; he wrinkled his lumpy nose and held it out at arm's length. "Call in the Haz-Mat team," he said.

When Irene returned, Alison was sitting up and asking for water—her throat was raw from screaming into the gag. Irene said she'd get it, and went back out into the hall to find the bathroom.

The first door she tried was a linen closet, its neatly folded sheets and towels lightly scented with lilac water. But the second door opened onto a spacious bathroom, nearly as large as Alison's bedroom. Inside, the body of a heavyset woman with a mullet hairdo lay jackknifed over the rim of the bathtub, head down, ass up; the acrid, new-penny smell of blood filled Irene's nostrils and brought tears to her eyes.

A few minutes later one of the first cops to arrive on the scene discovered Wally's body on the floor outside the downstairs bathroom, and the body count was complete.

Part Two

Mama's Place

CHAPTER SIX

1

The undersides of the fluffy clouds to the east were dawn-pink, the tops in bruised shadow as Lilith, stiff and sore after driving all night, trudged up an asphalt driveway so steep she felt like she should have been roped to something.

Her destination was a pink ranch house with a shingled roof and dormer windows, which appeared to have been airlifted from some 1950s-era suburb complete with hissing lawn sprinklers and little kids riding fat-tired bikes with bells and streamers on the handlebars, then plunked down precariously on the western slope of this scrubby hillside in the boondocks north of Redding.

Lilith paused on the front doorstep, trying to decide whether it was too early to ring the doorbell. Out of the corner of her eye she saw the living-room curtains rustling. She rapped lightly on the green door. "It's me," she called. "It's Lilith—open up."

The man—or was it a troll?—who opened the door was short, dark, and stocky, shirtless under Ben Davis overalls, with matted hair and beard, and a nose so flat and eyes set so far apart that his broad face seemed vaguely unfinished, like an underdone gingerbread man.

"Hey, L'il T.," said Lilith.

"Whaddaya want?" He kept one hand out of sight, behind the door.

Before she could reply, a woman's voice behind him cried out, "Well I'll be dipped in shit."

"Mama Rose?"

"No, honey, it's fucking Cher. I couldn't stand them dickless Hollywood phonies no more, so I come up here for a break."

Next thing Lilith knew, a six-foot-tall, orange-haired, two-hundred-pound white woman had shoved the troll out of the way, yanked her inside, and hugged her to an enormous bosom that smelled of cigarettes and cold pizza. "Hope you ain't still pissed off about . . . Weed," she whispered. "I'll tell you later how it went down—for right now, as far as anybody else is concerned the story is that you run into some folks you recognized, and split with 'em. Okay?"

"But—"

"Later." Mama Rose held Lilith at arm's length, looked urgently into her eyes. "Please?"

Lilith shrugged. "Yeah, sure, what the fuck."

Mama Rose pressed her palms against the girl's temples, drew her close again, planted a wet kiss on her forehead. *"Mmm-wwa!* Now let's get some breakfast into you, we'll catch up on old times, how's that sound?"

"We should probably get my car off the road first. The sooner we get it to the shop, the better." Referring to Carson's chop shop, where a surprisingly large percentage of Northern California's stolen vehicles were either parted out or given new identities.

Mama Rose licked her forefinger, touched it to an imaginary stove and made a sizzling sound, then raised her eyebrows inquisitively. When Lilith nodded, Mama Rose caught L'il T.'s eye and nodded toward the driveway. He asked Lilith for the keys.

"They're in the ignition," she said, adding hastily: "The thing is, though, I'm not exactly, you know . . . alone."

2

Why was Lily so angry at him all the time? Lyssy had asked himself repeatedly, during the course of the long drive. Only *angry* wasn't exactly the right word—it seemed more like she was disgusted or disappointed with him.

But if that was the case, why had she suddenly changed her mind and insisted he leave with her? "Are we escaping?" he'd asked her.

"Well, duh! Unless maybe *you're* looking forward to being locked up for the rest of your life."

Freedom, Lily: it was everything Lyssy had wished for, stretching out in front of him like the rainbow highway in the bonus round of the "Super Mario Kart" video game. He couldn't help thinking that deep down, even though he'd never be able to admit it to anybody, Dr. Al would secretly be happy for him.

So Lyssy had done as he was told (not exactly a novel experience for someone who'd been virtually raised in an institution): changed into the clothes Lily had found for him—baggy white T-shirt and button-fly Levi's with the cuffs turned up—then made himself small on the floor in the back of the big black Land Rover in the Corders's garage, covered himself with a scratchy, olive-green blanket, and kept his mouth shut unless he was spoken to.

Which hadn't been often. Around midnight Lily had asked him if he knew how to drive. He said he didn't think so; she said she hadn't thought so, either. And a few hours later she told him to stay out of sight and keep perfectly still under the blanket—they were stopping for gas. When he told her he had to pee she told him to hold it—it was another agonizing hour or so before she pulled over to the side of a deserted stretch of road so he could relieve himself.

But never mind, Lyssy had promised himself—sooner or later he'd win her over, just like he'd won over all the nurses and psych techs at the Institute. And who knows, maybe there'd even be a fire or a flood or a rabid dog he could save her from.

Eventually, despite the jouncing he was taking,

Lyssy had fallen asleep. When he awoke again the Rover had stopped—which was probably what had awakened him—and for once Lily hadn't barked at him to stay down. Instead she ordered him to wait for her in the car. "They don't take real well to strangers showing up uninvited," she'd told him. "Lemme just give 'em a little advance notice—and Lyssy?"

"Yes?"

"When you do meet them, don't say anything stupid."

When Lyssy said that wasn't very likely because, as Dr. Al had once told him, his IQ was so high it was practically off the charts, Lily rolled her eyes. "On second thought, maybe you shouldn't say anything at all."

"Very funny," he called after her—it had taken a few seconds to think up the retort. The sky was beginning to lighten; he could hear the birds starting to whistle and chirp, just like they did in the arboretum at dawn. Only this wasn't the arboretum, Lyssy reminded himself, closing his eyes to hear them better—it was the real thing. Awesome! as the ODDs and CODs used to say back on 2-East. Su-weeeeeet!

"Hey!"

Startled, Lyssy opened his eyes—a grotesque-looking creature with matted hair and beard, a flattened nose, and wide-set, off-kilter eyes was tapping on the car window. "Oh—hi."

The hairy stranger opened the driver's door and climbed in. "They said for you to go on up—I'll take care of the vee-hicle."

"Up there?" Lyssy pointed toward the pink house on the hillside.

"Good guess, Einstein." It *was* the only building within sight.

Openness, the astonishing absence of walls, the unsettling weight of the borderless sky—Lyssy's shoulders were hunched as he started up the asphalt mountain, as though he were expecting a giant roc to swoop down on him from that enormous, unprecedented firmament.

The climb, he estimated, was the equivalent of mounting the Japanese footbridge in the arboretum around twenty times. He was limping badly by the time he reached the front doorstep; several seconds went by before he realized the door was *not* going to slide open automatically. "Raised in captivity, released into the wild," he intoned, in the voice of a Discovery Channel announcer. "Can this magnificent creature adapt? Will he survive?"

It was Lily who answered the door, once he'd solved the dilemma of the doorbell. She led him back to the kitchen and introduced him to Mama Rose, the big redhead at the stove, who told him her casa was his casa, complimented Lily on having plucked a ripe one from the cutie-pie tree, then asked Lyssy if he was hungry.

"Starving," he said, taking a seat at the beat-up, burn-scarred kitchen table.

Mama Rose slid a chipped dinner plate heaped with scrambled eggs and bacon in front of him, filled a mug with steaming coffee. "Thanks." He lightened the coffee with half-and-half from a cow-shaped creamer and dumped in a few heaping teaspoons of sugar.

From the back of the house, they heard a toilet flushing loud enough to wake the dead. "One of these days we gotta get that fixed," said Mama Rose apologetically.

"The prodigal daughter returns," drawled a male voice from the doorway a few seconds later. A lanky man, handsome in a narrow-eyed Clint Eastwood sort of way, wearing flip-flops, a ratty bathrobe, and a khaki bush hat with the brim pinned up on one side, entered the kitchen, saw Lyssy for the first time, and turned back to Lilith. "Who the fuck's that? You know better than to—"

"Hi Carson." Lilith hurried over and threw her arms around him. He hugged her reluctantly, still glaring over her shoulder at the intruder. "That's my friend Lyssy. We were in kind of a jam, we thought maybe we could hole up here for a couple days."

Carson pushed Lilith away—but gently—and turned his glare from Lyssy to Mama Rose. In the way of old married couples everywhere, they exchanged a good deal of information in glance and gesture, the gist being: M.R.: *Be cool for now, we'll talk about this later.* C: *Goddamn right we will.*

Lilith intercepted enough of the message to understand she and Lyssy were out of danger for the time being. She hurried back to Lyssy, stood behind him with her hand on his shoulder. "Lyssy, this is Carson—he and Mama Rose saved my ass up in Sturgis."

"Pleased to meet you," said Lyssy.

"That goddamn well better not be the last of the bacon," was Carson's greeting. Lyssy quickly transferred the surviving bacon strips from his plate onto a paper napkin, which he handed to Carson.

"Sir, you are a scholar and a fucking gentleman," Carson said grandly, rolling the bacon up in the napkin, then gnawing sideways at the protruding strips as he pulled a chair out with his free hand, twirled it around, and straddled it backward, facing the table. "Any friend of Lilith's . . . had better watch his ass."

Sounded like humor; Lyssy forced a chuckle. He was more interested in why Carson had called her Lilith. It might have been a slip of the tongue, Lyssy told himself, or maybe a memory glitch—or perhaps Lilith *was* her real name, and Lily her add-a-Y nickname, like Wally for Walter, or Lyssy for Ulysses.

But deep down, he knew better. Because there was yet another explanation, one that accounted for all the discrepancies he'd been pretending not to notice and trying not to think about for the last twelve hours or so. Such as how the timid fawn he'd shown around the arboretum only a few days ago had been transformed into a bossy, fearless, outgoing, self-assured young woman with the vocabulary of a longshoreman.

"Lilith," he echoed, from around a mouthful of scrambled eggs. "Lilith, Lilith, Lilith."

"That's my name," she said, glaring daggers at him across the table. "Don't fucking wear it out."

3

On Thursday morning, Irene Cogan awoke disoriented, in a strange room. She heard snoring, looked over and saw, huddled under the covers of the queen-size bed next to hers, a mound that from the size and sound of it could only have been Pender—or possibly a hibernating bear. But this morning, unlike yesterday, everything came flooding back to her, from the hours under the spotlight at TPP Productions, to the slashed corpses in the living room, to the heartening discovery of the uninjured Corder girl, and the shock of finding the female psych tech's body draped over the rim of the bathtub.

She and Pender had missed their flight, of course. Naturally the police wanted to debrief them, and poor Alison had begged them to stay with her until her aunt and uncle arrived—they may have been strangers to her but they were all she had. The newly orphaned girl had clung especially close to Pender, who gentled her like a horse whisperer, encouraging her to talk when she wanted to and sob when she needed to. It was Pender who'd first learned that the girl believed Lily had saved her life, spiriting her upstairs when Lyssy (as Alison still thought of him) went berserk with his knife.

But there were so many questions still unanswered. Lily or Lilith? Accomplice or victim? If she was Maxwell's knowing accomplice, why had she bothered to save the girl from him? If not, why had she left Alison tied up on the floor of her closet instead of simply freeing her? And had she left voluntarily with Maxwell, or had he taken her captive? For Irene Cogan, who knew far too well what it meant to be abducted by Ulysses Maxwell, that was the most important question of all.

Rather than wait with Alison in the middle of a crime scene—a *wet* crime scene, in the cop lexicon—Irene and Pender had accompanied her to police headquarters. It had been close to midnight by the time her aunt and uncle arrived to pick her up; the girl hugged Pender good-bye so tightly he had to peel her off him like a limpet.

After dining, if such a grand word applies to a meal at an all-night Burger King, Pender and Irene had shared a room in the Holiday Inn Express near the airport. No thought of hanky-panky, of course—Irene was still half in shock from the horrors she'd witnessed, and worried to distraction about Lily—but even having to listen to Pender snoring all night seemed preferable to spending the night alone knowing Maxwell was at large again.

The snoring broke off with a choked snort. Pender took off his sleep mask and popped out his earplugs, then sat up, naked to the waist, his barrel-like chest surprisingly firm, his belly slopping over the covers like a slag heap that had reached the angle of repose. His torso was white as paper, but both arms were tan from the biceps down—a golfer's tan.

When he saw Irene looking over at him, he sang out a few bars of "Good Morning Starshine" in his surprisingly sweet tenor voice, then segued into "A

Day in the Life" as he padded into the bathroom wearing only his pajama bottoms. As one of his old friends used to say of the man who was rumored to know the lyrics of every pop song recorded between 1955 and 1980: "Pender doesn't just live his life, he also provides the sound track."

In the first half-decade of the new century, motel chains were still vying to see which could provide the biggest complimentary continental breakfast spread. Irene had coffee and orange juice and nibbled at a bagel with cream cheese, while Pender, humming "Food, Glorious Food," all but decimated the buffet.

And when his belly could hold no more, he filled the capacious side pockets of his madras sport coat with miniature muffins and pastries for himself and Irene—the rest of the passengers on the Southwest Airlines flight from Portland to San Jose would have to make do with salted peanuts and stale pretzels.

"A little pocket lint never killed anybody," Pender assured Irene as they joined the line shuffling sullenly toward the airport security checkpoint.

"I'm sorry, what?"

"Never mind—nothing important." He transferred his carry-on to his other hand, slipped his arm around her, gave her shoulder a squeeze. "How're you holding up there, scout?"

She looked up at him, her eyes bloodshot from worry and lack of sleep, her complexion drained of color save for a tubercular spot of red high on either cheek. "Do you think Lily killed that woman in the bathtub?" Alison hadn't been sure one way or the other—while continuing to insist that the girl had saved her life, she had admitted reluctantly to a vague recollection of Lily saying she had to visit the john, and of her mother giving her and her escort directions to the guest bathroom upstairs.

Pender shrugged. "Let's wait for the forensics."

Something in the way he said it, perhaps the impersonality, set off a spark in Irene. "Well I don't *care,"* she whispered fiercely. The line had started moving forward again, but Irene stayed rooted in place, her fists clenched at her sides. "I don't care what she's done or how involved she was, I won't let them put her in prison, Pen. I won't let them put her away again if I have to . . . I don't know, if I have to sneak her out of the country myself."

"Let's hope it doesn't come to that," said Pender—but he knew that if it did, he'd have himself one hell of a conflict of interest.

4

Lilith followed Lyssy, spotting him for safety as he stumped unevenly up the swing-down ladder and through the trapdoor into the attic dormer, a low-budget add-on consisting of one long, low-ceilinged room built of cheapjack pine and press-on veneer siding, running almost the length of the roof. Two dormer windows faced front, each housing a bulky air conditioner, only one of which still functioned.

The cracked and faded *Teenage Mutant Ninja Tur-*

tle–themed linoleum, along with the twin beds, the twin child-size dressers, and a spray-painted baby-blue bookcase, suggested even to Lyssy's inexperienced eyes that the room had once housed children. He asked Lilith if Carson and Mama Rose had had any kids; she told him no, that they'd bought the place furnished.

"They seemed like nice folks," said Lyssy, sitting on the bed nearest the trapdoor.

"Actually, they're stone killers, both of them. And Mama Rose already sold me out once don't think she won't try it again, first chance she gets."

"Then why did you bring us here?"

She sat down next to him, put her hand on his flesh-and-blood knee, and lowered her voice to a whisper. "For the same reason people rob banks—because that's where the money is."

Lyssy's eyes widened, the gold flecks dancing in the dim morning light. "We're gonna *rob* them?"

"We're gonna need lots and lots of cash to live on the lam. You got a better idea?"

"No, but—"

"I didn't think so," she said wearily. The lack of sleep was starting to catch up to her. She closed her eyes and felt the room swaying; when she opened them again Lyssy was staring at her in alarm.

"Are you okay?" he asked her.

"Fine—I'm fine," she mumbled, swinging her legs up onto the bed. "Just need . . . couple hours . . . good as new."

She was asleep atop the covers by the time her head hit the pillow. Lyssy took off her sneakers for her, then limped over to the other bed, stripped off the blanket, covered her with it, and sat down again on the edge of the bed to watch over her while she slept.

5

Mama Rose barely made it to the stove in time to save the bacon from burning. "Sweet Jesus forbid you should get up from the fucking table," she muttered to Carson as she set the plate down in front of him.

"One of these days, woman. . . . " He made a fist, brandished it threateningly.

"You and what army?" she replied, sliding into the chair across from him. Both threat and response were pro forma—he'd only struck her in anger one time, when they were newlyweds. She'd bided her time, then whacked him across the back of the head with a shovel. Concussion, no fracture. Lesson taken.

"That gimp Lyssy, he look familiar to you?" she asked Carson.

"Kinda."

"I could swear I've seen him before someplace."

"I know what you mean. You get his last name?—we could Google him."

"He wasn't very talkative."

"And she didn't tell you who or what they were on the lam from?"

"Whoever owned that Rover, I'm guessing." Mama Rose pushed herself back from the table. "Listen babe, I'm beat, I'm gonna turn in. Just leave the dishes in the sink, I'll take care of 'em later."

A cavernous yawn from Carson, a phony-looking, ham-actor stretch. "I think maybe I'll join you—I'm getting too old for these fucking all-nighters."

In addition to running the chop shop to which the Rover had been removed, the Redding Menace were mid-level players in the new triangle trade—drugs, firearms, and cash. All night long, on any given evening, dealers and couriers came and went, arriving with large quantities of one of the aforementioned substances, and departing with (ideally) smaller quantities of another.

It was often a complicated dance: player A might have to be hooked up with players B and C, while B had to be kept apart from C, with D waiting in the wings, and so on; meanwhile all the players had to be entertained, plied with weed or coke or brandy, topped up with coffee.

So the exhausted hosts had been on their way to bed when their last two visitors arrived unexpectedly. And now Carson, who hadn't approached his wife with amorous intent for ages, wanted to make love. Mama Rose was no fool: she knew what was up, and why it was up—he'd had a letch for Lilith ever since Sturgis—but reminded herself that it didn't matter where a man worked up his appetite, so long as he ate at home.

She grabbed a quick shower and changed into

her sexiest nightgown, making only one concession to jealousy: If Carson even closed his eyes, much less called out Lilith's name, Rose would have his nuts for earrings.

When Mama Rose emerged from the bathroom, Carson was at the computer. Like many another twenty-first-century wife, her first thought was that he was surfing for porn. Not that she minded—that appetite thing again.

"Hey babe, look at this."

Mama Rose crossed the room, and standing behind him, resting her right breast on his left shoulder, she saw a picture of their new houseguest plastered across the front page of the cyber edition of the *Oregonian*. "Looks like we have a celebrity in our midst."

She read past the headline to learn that the infamous serial killer Ulysses Maxwell had escaped from an asylum, leaving four dead bodies behind; a fellow patient, a minor, name withheld, was either a hostage or an accessory. "Got any bright ideas?"

"Fuckin' A." Carson leaned back in his chair, laced his hands behind his head. "Way I figure it, if there ain't a reward for him yet, there will be; if there is, it'll get bigger. So we find somebody we can trust, somebody with a clean record, that somebody takes Maxwell . . . shit, I don't care, someplace far enough away from here, blows him away, makes up a good story for the cops, we split the reward. What do you think?"

"It might work," said Mama Rose. "But what about the girl?"

"What do *you* think?" Same four words, but this time they chilled Mama Rose to the marrow.

6

No lights, mailbox stuffed, four days' worth of rubber-banded *Monterey Heralds* on or around the porch steps—Pender might as well have put up a sign on his postage-stamp front lawn: Attention burglars: nobody home.

But burglaries were almost unheard of in The Last Home Town, as Pacific Grove officially styled itself—its other nickname was Butterfly Town, USA, for the monarchs that wintered over every year—and the annual murder rate hovered just above zero.

So Pender's jet-black '64 Barracuda was still in the short, weedy driveway when he hauled his bags up the mossy brick walk (he and Irene had taken the shuttle bus from San Jose to Monterey, then shared a cab from there) and his new flat-screen plasma TV was still on the wall of the front room—other than that, there wasn't much worth stealing. (The kind of music Pender enjoyed sounded best in a car, second best on a boom box, the cheaper the better.)

Built in 1905, the cottage originally contained only three small rooms—parlor, bedroom, kitchen—lined up shotgun-style, front to back; a tiny bathroom with toilet, pedestal sink, and stall shower had been added on off the kitchen. Pender carried his luggage through the front room with its secondhand velour love seat, non-matching Naugahyde recliner, and hooked oval rug, dropped it off in the bedroom, where a queen-size bed took up most of the floor-space, grabbed a beer in the kitchen, and carried it out into the backyard.

Too small to qualify as postage stamp, Pender's tiny yard was overhung and walled in on three sides by a gnarled and ancient fig tree, a spreading giant that also supported Pender's only outdoor furniture, a low-slung, dispirited-looking mesh hammock. Lying in it, his big ass barely clearing the ground, Pender was still steaming about the disrespect with which the Portland police had treated him the night before. As a federal agent, he'd grown used to being regarded with suspicion or resentment by the local constabulary—but not with contempt, never with contempt.

And never mind that he and Irene had probably saved the Corder girl from death by suffocation—whatever happened to plain old professional courtesy? Even after he told the officer in charge who he was, all the supercilious sonofabitch had to say was that in that case, he should have known better than to even *enter* a possibly dangerous crime scene on his own, not to mention dragging a civilian through it—and are you *sure* you didn't touch anything in the living room, Pops?

As for getting one of the Nike-town cops to listen to his theory that the fugitives might well head for "Lilith's" old stomping ground in Shasta County, CA, lots of luck. Once they'd taken his statement, it was thanks for your cooperation and don't let the door hit your fat ass on the way out. Even if you're the world's leading expert on Ulysses Maxwell *et al.* Even if you know that Maxwell had been locked up for the last three years, and isolated up on Scorned Ridge with his now-deceased stepmother/lover/accomplice for a dozen or so years before that. And that the only friend he'd made at the Juvie Ranch was also three years dead. So who the hell was *he* going to run to?

But according to Irene Cogan, the world's leading expert on Lily DeVries *et al.*, Lilith had almost certainly been running the show for *her* syndicate last night—Lily, the original personality, would have turned into a basket case at the first sign of trouble. And what was it she'd said about Lilith the night before last? Something about Lilith serving as a protector alter?

King-hell of a job she'd done too, thought Pender, if she'd managed to keep both herself and Alison alive through last night's massacre. And Lilith the protector did have someone to run to—those bikers.

The more Pender thought about it, the more sense his theory made. But how to act on it? He'd just about decided to call the Shasta County Sheriff's Department and lay it out for one of their homicide detectives when he realized that except for his own eyeballing of a redheaded, middle-aged biker mama, he had almost no information about the bikers to pass on to said homicide dick.

That was because Mick MacAlister, the brilliant, if perpetually half-stoned skip-tracer who'd set up the rendezvous in Weed, operated on a strictly need-to-know basis, and as far as MacAlister was concerned, all Pender and Irene had needed to know was the location of the coffee shop and what time to be there. "Trade secret," MacAlister would say if pressed for details—now Pender decided it was time to pay MacAlister a visit and persuade him to cut loose with a few of his trade secrets.

Assuming he could fight his way up from the hammock, of course.

7

Lilith awoke to the hum of the air conditioner. Lyssy lay asleep on the other bed, an open book resting facedown on his chest, rising and falling with every baby-soft breath.

Seeing him vulnerable like that, Lilith was overwhelmed by a strange new sensation, a feeling of tenderness so intense it was almost painful. "Don't worry, I won't let anything bad happen to you," she whispered, unconsciously—or perhaps subconsciously—echoing Irene Cogan's broken promise to Lily.

Lyssy opened his eyes and smiled when he saw her watching him. "Hi."

"Hi. Whatcha reading?"

He looked confused for a moment, then discovered the book on his chest. "Something about the Hell's Angels—I found it in that bookcase over there."

"Oh yeah, I read that one when I was here before."

Lyssy sat up. "How long were you here?"

"I dunno, couple weeks I guess."

"And before that?"

"I joined up with Carson and Mama Rose at the big rally in Sturgis in July."

"But when I met you, you were Lily, right?"

"How the fuck should I know? When I met *you,* you were Max."

Lyssy groaned—more of a grunt, really, like somebody'd just kicked him in the nuts. A phrase he'd heard or read someplace started bouncing around in his head: *Don't ask, don't tell.* But he had to know. "Did I tell you I don't remember anything that happened last night? Before you came down the stairs to get me, I mean?"

"I figured as much."

"So where was everybody? Didn't we have escorts? How come they let us just drive away?"

She sat down beside him on the edge of the bed and rested her hand just above his prosthetic knee; the quadriceps muscle was quivering like an idling engine. "Me and Max, we did what we had to do, Lyssy." Remembering the terrible gurgling noise as Patty lay jackknifed over the rim of the bathtub while Lilith was washing her hands at the sink—luckily, Lilith hadn't seen the dying woman's face. "And if I had to, I'd do it again."

"I want to know everything that happened," said Lyssy. "Everything."

Lilith, singsong: "I don't *think* so."

"Okay then—I *have* to know."

She took awhile to think it over. Contrary to Irene Cogan's opinion—that alters were basically single-faceted identities—Lilith's personality, less than a month old, was accruing in complexity with every decision and every human interaction, the way crystals magically form themselves around a starter-seed.

Of course, *protect yourself at all times* was still her prime directive, but she was beginning to understand that sometimes other people's lives got so mixed up with yours that in order to protect yourself, you had to consider what was best for them as well. Even more confusing, sometimes what was best for somebody might also be hurtful to them. "You're not gonna go all weepy 'n' shit, are you?"

Lyssy shook his head.

"And you understand, no matter what happened, there's no sense freaking out about it, 'cause there's nothing you can do to change it?"

To Lyssy, that sounded like an equally good reason *to* freak out. But he nodded and listened, interrupting only twice. They were lying on their backs on the narrow bed, their bodies pressed together from shoulder to thigh. "Kinch," he said, when she got to the part about Max going crazy with the knife.

"Kinch?"

"That's who went crazy with the knife—Kinch, not Max. Max would have wanted to kill them slowly."

And when she told him how she'd hidden Alison from the berserk alter, he broke in to thank her.

"I didn't do it for you," she said.

"I wasn't thanking you for me."

When she'd finished, they rolled over onto their sides, facing each other. "Is there anything more?" he asked.

"That's about it. How're you doing?"

"I don't think it's completely sunk in yet—I'm not even sure I want it to." There was so much to *process,* as Dr. Al would have phrased it. He *missed* the Corders, especially Dr. Al—it hurt to know he'd never be seeing him again, and hurt even worse to realize that he'd been at least indirectly involved with their murders. If he'd been honest with Dr. Al about the dark place and the occasional voice in his ear, his surrogate father would still be alive.

But on the other hand, he, Lyssy, would still be locked up, and facing a lifetime of incarceration at best, so what was *that* all about?

Then there was the whole question of his relationship with the alters. He'd always gotten mixed signals from Dr. Al, who'd tell him in one breath not to feel guilty about the terrible things the alters had done, and in the next breath assure him that the alters were *not* separate beings, but dissociated aspects of his own personality.

He explained all this to Lilith as best he could (it probably would have been easier for Lily to understand), concluding with the biggest paradox of all: even knowing how their escape had been accomplished, and at what cost, Lyssy told Lilith he couldn't honestly say he wished that he could take it all back, that it had never happened—not if it had brought him here to this room, to this bed, with her.

She told him it was the sweetest thing anyone had ever said to her. Their first kiss, though it took forever for their lips to come together, had an inevitability about it nonetheless; afterward, for instance, neither of them would recall having intentionally closed the distance between them.

8

Mick MacAlister worked out of a one-room, second-story walk-up located above a bowling alley only a few blocks from the Santa Cruz Beach Boardwalk.

Pender parked the 'Cuda in front of the bowling alley and walked around to the side of the building, the wall of which had been given over entirely to graffiti—*Death to the Ass-Licking Sons of the Dying Regime* was the predominant sentiment.

MacAlister & Associates
Private Investigations
Discreet and Effective

read the business card taped next to the button marked 2-C, one of three set into the side of the recessed doorway. Pender pressed the buzzer and a few seconds later the door lurched open a few inches.

The smell of urine faded as Pender climbed the stairs, wearing a single-breasted sport jacket of grass green and mustard brown over a lavender polo shirt and plaid slacks; a brown Basque beret, argyle socks, and beige Hush Puppies completed the ensemble. He knocked on the wooden door marked 2-C, then let himself in.

The office walls were covered with Grateful Dead posters, and though there was nothing burning at the moment, the air was still layered with tobacco/cannabis smoke and cheap strawberry incense. MacAlister, seated at a rolltop desk placed sideways to the room like an upright piano on a stage, was a charter member of the gray ponytail brigade; a burgeoning belly strained his tie-dyed KPIG T-shirt. "Sorry, no refunds," he said. "How about a cigar instead." Nodding toward a cherrywood humidor.

"Try one of mine." Pender offered MacAlister one of his Green Iguanas, a mild, stubby Dominican cigar named for its olive-green *claro* wrapper. He had started smoking cigarettes again during his second wife's illness. After her death he had switched to cigars in an effort to wean himself from the cigarettes—Pender's doctors had been promising him a coronary for years if he didn't lose weight, get more exercise, and give up the gaspers—and wound up hooked on stogies.

Giving the Iguana a dubious glance, MacAlister instead flipped back the top of the humidor and turned it so Pender could see inside. It was full of Macanudos, genuine *hecho a mano* Havanas, each of which probably cost as much as a twenty-stick box of Pender's Dominicans. "Gift of a grateful client," he said.

"Go ahead, twist my arm," murmured Pender, dragging a wooden chair closer to the desk.

The snip of the cutter, the snick of the lighter, cigar heaven. They smoked wordlessly for close to a minute; then through a haze of blue smoke MacAlister asked Pender what he wanted.

"I need to know more about those bikers."

"Sorry, trade—"

Pender cut him off. "Not today, Mick—four people died last night."

MacAlister blew out a perfect smoke ring, waited for it to break up. "Aw, what the hey—why hide my light under a bushel?"

"Why indeed," agreed Pender, holding the cigar between his teeth while he took out his pocket notebook and a stubby pencil.

"Okay," MacAlister began. "Second week of the search, I get a credit card hit in Sturgis, South Dakota. That's where they have the big motorcycle run every summer. I'm there the next day. Nobody at the restaurant where I got the credit card hit remembers anything, so I paper the town and the encampments with flyers, and hook up with the Wharf Rats—that's a gang of clean-and-sober Deadhead bikers I knew back in Berkeley, in the old days.

"One of the Wharf Rats tells me this story that's going around, about some girl who bit the nose off some shit-heel during a gang bang. It never occurs to me that it's our gal from Pebble Beach—I mean, Pebble Beach, gimme a break!—but the next day, the last day of the run, I'm out pounding the pavement, where there *is* pavement, and two gals who put up a hot dog and loose joint stand in Sturgis every year tell me about a girl who looks "kinda like" the girl on the flyer, and how somebody with her made that old joke about "you don't want to see laws or hot dogs being made," and how the girl joked that at least it tastes better than that asswipe's nose.

"I figure it's worth a trip to the county hospital, where of course everybody remembers the guy who got his nose bit off. Turns out he gave a phony name and address, but I track down the triage nurse, and she remembers their colors. The Redding Menace. One-percenters out of Shasta County. Head of the gang is a mucho mysterioso figure named Carson. Sumbitch keeps a lower profile than a snake in Death Valley. Dirty as can be, has his fingers in everything from meth to money laundering, and forget about finding him—the local cops don't even know whether Carson is his first name or his last name. So I decide to let him find me. I rent a motel room in Weed, put the word out in every bar and biker hangout in Shasta County that I'm looking for him."

Gently, he broke off the silvery, inch-long ash from the Havana into a blackened glass ashtray on his desk. "I tell you, a week in Redding in August is enough to make a man turn religious."

Pender flicked the ashes off his stogie with his ring finger, George Burns style, and like Burns was quick with the straight line. "How so, Mr. MacAlister?"

"Because after it, Mr. Pender, you've had enough hell to last you an eternity. (Thank you, no applause, just throw money.) Anyway, on Saturday I finally get the call I've been waiting for. Woman asks me why I'm trying to find Carson. I tell her. She says maybe she knows something, maybe she don't, what's it worth? I tell her about the ten-G reward. All of a sudden she's pretty goddamn sure she can work something out, only the reward's gotta be in cash—no checks, no money orders, no paper trail. We set up the meet for the motel coffee shop on Monday morning, and the rest is skip-tracer history."

"Did you get a phone number from her?"

"Negatory—she always called me from a pay phone."

"License plate on her Harley?"

"Sorry."

Pender looked down at his notebook, where he'd scribbled *Sturgis, Wharf Rats, Man w'out nose, Menace, Redding,* and *Carson.* Not much to go on, but perhaps it would mean more to the Shasta County sheriff. "Thanks, Mick, I appreciate the help."

"No problemo. Here, take one for the road." He tilted the humidor toward Pender.

"Don't mind if I do," said Pender. "You'll call me if that woman gets in touch with you again?"

"You bet. Drop by anytime."

MacAlister showed Pender to the door and locked it behind him, then retrieved Alice, the office bong, from her customary hiding place inside a hollowed-out boxed set of *Remembrance of Things Past,* selected for the honor because nobody but nobody ever browsed Proust. Shaped like a voluptuous nude with a carburetor hole in the side of her headless neck, Alice had been banished from the MacAlister domicile by wife #3.

Mick was on his second toke when the phone

rang; he coughed out the hit and answered it as his nonexistent French receptionist. "MacAlister and Associates, zis is Gabrielle, 'ow may I direct your call?"

"Mr. MacAlister, please."

" 'Oo may I say is calling?"

"He wouldn't recognize my name."

"What is zis in reference to?"

"Just tell him it's about Lily DeVries."

" 'Old ze line, please." MacAlister, a little surprised at how little surprised he was, put the phone down while he filled his KPIG mug with lukewarm black coffee from the thermos on his desk. "The monkey's got the locomotive under control," he whispered to Alice before picking up the phone again. "MacAlister here. What can I do you fer?"

9

Lyssy stared in wonder at the naked, sleeping girl. He thought back to the first time he'd laid eyes on her in the arboretum. He felt as if he'd known even then that she was fated to be a part of his life.

But how deep a part, he could never have guessed. Since they'd made love, clumsily at first, then with increasing skill as instinct and muscle-memory took over (for both of them), every inch of her had somehow become precious to him, verging on holy, the curve of her breasts and buttocks no more or less so than the curve of her calves or earlobes.

She stirred and rolled over onto her side; a snore bubble formed and popped on her perfectly shaped lips. In this position, he could see the dark shadow between her legs. Lyssy grew aroused again, realized he had to pee.

The bathroom facilities in the attic consisted of a toilet and a low sink hidden behind a blanket at the far end of the room. Before Lyssy could put on his prosthetic leg—he'd taken it off earlier, at Lilith's insistence; she'd said it was like having somebody else in bed with them—Lilith sat up and hugged him from behind.

"Is that a bullet hole?" she asked him sleepily, gently tracing the round, indented scar in the hollow of his left shoulder with her fingertip.

"Nine millimeter, they told me in the hospital."

"Does it hurt real bad, getting shot?"

"I don't *remember* getting shot—just waking up in the hospital with this shoulder all bandaged, and a thing like an upside-down basket over my knee."

Lilith changed the subject. "If you want, we could do it again. There's lots of ways, you know."

Lyssy could feel himself blushing. "Sure, maybe. I have to pee first, though."

"No you don't," said Lilith mischievously.

"I don't?"

"No, you have to pee *second,"* she told him, hopping out of bed butt-naked and racing for the toilet.

"Hurry up," called Lyssy, frustrated but laughing; obviously, sharing a bathroom was something else he was going to have to get used to.

* * *

Carson was still in bed when Mama Rose called from town. He smiled when he heard her voice, remembering their spirited romp that morning. Whoever said more than a handful of titty was a waste must have had some big goddamn mitts, he decided. But despite the conjugal workout, he still hadn't changed his mind about tucking into that sweet Lilith at least once before he had to kill her—now *that* would have been a *real* waste.

"Hey babe, what's up?" he asked his wife.

"Everything okay on the homefront?"

"So far, so good—they don't even know they're locked in yet."

"Good, good. Listen, I ran into Dennie in town." Dennie, half full-blooded Aleut, half Okie pipeline worker, was Li'l T.'s immensely pregnant ol' lady. "We're thinking about grabbing some dinner."

"No problem, long as you get back before nine o'clock."

"Why nine o'clock?"

"That deal with those guys from San Berdoo? Remember, me and Li'l T., we're supposed to meet 'em in town, drive 'em up to the shop?"

"Oh, right," said Mama Rose. "It completely slipped my mind." A purposeful lie—she'd needed to verify that Carson was still planning to go out that night, but had been afraid that a direct question might have aroused suspicion on his part.

"It's just I don't think we want to leave our friends in the attic home alone."

"Don't worry, I'll be back in plenty of time."

"Okay, see ya then."

"Love ya," said Mama Rose.

"You bet," said Carson, whose thoughts had already turned back to the girl in the attic.

"Lyss?"

"Hmmm?"

"Want to get some fresh air?"

"I thought you'd never ask." Lyssy sat up—they'd moved the two beds together for the second go-round—and started looking around for his leg, while Lilith slipped on her jeans, her brown cashmere sweater, and her sneakers, then bent over and grabbed the handle to the naked-looking wooden trapdoor set into the linoleum. It wouldn't budge.

"Fuck a duck, it's locked. They never locked it when I was here before." She stomped on the closed hatch like a three-year-old having a temper tantrum. "Hey! Hey, the fucking door's locked."

They heard footsteps on the ladder, the click of a padlock. "Go ahead, open it." Carson's voice.

Lilith yanked. The trapdoor swung up and over, crashing top down against the linoleum; years of such abuse had worn a harelip-shaped gouge in the face of the Ninja Turtle with the blue headband. "You first, lamb chop," called Carson, still wearing his bush hat, bathrobe, and flip-flops.

The ladder was steep, but the rungs sturdy and wide, of the same unfinished wood as the trapdoor. Lilith scrambled down, but before Lyssy could follow—he hadn't found his pants or his leg yet—Carson sprang up the ladder. Waist-high in the attic, he waved a stubby-looking revolver in Lyssy's direction.

"One customer at a time," he said, keeping his eyes and the gun trained on Lyssy, while he felt around for the handle of the trapdoor. He raised the hatch to the vertical and held it up with one hand, dropped the gun into his bathrobe pocket with the other, then let go and ducked simultaneously. The trapdoor came crashing down, nearly crushing his jaunty bush hat.

Lilith watched from below while Carson reattached the padlock and snapped it closed.

"Lilith? Lilith, what's going on?" There was panic in Lyssy's voice.

"It's okay," she yelled, as Carson scooted nimbly down the ladder, skipping the last few rungs and landing lightly on his flip-flops. "We'll get it straightened out, I promise."

Carson laughed. "Oh, we'll get it straightened out all right," he said. "We'll get it good and straightened out."

CHAPTER SEVEN

1

No rewards for Maxwell had been posted by the time Mick MacAlister and E. L. Pender left Santa Cruz Thursday afternoon in a red Cadillac convertible with white upholstery and a Grateful Dead skull-and-roses bumper sticker. But Pender had already called Lily's uncle to tell him they had a line on Lily's whereabouts, and might need to offer a reward, and Rollie DeVries had informally agreed to pony up another ten grand.

This one wasn't about the money for MacAlister, though. It was about glory—or its modern equivalent, celebrity. Bringing in Maxwell while the hot white glare of the media spotlight shone full upon him would all but guarantee Mick his allotted fifteen minutes of fame, which nowadays could be extended almost indefinitely.

As for Pender, who'd been driving through Moss Landing—quaint fishing village on one side of the two-lane highway, hellish power plant, like something out of *The War of the Worlds,* on the other—when MacAlister reached him on his cell phone, it had been a mixed bag of motivations, none of them financial, that inspired him to turn around and head back to Santa Cruz.

Rescuing Lily was foremost in his mind, of course. And capturing, or rather, recapturing Maxwell was high up on Pender's list as well, but not for the publicity. Pender had already had his Warholian fifteen minutes of fame several times over, and had always been more relieved than disappointed when the spotlight had moved on.

Instead, Pender looked on the opportunity to bring Maxwell in again as a chance to redeem two of the worst mistakes of his FBI career. Through a moment of inexcusable carelessness on Pender's part three years earlier, the psychopath had escaped from the Monterey County jail, at the cost of half a dozen additional lives. Then after the shootout on Scorned Ridge, when Maxwell lay injured, every instinct Pender had developed in three decades of chasing serial killers cried out for him to end it with a coup de grâce, or by letting Maxwell bleed out on the floor of the barn.

But although it was Irene Cogan who'd talked him out of it, then tied a tourniquet around Maxwell's thigh, thereby saving his life, Pender still blamed himself. Witness or no witness, there were dozens of ways for a determined special agent *not* to bring his man in alive—and if he'd employed any of them, Patricia Benoit, Walter Smets, Alan Corder, and Cheryl Corder would still be alive.

Pender's remaining motivations were less conscious. Chief among them were resentment for his treatment at the hands of the Portland cops—your basic "I'll show *them*" state of mind—along with a severe action jones: at fifty-seven Pender was no better prepared to slip gracefully into his golden years than he had been when he reached the FBI's mandatory retirement age two years earlier.

They drove with the top down and the CD player blaring Grateful Dead tunes. Pender, still wearing his grass-and-mustard-checked sport coat, nearly lost his hat when Mick put the hammer down on the superhighway running the length of California; he reached out to make a last-second, one-handed grab as the beret flew off his head. A few minutes later, Mick, wearing a casually matched jacket and jeans outfit of faded denim, took a joint-filled Sucrets tin from his pocket, and fired one up with a windproof butane torch.

"Don't worry, I drive better stoned," he told Pender, with the dangling joint glommed securely to his lower lip.

"You're under arrest," Pender replied.

"You got me fair and square, copper," said the portly private eye, raising both hands over his head—at eighty-plus miles an hour, on a far-from-empty eight-lane highway.

"On second thought, maybe I'll let it slide just this once," Pender decided.

They made good time, stopping once for gasoline and a convenience-store chili dog that reminded Mick, a native New Jerseyan, of the sign on the old roadside greasy spoon/gas station in Tuckahoe: EAT HERE AND GET GAS. As they passed Sacramento, he lit up a second doob. Pender remonstrated, reminding him they still had a potentially hazardous job in front of them.

"What, you think I'm goin' up against a psychopathic serial killer *straight*?" said MacAlister.

Which made so much sense to Pender that he found himself wondering whether he hadn't inhaled a little secondhand smoke himself.

2

Alone now in the attic, Lyssy searched wildly for his leg, which proved to be under the bed.

Yeah, like that's going to do a lot of fucking good, said the voice in his head.

"Max?"

No shit, Sherlock. Now be a good little boy and go to sleep—I'll take it from here.

"I'm not a little boy anymore."

You'll always be a little boy to me.

Lyssy clapped his hands over his ears. Max chuckled slyly. *I'm not out there, sonny, I'm in here. Now you know what you have to do—don't make it any harder on yourself than it has to be.*

"Never," said Lyssy. "Never, never, never again."

Okay, buddy-bud, you asked for it.

Lyssy heard the crackling sound, saw angry orange flames leaping up all around him. To fight them, he pictured Lilith—her hair the color of rich dark chocolate, her eyes big and dark in her sweet round face, her sweetly curved lips, her soft white rosy-tipped breasts, her velvet-soft belly, her creamy thighs and the dark mystery between them, her dimpled knees, strong calves, her toes arching in ecstasy. Then he worked his way back up, past her calves, thighs, bush, belly, breasts, and back up to her face, and he held her face there, he made himself *see* it, ten times larger than life, backlighted by the leaping flames. Which weren't leaping quite as high now, or burning quite as hot.

You're making a mistake, said the voice, sounding less sure of itself. *You're nothing without me. Nothing. Nothing. Nothing. Nothing. . . .*

The flames were gone. Lyssy found himself alone in the tiny attic room, sitting on the edge of the bed with his prosthetic leg in his hands. "Who's nothing now?" he said aloud. But for all his bravura, he couldn't help cocking his head to the side and listening, as if he weren't at all sure there wouldn't be an answer.

3

The problem was, Mama Rose *liked* the girl, had liked her from the moment she'd first set eyes on her, snapping and snarling like a she-wolf in a trap as she faced down the bikers back in Sturgis. And having a surrogate teenage daughter around, especially one who was as tabula rasa as Lilith, had meant a lot to the childless older woman. She'd had fun during that first visit, showing Lilith the ropes, passing on a little hard-earned practical wisdom.

But Mama Rose was nobody's fool: she had seen her walking hard-on of a husband growing more infatuated with the kid every passing day. Not that the prospect of Carson knocking off a quickie had her particularly worried—but what if it turned into a full-blown midlife crisis? He wouldn't have been the first man to trade in a middle-aged wife for a firm young mistress.

So she'd quietly cut a deal with the private eye, MacAlister, put the reward money into her secret "Fuck You" account—a safe-deposit box at the Bank of America down in Redding—and told Carson that Lilith had gone off with some folks she'd met in Weed. And while Mama Rose *had* missed her company—the warmth of her greeting this morning had been genuine enough—she was more determined than ever that Lilith had to go.

But not to *die*—that seemed a little extreme to Mama Rose. In the absence of a compelling threat to herself or Carson (Lilith had already proved she could be trusted to keep her mouth shut about the chop shop and the little pink house, if only because Swervin' Mervin was buried in the nearby woods, and both Carson and Mama Rose had witnessed his death) Mama Rose could not allow Carson to kill the girl.

As for Lilith's boyfriend, though, Mama Rose had no objection to terminating *him*. They certainly couldn't let him go: if captured, he could lead the cops straight back to them the same cops who'd been trying in vain to find Carson for fifteen years. And never mind how sweet Lyssy had seemed to be during breakfast: judging by what she'd read about him in the newspapers, anybody who knocked off Ulysses Maxwell would be doing the world a favor.

Hence the tangled web Mama Rose had been weaving all afternoon. First she'd cut another deal with MacAlister in return for another contribution to the Mama Rose Fuck You fund. The private eye and the backup he'd insisted on bringing along were to rendezvous with Mama Rose at a coffee shop in Mt. Shasta, follow her to an undisclosed location out in the boondocks, lend her two pairs of handcuffs, and wait for her to return with a manacled pair of fugitives.

And the only difference between their relative expectations, Mama Rose's and MacAlister's, was that *he* assumed that both fugitives would be alive when she handed them over.

4

Lilith's breasts, white and round as scoops of meringue, floated above the burbling, steaming water of the redwood hot tub on the narrow patio behind the house. On the other side of a trellis twined thinly with haphazardly blooming rose vines, the hillside rose sharply, buttressed by old tarry railroad ties. The late afternoon sun was hot as ever as it sank toward the crest of the hill, but the shadows were lengthening rapidly.

Carson slipped the revolver, a snub-nosed .38, under a pile of clean towels on the whitewashed, round wrought-iron patio table, and switched on the boom box. This radio, although it was connected to a long orange extension cord plugged into the same outlet that powered the Jacuzzi motor, was kept on the table, out of arm's reach of the tub, to prevent stoned bathers from accidentally electrocuting themselves. Carson fiddled with the dial until he found his favorite heavy metal station, then with the radio blaring post-Sabbath Ozzie, he took off his bathrobe and climbed in after her wearing only his bush hat. Groaning long and loud, he lowered his dangling privates into the steaming water until he was submerged to his neck, beads of sweat already forming on his brow.

Lilith held her nose, bent her knees, and submerged herself. Underwater, the echoic rumble of the Jacuzzi jets sounded almost peaceful. Hearing a distant splashing sound, Lilith opened her eyes underwater, found herself staring down the barrel of Carson's hard-on. She rose like Venus, hair plastered flat against her sleek round skull, water dripping from her full, round breasts. "I like your cock," she whispered, pressing the length of her body against his, front to front.

"Me too," he replied hoarsely.

"Could I change the fucking station?" The radio was blaring that annoying McDonald's jingle: *I'm loving it, I'm loving it.*

"Hunh, what? Oh—sure."

She climbed out hurriedly, before he could change his mind, and trotted over to the table shivering, with her arms crossed in front of her. "Where's a good station?"

"Try the FM band," he said easily—but his glance had flickered briefly to the pile of towels on the table. Shit, she thought: obviously he'd remembered where he'd left the revolver. Which meant her chances of grabbing the gun, finding and releasing the safety, pulling back the hammer, and squeezing off a shot before he could leap from the tub and cross the five or six feet to the table, were not exactly encouraging, Lilith decided, as she absentmindedly fiddled with the radio dial.

Then suddenly it dawned on her, with all the force and clarity of revelation, that the revolver wasn't the only weapon on the table. Or even the deadliest—pistols misfire, bullets miss their targets. She turned her face away, hiding a savage grin as she traced the length of the orange extension cord with her eyes to make sure it lay free, with enough slack so it wouldn't tangle or catch on anything. Picking up the boom box in both hands, she raised it over her head.

Mentally and emotionally drained after the struggle with Max, Lyssy strapped on his leg, still in its gray sock and black sneaker, then dressed hastily in the same oversize white T-shirt and button-fly jeans Lilith had given him before they left Dr. Al's. After tying his other sneaker, he tried to raise the trapdoor, again to no avail.

There has to be another way out, he thought, glancing around the long, narrow attic—there just *has* to be. He examined the double-sashed dormer windows jutting out onto the roof in the front of the house. They were both nailed shut on top and sealed so tightly around the air conditioners below that no light showed around them. But only one of the machines was running; the short three-pronged power cord of the other dangled limply.

Lyssy seized hold of the unwieldy gray-brown box with his fingertips, and began rocking it. It was lighter than it appeared to be, and held firm at first. But as Lyssy continued to rock it back and forth to the pounding rhythm of the ungodly music blaring from around the back of the house, lengthwise cracks like miniature geological fissures began to form in the dessicated gray putty that held the box in place.

Encouraged, Lyssy threw all his weight into the effort, working the awkward load up and down, side to side, until it was loosened enough for him to get a good grip with his clawlike hands. After three strong heaves it broke free, tilted, and began sliding back into the room. Lyssy stepped back just in time to avoid getting his toes crushed when the air conditioner crashed to the floor, corner first, gouging a furrow in the linoleum.

Listening for a response to all the racket he'd made, Lyssy heard only the infernal howling of the radio. He cleared the gaping hole of clinging cobwebs and active spiderwebs decorated with mummified flies and sticky egg sacs, stuck his head through, looked down, and beheld his next challenge: though the drop to the roof was only four or five feet, there were but eighteen inches or so of steeply pitched composition shingles between the base of the dormer and the edge of the roof to use as a foothold, then an eight-to-ten-foot drop to the ground, or rather, the front doorstep.

Lyssy lowered himself backward through the hole. His left foot, arching downward, touched the slanting shingles first. Gripping the window frame with his deformed hands, he began to sidle to his left, keeping as much weight as possible on his real foot. It seemed to take forever, but at last he rounded the corner of the protruding dormer, and had room to drop to his hands and knees.

The heavy metal music from the radio had given way to a McDonald's commercial by the time Lyssy reached the apex of the roof. He spread-eagled himself against the shingles and crept with a sort of swimming motion headfirst down the other slope. Just as the patio came into view, he heard the *urp-beep-fleep-floop* sound of someone dialing swiftly through the channels on a radio. Peering over the edge of the roof, he saw Carson directly below him, reclining naked in a hot tub; Lilith, also nude, stood a few feet away, holding a boom box above her head with both hands.

Carson had only an instant to realize what was coming. He struggled to his feet, opened his mouth to scream. Lyssy's own scream caught in his throat as the radio sailed through the air, then everything was blue sparks, popping noises, bubbling water, and a weird, high-pitched shriek, like a lobster makes when you drop it live into a boiling pot.

Suddenly hatless, his hair sticking straight out from his head and his body jerking like Sonny Corleone at the tollbooth, Carson lurched around the tub with his arms extended—think Frankenstein's monster—until the strain on the circuits blew the fuses.

Seconds later, all was quiet. Carson floated faceup, hair fanned out and bobbing gently, with an erection you could have pitched horseshoes at. Lilith lay naked, crumpled on her side at the edge of the patio, a good fifteen or twenty feet from the tub.

Lyssy scrambled frantically across the length of the roof, grabbed the aluminum rain gutter with both hands, and lowered himself over the edge, bracing himself for a nasty fall. But instead, the gutter began to bend, nails and rivets popping as it pulled free from its moorings and swung him down gradually.

When his flailing feet touched the concrete, he let go, swaying unsteadily for a moment, then regained his balance and limped across the patio to Lilith. He knelt beside her and rolled her onto her back, relieved to see that she was breathing. "Lilith? Lilith, you okay?"

Her eyelids fluttered open. He stroked her cheek with the back of his hand; she jerked her head away sharply, looking not at him, but past him.

"Lilith? It's Lyssy. Talk to me—can you talk to me?"

She might as well have been deaf and dumb. Blind too, as far as Lyssy was concerned—try as he might to insert himself into her line of vision, her eyes failed to focus on his face.

Lyssy said her name a few more times—no response—and was trying to figure out his next move when he heard the roar of a downshifting Harley growling as it climbed the steep asphalt driveway in low gear. Panic mounting, he glanced around wildly, wadded up one of the white towels strewn around the patio to cushion Lilith's head, and covered her with another—he couldn't just leave her lying there like that.

Someone was coming around the side of the house. As he climbed to his feet and looked around for a place to hide, Lyssy spotted Carson's revolver lying on the cement, a few feet from the overturned patio table. He snatched it up, slipped it into the waistband of his jeans, limped around the hot tub, keeping his eyes averted from the sickening sight of Carson's scalded corpse, and crouched behind the tub.

"Fuck, it stinks back—" The bearded troll Lyssy had met that morning—felt like a whole lifetime had passed since then—rounded the corner of the house. He saw Lilith first, broke off in mid-sentence, started another sentence that began with "What the . . . ?" and trailed off when he caught sight of the hot tub with its grisly contents.

What happened next would seem strange only in retrospect: Lyssy, who'd never knowingly handled a gun before, drew the .38 from his waistband, flicked off the safety, cocked the hammer, and rose, calling, "Put your hands up," in as deep a voice as he could manage.

"You!"

"I said, put your hands up!"

"You killed Carson."

"Darn right," said Lyssy, happily taking on Lilith's guilt. "And I'll kill you too if you don't put your stupid hands up."

"Fuck you," said the troll, so Lyssy shot him. Not a whole lot of thinking had gone into it—he'd pointed the gun toward the troll's knee and tightened his finger experimentally, just a hairsbreadth or so. Apparently that was far enough.

But Lyssy hadn't counted on the upward kick—the bullet struck at the intersection of leg and groin, severing the troll's femoral artery, and blew a fist-size hole in his buttock on its way out. The troll didn't seem to realize at first that he'd even been hit. He took a step toward Lyssy, frowning and reaching behind himself to grab his ass, as if he'd pulled a glute. His hand came away wet; only then did he look down to see dark arterial blood spurting from the hole in his overalls.

"You should have put your hands up," said Lyssy as the bearded man took one more step, then crumpled to the ground. It took the puzzled-looking troll only a minute or so to bleed to death, unnoticed by Lyssy, who stood frozen in place, staring at the spot where Lilith had been lying, and from which she had somehow magically disappeared, leaving him alone on the patio with two dead bodies.

5

With a little help from her very pregnant friend Dennie, Mama Rose had manged to kill the rest of the afternoon and the early evening hours smoking dope, hitting the thrift shops, dining at a Mexican restaurant on Mt. Shasta Boulevard—but the time had died slowly.

It dragged even more slowly after Dennie left. Sipping espressos on the patio of the coffee shop where MacAlister was to meet her, Mama Rose couldn't get her mind off the unpleasant task which lay before her: shooting Maxwell in cold blood. Very cold blood: her plan was to handcuff him first, walk him around the side of the house, then shoot him in the head.

But nasty as that was to contemplate, it still beat thinking about what she'd tell Carson when he came home later that night and discovered that Lilith and Maxwell were gone. In a way, she thought, it might have been better to let Carson fuck the girl at least once—at the very least, it would have made it more difficult for him to lay any self-righteous guilt trips on her.

The sun was low in the sky when Mama Rose caught sight of a red Cadillac convertible pulling up in front of the coffee shop. As MacAlister had requested earlier, she made no sign of recognition, but she did make such a show of "casually" finishing her coffee—smacking her lips, shaking her head regretfully, and patting her lips with a paper napkin before pushing her chair back from the sidewalk table, pulling on her helmet, and zipping up her leather jacket—that if *he* had had her under surveillance, Pender whispered to Mick, he'd have been looking around to see who'd just arrived.

Just in case, MacAlister waited a full minute before following her. They caught up to the baby-blue Sportster waiting at a stop light at the edge of town and followed it discreetly for four and a half miles, to a derelict wood-frame gas station with two red, round-shouldered pumps out front, from which the hoses had been cruelly amputated. She rode around the back of the barnlike building; by the time they pulled up she was already off the bike, shaking out her thick red hair and combing it with her fingers.

"You made good time," she said, as Mick climbed out of the Caddy—Pender waited in the car, his face averted, his beret tugged low over one eye.

"Zoom, zoom," replied Mick.

"Any progress on the reward?"

"Ten thou, same as last time. Only thing is, I don't have the cash with me this time—you're just going to have to trust me."

"How do I know you won't try and screw me?"

"Lady, if I wanted to screw you—in that sense of the word—you'd have found a Michigan sandwich in that bag the other day." A Michigan sandwich, also known as a Michigan roll or brick, was a thick sheaf of bills with twenties or hundreds on the outside, depending on the size of the con, and singles or green paper cut to the size of currency on the inside.

"Okay, here's the situation," said Mama Rose. "You're gonna have to wait here for a couple hours. Carson's going out around nine—as soon as the coast is clear, I'll get Maxwell and the girl out of the attic, bring 'em back here, then they're all yours. You can make up any story you want for the cops, as long as you leave us out of it. If you rat us out, though, you're a dead man."

"Don't worry, I won't rat you out. But are you sure you can handle them?"

"I can handle them."

"Then we've got a deal." MacAlister shook Mama Rose's hand, then turned his attention to the Sportster. "That's a beaut," he said, walking around the bike, squatting to admire it at close range. "What year?"

"An original '57."

"Engine?"

"Fifty-five-cubic-inch overhead valve XL."

"Wow," said Mick, standing up and stepping back after surreptitiously affixing the miniature, magnetized GPS transponder to the underside of the teardrop-shaped gas tank. He handed her the two sets of handcuffs she had asked him to bring.

"Zoom, zoom," Mama Rose replied, donning her helmet, zipping her jacket, and kick-starting the Sportster on the first try.

Mick bustled back to the car, grinning. He grabbed a laptop computer from the backseat, balanced it on the center console. Pender leaned in from the other side and together they followed the Sportster's progress via a green dot superimposed over a scrolling onscreen map. Seventeen minutes later the signal went stationary; Mick tapped a few keys to save the coordinates in case Mama Rose failed to return.

By then the sun was nearly at the horizon. Mick and Pender climbed the rise behind the garage, where somebody—another pothead, Mick would have been willing to bet—had dragged the backseat of an old Chevy and positioned it facing due west in order to catch Mother Nature's crepuscular light show. Mick sat down, took his Sucrets tin from the pocket of his Levi's jacket, fired up a joint, offered Pender a toke.

"Maybe you ought to lay off that shit til this is over," said Pender.

"C'mon, it's gonna be shooting ducks in a barrel."

Pender reached into his sport coat pocket, took out the Havana Mick had given him earlier. Patting through his trouser pockets, he found his oval-shaped, double-bladed cutter, clipped the cap of the Macanudo. "Why do you think they call it dope?"

"Why do they call anything anything?"

Pender patted through his pockets again, took out an orange Bic. He rotated the cigar as he held the flame to it, puffing vigorously until the tip was a uniform cherry red. "Forgive him, Harry J. Anslinger," he said between puffs. "He knows not what he does."

MacAlister made the sign of the cross at the mention of the man who had almost single-handedly caused marijuana to be declared illegal in America, and while great clouds of cigar and cannabis smoke drifted over the meadow, glowing pinkish-brown against the backdrop of the setting sun, the retired FBI man treated the hippie-dippie private eye to a flawless rendition of Brewer and Shipley's "One Toke Over the Line."

Alone on the patio, kneeling next to the dead troll, Lyssy experienced an upwelling of despair so acute it was almost physically painful. For a few wild seconds he considered putting the gun to his head and pulling the trigger; then he heard the homely, familiar sound of the loudest toilet in northern California.

"Lilith? Lilith, where are you?"

No answer. He opened the sliding-glass door and hurried into the living room, which was dominated by a huge flat-screen television. With the power off, the house was so quiet he could hear the gurgling of water through the pipes as the noisy toilet refilled itself. He followed the sound down a corridor and through a bedroom, and found Lilith standing naked next to the toilet, looking down into the tank, from which she'd removed the heavy porcelain cover.

Seemingly unaware of his presence, she pushed the lever to flush the toilet, staring intently down into the bowl, fascinated by the swirling water, then turned her attention to the tank, to watch the red rubber ball bobbing atop the rising water level. Then, when it was high enough, she pushed the lever, and the process began again.

"Lilith, we have to get out of here."

There was still no indication that she was aware of Lyssy's presence, and when he grabbed her elbow and began tugging her away from the toilet, her resistance—she leaned her full weight in the opposite direction—was disturbingly impersonal, as if she were pulling against a rope tied to a cleat.

He tugged her as far as the bedroom, but as soon as he released his grip on her arm, she darted back into the bathroom. "Okay, just stay there," he called, limping for the doorway. "Don't go anyplace—I'll be right back for you."

Ka-wooooshhh!

* * *

The trick to climbing the macadam driveway on a motorcycle was to maintain enough speed coming out of the turn to carry you up the slope without having to downshift. Mama Rose executed it perfectly, slewing the Sportster to a stop at the relatively level top of the driveway, next to a red GMC pickup recently released from the chop shop.

The house was completely dark. Must have had another power outage, she told herself. Rather than try to raise the electric door manually, she walked the Sportster around to the side of the garage—leaving a bike visible from the road was a definite no-no—and parked it next to Li'l T.'s custom chopper.

"Power out again?" she called as she lowered the kickstand and hung her helmet from the handlebars. No answer. She continued around the side of the house, heard a toilet flushing inside, smelled something burnt and nasty, then saw Li'l T. lying in a pool of blood on the cement patio.

Reality took a sudden lurch; slowly, with a nightmarish sense of powerlessness, Mama Rose raised her eyes to the hot tub and saw the thing that had been Carson floating motionless on the still surface of the water.

Now that he too knew what it was like to love someone, Lyssy, concealed behind the living room curtains, felt awful for Mama Rose. He wondered whether it would be a bad thing to just shoot her right then and there and save her a truckload of heartbreak.

But his first responsibility was to himself and Lilith. "Don't move," he called, stepping out onto the patio, gun in hand.

"You did this?" she said unbelievingly.

"Where do you keep the money?"

Mama Rose's lips pulled back in an uneven snarl. "Not a chance in hell, you dickless piece of shit gimp motherfucker."

"Look, I understand you're upset, but we really need the money, so please, if you could just tell me where you keep it, and give me the keys to that pickup out front, we'll get out of your hair."

"Jesus fucking Christ, you're even crazier than they said you were."

"Actually, I test more or less normal," he said, limping toward her.

"Normal? You're a nut job, you're a fucking wacko. And as for that fucking cunt that brought you here, when I get my—"

This time he was ready for the kick of the .38; the shot whanged off the concrete at Mama Rose's feet, sending up a puff of cement dust. "There's no use calling names. It's *his* fault." Tilting his head toward the hot tub. "If he hadn't tried to rape Lilith, none of this would have happened. And now *I* have to take care of *her*. And *you* have to tell me where the money is, because if you don't, I have to do some stuff to you I don't even want to *think* about. Because I really don't want to hurt you. Really."

It wasn't that she didn't believe him—she simply

didn't fucking care. Like an incoming tide, shock and anger had carried her as far as they could, then receded, leaving her high and dry on a desolate beach. "Eat shit and die," she said without heat.

The usage was new to Lyssy. Eat, shit, and die, he thought—what's that, everybody's life story?

Inside the house, the toilet continued to flush.

6

After sunset, Pender and MacAlister strolled back down the hill to the Cadillac. Mick raised the top to protect the leather upholstery from the evening dew, then opened his laptop again to keep an eye on the Sportster.

For most people, sitting in a parked car for two hours would have been stultifying, but for the ex-cop and the private investigator it was just another day at the office. They watched the green dot not moving, talked about sports, about old girlfriends and even older cases, then watched the green dot not moving some more.

At nine forty-five, MacAlister turned to Pender. "I sink ve've got ein problem, Professor," he announced in a stagy German accent.

"Give it another few minutes—and why are you talking like Dr. Strangelove?"

"Was I? Maybe I *should* lay off the weed for a while."

At ten o'clock—the transponder was still broadcasting the same coordinates—they agreed that a look-see was definitely in order.

With MacAlister driving and Pender navigating by the green glow of the laptop screen, they rolled slowly along the back roads of Shasta County for close to half an hour. As they neared the designated axis, Mick pulled over to the side of the road and turned off his headlights. All was darkness—no lights, no dwellings. He double-checked the coordinates on the laptop against the Caddy's onboard GPS system, looked over at Pender, and shook his head, baffled. State-of-the-art technology was assuring him they were within two hundred feet of the transponder, while his eyes were insisting they were alone on a dark country road.

"Mama Rose probably spotted the bug, tossed it into the weeds," said Mick.

"Ssh!" A faint noise from the hillside looming up on their left had caught Pender's attention. He signaled for Mick to turn off the engine, then closed his eyes and held his breath, listening for all he was worth and hearing at first only the rasp of crickets and the soughing of wind in the treetops. "Never mind, you're probably right," he whispered—then he heard it again, a faint groaning sound, like water rushing through pipes.

So did Mick—he reached across Pender, unlocked the glove compartment, took out a nine-millimeter Czech automatic with a flat black Stealth finish, popped in a fifteen-round clip, and jacked a round into the chamber, but left the safety on.

"Does your friend have a friend for me?" Pender asked him, nodding toward the pistol.

"You're not packing?" It was too dark to see MacAlister's face, but he *sounded* surprised.

"I'm retired, remember?"

"What's that got to do with anything? This is America, goddamnit—*everybody*'s supposed to have a gun. It's in the constitution or something." MacAlister handed Pender a long, heavy six-cell flashlight. "Here, take this."

Pender hefted it. "You call this a weapon? What am I supposed to do, hit him over the head?"

"Actually, I call it a flashlight—I was hoping maybe you could sort of shine it around so we could see where we're going."

"Wise guy," muttered Pender. He climbed out of the car, closed the door quietly behind him. The piney air was cool and thin; somewhere out there a cricket was going batshit. Shielding the beam with his palm, he shined it back and forth, waving it slowly and carefully like a Geiger counter, until it picked out a dark paved surface climbing steeply upward from the road. Leaning forward against the pull of gravity, Pender preceded Mick up the face of the asphalt mountain. When he next heard the noise, he was close enough now to identify the sound of a toilet flushing—he was reminded of Archie Bunker's noisy crapper in *All in the Family*—and water groaning through old pipes.

Neither Pender's rubber-soled Hush Puppies nor Mick's rubber-soled, negative-heeled Earth Shoes made any noise as they padded up the asphalt. There was a pickup truck parked at the top of the driveway, but no sign of Mama Rose or her bike. The garage door was locked. They walked around the side of the garage, saw Mama Rose's Sportster parked next to a much larger Harley. Mick stooped to retrieve the transponder from the gas tank, then followed Pender around to the back of the darkened ranch house.

Pender shone the flashlight around the narrow patio, illuminating, in turn: a trellis twined with pink roses, a wrought-iron patio table lying on its side, a redwood hot tub with a plywood cover, and when he trained the flashlight straight down, a puddle of some thick, black, half-congealed substance pooled in a shallow declivity in the concrete at their feet.

Pender stooped, touched his forefinger to the sticky stuff, and brought it to his nose. The smell of blood was dreadfully familiar—his head jerked away from it so violently he almost sprained his neck.

Ka-whoooshhh! The toilet again. Mick signaled for Pender to turn off the flashlight, then sidled through an open, sliding-glass doorway flanked by curtains. Pender followed. The house was even darker inside than out. From the end of a short hallway to their left came an indistinct grunting sound. Moving in lockstep, one behind the other like a baggy-pantsed vaudeville team, MacAlister and Pender followed the noise to the open doorway at the end of the corridor on the left.

Inside, candlelight flickered. Mick signaled for Pender to wait in the hall, then slipped into the room sideways to present a slimmer target profile. A fat candle burned on a saucer on the bedside table; Mama Rose lay mummified on the bed, cocooned in winding sheets from neck to ankles, with a strip of torn linen serving as a gag, through which she grunted frantically, rolling her eyes toward the adjoining bathroom.

Ka-whoooshhh! Mick held his pistol in a braced, two-handed firing position as he approached the open bathroom doorway. The DeVries girl, all but lost in an orange, hibiscus-pattered muumuu several sizes too large, was standing over the toilet, aiming a pencil flashlight straight down into the tank and watching in rapt fascination as the water level rose. She didn't appear to have noticed Mick.

"Pender, in here!"

Pender hurried into the bedroom, caught sight of the girl in the bathroom. "Lily," he called. No response. "Lily, it's Uncle Pen."

Still no response. Pender put his arm around her and gently ushered her out into the dim light of the bedroom, where Mick had put his gun down, and was sawing through Mama Rose's gag with his pocket jackknife.

Goddamn pothead, thought Pender, seeing the gun lying useless on the bed. "For shit's sake, Mick—"

But it was too late. "Hands up, please!" called a high-pitched male voice, from the doorway.

They all froze in place like a kid's game of Statues, their shadows dancing nervously in the flickering candlelight. "Take it easy there, son," said Pender, standing just outside the bathroom door with his arm still draped around Lily's shoulders.

"I *said,* everybody put your hands *up,*" Lyssy

called petulantly, turning the gun from MacAlister to Pender and the girl, then back to MacAlister. But when Pender raised his hands, the girl darted into the bathroom and slammed the door behind her. Lyssy's eyes flickered toward the sudden movement and noise. Seeing him distracted, Mick dropped the jackknife and dove for the gun.

Lyssy whirled, his finger tightening on the trigger. *Blam, blam, blam, blam*—four shots. Blue flashes like lightning lit the room. A gobbet of something wet flew past Mama Rose's head and hit the candle; the flame sizzled and died.

"How come nobody ever *listens* to me?" Lyssy whined in the darkness, as the toilet began flushing again in the bathroom. "Nobody *ever* listens to me."

7

Irene had no appointments scheduled for Thursday afternoon—according to her original schedule, she was still supposed to be in Portland. Her spirits somewhat buoyed by Pender's mid-afternoon telephone call (from what she'd been able to make out over what sounded like the roar of a hurricane, he and MacAlister had an extremely promising lead and were driving up to Shasta to check it out), she'd spent the day catching up on a myriad of chores—correspondence, revisions for the new edition of her textbook on dissociative disorders, a little dusting, a little gardening.

After supper (a prepacked salad of wilted baby greens, glazed pecans, crumbled feta, and dried cranberries from Trader Joe's that had been in her fridge since Sunday—hence the wilted greens), Irene went outside to water her prize-winning Cecil Bruner roses, then ran the vacuum cleaner and did a load of laundry: as an eco-conscious, energy-saving Californian, she always did her watering and ran her major appliances in the evening.

Irene locked up the house and went upstairs to bed around ten o'clock. She set her alarm, laid out her jogging outfit, changed into her last surviving pair of Frank's oversize pajamas—she had to turn the sleeves and legs up several inches—and climbed into bed with the new issue of *Psychology Today,* which for her constituted light reading.

At eleven, she switched off the light and turned on the TV at the foot of the bed to watch the news. KSBW, the NBC affiliate in Salinas, led with the story of last night's murders in Oregon, hitting hard on the two local angles—Lily's Pebble Beach address and Maxwell's previous rampage in Monterey County.

But there was no real clarification of Lily's status. "Portland police say they still aren't clear as to whether the young woman from Pebble Beach was involved directly with any of the killings, but stressed that until they know more, both fugitives should be considered armed and dangerous," cautioned the sad-eyed, folksy anchorman with the David Letterman widow's peak.

"Oh, shut up," said Irene, switching off the television. She lay there in the dark for another few minutes, then climbed out of bed and went back downstairs to double-check whether she had indeed locked both doors.

As it turned out, she had—for all the good it would do.

8

"C'mon, Lilith, we have to find that money and get out of here."

Although she seemed to be unharmed physically, the girl's repetitive, almost robotic preoccupation with the workings of the toilet had continued while Lyssy cuffed Pender to the brass rail of the headboard ("Is that too tight? Let me know if it's too tight."), gagged him with torn strips of sheeting ("I know it's uncomfortable—there, is that better?"), then wrapped him with winding sheets ("Here we go round the mulberry bush.") and left him lying there next to Mama Rose, similarly gagged, cuffed, and bound; they looked like two mummies lying with their hands raised in surrender.

"C'mon, please?" There was no indication that Lilith recognized Lyssy. She seemed scarcely aware of his existence, or rather, of his existence as a fellow sentient being—for all the notice she took of him as he tugged her out of the bathroom, he might have been a mechanical device to which she was attached, a winch or a block and tackle.

He closed the bathroom door, led her into the middle of the bedroom, and let go of her, just to see what she'd do. With the door closed, she appeared to have forgotten about her beloved toilet—out of sight, out of mind. Instead she glanced around the bedroom, where half a dozen candles now flickered and glowed, then made straight for the antique brass apothecary scale on the dresser, stepping over the denim-clad, ponytailed body of the dead interloper as if it were a log.

Soon she was engrossed in balancing the counterpoised trays with the tiny brass milk-bottle–shaped weights; everything else, including Lyssy, had apparently ceased to exist for her.

"Lilith, we have to go," he said again, dumping the scale and weights into the pillowcase, along with Carson's revolver, which he'd reloaded from a box of shells he'd found in the drawer of the bedside table. There was another pistol with a wooden handle in the other bedside table, but Lyssy decided to take the dead man's gun instead. It was lying where it had fallen, inches from the outstretched hand of the now-faceless corpse. He picked it up and popped the clip to see how many rounds were left. There were fourteen, with another round in the chamber: Mick hadn't fired a single shot.

The girl watched from the bedroom doorway, fascinated, as Lyssy worked the pistol's mechanism; now she held out her hand, making that mewing noise again, and stamping her bare foot on the doorstep.

"Sorry, Charlie," he told her—one of Dr. Al's

corny sayings. "These things are dangerous if you don't know how to . . . holy cow." He looked down at the gun in his hand—it had finally dawned on him that for all his demonstrated expertise, before this evening he himself had never fired a gun, never even held a pistol. And yet handling one seemed to be second nature to him. Which meant . . . what?

His mind working at warp speed, he came up with three possibilities. The first was that he'd picked up his knowledge of firearms unconsciously, maybe from all the videos and TV shows he'd watched, and had proved to be a natural.

Another possibility was that since he and his alters shared one brain, perhaps as the original personality he was able to draw upon the knowledge and experience of the alters without even being aware of it—which was a little scary.

But there was a third possibility, even more frightening: that *he* was the one being used. By Max. Or guided, or controlled, or whatever you wanted to call it. A jolt of terror coursed through him at the thought. It was like that bad dream he used to have when he first came to the Institute, a nightmare where he's running from a monster, and finally reaches a safe place. Only there's a mirror there, and when he looks into it, he sees the monster's face looking back at him and realizes he hasn't escaped at all. And never would, because he was the monster and the monster was him.

Then he heard that faint mewing sound again. He looked up, saw Lilith standing in the doorway wearing that ridiculous orange muumuu, looking for all the world like a little girl playing dress-up in Mommy's clothes, and suddenly all that mattered to him was taking care of her.

Earlier that evening, he'd found himself unable to carry through on his threat to torture Mama Rose until she told him where the money was. After running out of verbal threats, he'd settled for tying her up, covering the still-naked Lilith with a muumuu from the closet, and leaving the girl to entertain herself with the endlessly fascinating toilet while he disposed of the troll's body, dumping it into the hot tub and dragging the plywood cover over the tub. Then he began his search of the house and grounds.

He'd been going through the living room for the second time when he heard the two men out on the patio. He'd ducked behind the sofa, followed them into the bedroom, caught them by surprise.

And now it was time to try playing the Spanish Inquisition game again. It occurred to Lyssy that he might be less inhibited if Lilith weren't within earshot.

"C'mon, let's go find your own clothes," he told her, dropping the second gun into the pillowcase sack, then holding it over his head and shaking it alluringly as he brushed by her on his way out of the room. Zombie-like, she turned and followed him down the short hallway, through the living room, and out onto the patio.

The moon had risen since he'd last been out here, illuminating the overturned table, the scattered furniture, and the dark pool of blood. He righted the table, then dumped the scale and weights out for

Lilith to play with while he snatched her sweater and jeans off the trellis where she'd draped them earlier.

She neither resisted nor assisted him as he took off the muumuu. His breath caught in his throat to see her naked in the moonlight. He wrestled the sweater over her head, somehow pulled her arms through the sleeves, then knelt at her feet and lifted her legs one at a time, as if he were shoeing a horse, to get her jeans on. As he tugged them up past her knees, the back pocket turned inside out and a small white card fluttered to the ground.

Lyssy picked it up, turned it over, shined his flashlight on it, and whistled under his breath. There, spelled out for his convenience, were the name, address, and phone numbers of Lily's original psychiatrist, Dr. Irene Cogan, the woman he remembered from their stroll through the arboretum Monday afternoon.

"You know what, I'm starting to think things might be turning our way," he told Lilith, slipping the card into his own pocket. "You stay here, have fun with your new toys. I have to go talk to Mama Rose—I'll be back soon."

Lyssy limped back inside to the bedroom where Pender and Mama Rose were tied up, pulled a chair over to Mama Rose's side of the bed, leaned over, and tugged the gag from her mouth. Her face and hair were still spattered with gobbets of blood and brain matter, none of it her own. "I'm trying to be polite about this, ma'am. Dr. Al always said you catch more flies with honey than with vinegar. And I'm sorry about what happened to your husband. I wish I could bring him back, I really do. But I have responsibilities now. I have Lilith to think of. And we're going to need that money to have even a chance of surviving out there. So either you tell me where it is, or I have to . . . to . . ."

His glance had fallen upon the mother-of-pearl-handled jackknife lying open on the bed.

Sudden flash: a knife in a hand scarred and crippled like his own hand rises and falls, rises and falls against a backdrop of bright bunting and bobbing birthday balloons. Confusion—he is neither here nor there, neither himself nor someone else. The bed is an island, floating in a sea of darkness. There is only the knife in his hand and the redhead laid out before him, mummified like some kind of ritual sacrifice.

Mama Rose, upon seeing him pick up the knife, shut her eyes. Her body tensed, waiting for the first blow to fall. And waiting. And waiting.

"No!" Lyssy's shout broke the silence, broke the spell. He flung the knife away. *You can go to hell,* he told them—Kinch, Max, whoever was listening. *You can all go straight to hell.*

"The attic," said Mama Rose weakly, without opening her eyes.

Lyssy slumped back in his chair. "What?"

"The money—it's in the air conditioner in the attic."

"Oh." Lyssy was so drained, it took a few seconds for the victory to soak in.

Who's nothing now, Mister Max? he thought, popping the gag back into Mama Rose's mouth before leaving the bedroom; seconds later he was back, removing it again. "The lock on the trapdoor—what's the combination?"

She told him; back went the gag. It took Lyssy several tries—he'd never used a padlock of any sort—but eventually it popped open. He pushed the trapdoor up and over, boosted himself up into the attic. A cool night breeze wafted through the now-empty dormer window. Lyssy's flashlight beam illuminated the dark hulk of the air conditioner on the floor.

The fall had cracked the case and sprung the frame. Lyssy's fingers pried loose the plastic panel in the back, which was held in place by four recessed screws. One last yank snapped off the corner of the panel, and a quick inspection with the flashlight ended the search: the air conditioner was indeed hollow, and stuffed with rubber-band-bound stacks of currency, as well as a hand-cranked clear plastic coin sorter and a sack of loose change.

Half an hour later, with the cash in the trunk of the Cadillac at the bottom of the driveway (the keys had been in the ignition), Lyssy returned to the patio, where Lilith was still happily engrossed with her scale and weights, and lured her down to the car and into the backseat with the even more fascinating coin sorter.

So far, so good, he thought as he fastened Lilith's seat belt for her, slammed the back door, and limped around to the driver's side of the car. But there was something nagging at the back of his mind—something undone or forgotten, some vague, inchoate misgiving. He tried to focus, tried to close his mind around it as he slid behind the wheel and turned the key, but nothing came to him.

The engine roared to life. Lyssy experimented for a few seconds and discovered that he could work the accelerator by planting the heel of his prosthetic right foot on the textured rubber floor mat and the toe on the gas pedal, then pushing down with his thigh to rock the foot forward, using the ankle spring as a fulcrum. He turned on the headlights, planted his left foot on the brake pedal, and shifted the Cadillac into gear.

Lurch, *screech,* lurch, *screech*—it took a few minutes of trial and error, but eventually he got the hang of driving two-footed, and from then on, it was smooth sailing. And not only that, but by the time he figured out what had been nagging at him subconsciously—a minor detail: he'd never driven an automobile before—the point was utterly moot.

I guess it just proves that whatever happens, I can handle it, Lyssy told himself. I can handle whatever happens.

CHAPTER EIGHT

1

After struggling against his bonds for hours, the only tangible progress Pender had made was in loosening his gag in order to breathe around it. But that was a not-unimportant achievement: it meant he could allow himself to fall asleep without having to worry about suffocating.

Or not so much fall asleep as doze off for a few minutes before being jolted awake by the apnea that had prevented him from sleeping on his back for the last five years or so. It was an uncomfortable, even frightening feeling, awakening with the sound of your own snort still echoing in your ears, and realizing that the back of your throat had swollen shut, blocking both airways—but then, being awake was no goddamn picnic either.

When he wasn't thinking about the possibility

of never being rescued, of dying here either of thirst or suffocation—which was *not* all that likely when you considered the situation rationally, he had to keep reminding himself—Pender had time to wrestle with his own shame and grief. He'd come to like Mick MacAlister in those last few hours—his mind-projector kept screening the clip of the two of them sitting on that old automobile seat on the hill behind the barn, harmonizing on a medley of pot songs—"One Toke Over the Line," "The Joker," and of course "Puff the Magic Dragon"—before the gnats and mosquitos chased them back inside the car.

But oh what a fiasco (Fucked In All Seven Common Orifices, as the folk etymology had it) the two of them had perpetrated. They couldn't have blown it any worse if they'd been on Maxwell's payroll—and Pender didn't even have the excuse of being stoned. Yes, it had been Mick who'd put the gun down so he could free Mama Rose, but surely Pender should have been watching for Maxwell instead of hurrying to Lily's side.

Then when the firing began, Pender remembered with deep shame, his response had been to hit the floor. If only he'd done *something, anything:* charged Maxwell, thrown the flashlight at him, run for the door, dived for the bedroom window. Mick might still be dead, but Pender wouldn't be tied up here like a Christmas goose—and Maxwell wouldn't have a six-hour lead. Or twelve, or twenty-four, or however long it took before *somebody* dropped by the pink ranch house.

* * *

Lying next to Pender with eighteen inches or so of space between them, Mama Rose lost the battle with her bladder in the first few hours, which meant that in addition to the dire thirst, the muscle cramps, the headache from rebreathing stale air, and a rapidly worsening case of claustrophobia—a disorder that had never troubled her before—she now had a new problem to worry about. *Diaper rash,* she told herself, with a harsh mental laugh. Okay, Rosie, what's next?

But although she had, like Pender, managed to loosen her gag far enough to be able to breathe through her mouth, unlike Pender Mama Rose never stopped struggling with it, worrying at the fabric, until eventually—around two or three in the morning, at a guess—the linen strips had gone damp and slack enough to enable her to shove the gag out of her mouth with her tongue.

"Hey," she said.

"Mmmf," replied Pender.

"I got an idea."

"Mmmf?"

"Can you get any closer?"

Wriggling, writhing, he humped sideways as far as the cuffs securing his hands to the headboard would permit. Mama Rose did the same; they met in the middle of the bed. "Try to turn onto your side," she told him.

He couldn't, not without dislocating his shoulders. "Okay, just your head, turn your head toward me."

He did, and discovered that she had succeeded where he'd failed, and was lying on her side. They looked into each other's eyes for a few seconds—her eyes were a darker blue than his, puffy and red-rimmed from crying for Carson; she had a tiny white scar on the bridge of her nose. She strained toward him. Her face came closer, closer, her mouth open, her teeth bared, her breath foul. For a few seconds he thought she'd gone bonkers and was going to start kissing or biting him; he flinched away.

"Hold still," she told him, then seized his gag in her teeth and started chewing.

2

Irene Cogan rarely dreamed about her late husband. When Frank did make an appearance, it was as a nebulous figure on a busy sidewalk, or across the room at a crowded party, his face in deep shadow. Sometimes she'd realize he was there and try to fight her way across the room, or catch up with him as the current of the crowd swept him along, but always in vain.

Until tonight, that is. The party scenario again. Just as she recognizes Frank, he turns away and starts for the door. Frantically, she calls his name, struggles to catch up to him. He turns back just as she reaches him. His face is blue with cold, his beard rimed with frost.

"Frank! I thought you were—"

"Zip it," he whispers harshly, touching his skeletal forefinger to his lips.

She turns to scream; the hand clamps over her mouth.

"Don't be scared, I'm not going to hurt you."

A boyish voice. The dream hand was still clamped over her mouth. Irene opened her eyes, saw Ulysses Maxwell's face floating above her, filling her field of vision.

"Promise me you won't scream?"

She nodded. He removed his hand from her mouth; she took in a great gulp of air. The bedside lamp was on, the bedroom curtains closed. Next to the clock-radio on her bedside table, the cradle for the cordless phone lay empty.

"Remember me, Dr. Cogan?"

Panic rose like a swelling tide; part of her yearned to lose herself in it, to make a clean psychotic break. But something in his pleading tone, in the earnestness with which his gold-flecked brown eyes searched her own, encouraged her to hold on just a little longer. "Yes, of course, Lyssy. How did you get in?"

"I squeezed through that little sliding window in the downstairs bathroom. You're Lily's doctor, right?"

"Ohmigod, Lily!" Irene sat up, fully awake. "Is she all right? Where is she?"

"In the next room. But there's something wrong with—"

Irene, still wearing Frank's pajamas, scrambled out of bed and hurried into the spare bedroom with Lyssy close behind.

Lily was sitting cross-legged on the floor, her back to the door, busily cranking the handle of a plastic coin sorter. Irene knelt at her side. "Lily? Lily, it's Dr. Irene."

When there was no response, she passed her hand across Lily's line of vision. The girl's dark eyes failed to track. "How long has she been like this?"

"Since last night."

Irene kept her eyes trained on Lily—it was easier to fight off the panic if she didn't look at Maxwell. "Was there something in particular that set her off?"

"A shock—she got an electric shock. Can you help her?"

Irene saw a glimmer of hope. "Y-yes—but we have to get her to a hospital right away," she lied, after a short hesitation.

"Why?"

"Why?"

"Yeah, why? Why a hospital? What are they going to do for her?"

"A brain scan, for one thing."

"You know the police are after us, right?"

"I—yes, I know."

"Both of us."

"Yes."

"Do you know what they'll do if they catch us?"

"Send you back to Reed-Chase, I imagine," replied Irene, after another telltale hesitation.

"You're not a very good liar, are you?" said Lyssy.

"I suppose not."

"Me neither. Can you help her?"

"I think so, but . . . " Her voice trailed off.

"But what?"

Irene forced herself to look directly into his eyes. "I'm not sure I'd be doing her much of a favor."

3

Talk about your Odd Couple: compared to Pender and Mama Rose, Oscar Madison and Felix Unger were practically clones. But lying next to each other during the course of that endless night, the former G-man and the biker mama discovered they had something in common after all.

"I lost my wife a little over six months ago," confided Pender, after learning about Carson's death.

"How long were you together?"

"Not even a year—she was diagnosed with pancreatic cancer not long after we were married."

"Over twenty years for me and Carson," said Mama Rose. "I don't even remember what it felt like to be single."

"I know it sounds stupid, but I sort of envy you," Pender mused.

"What do you mean?"

"I'd have sold my soul for twenty more years with Dawson—no matter how it had to end."

"Did she . . . ?" Her voice trailed off.

"Did she what, suffer?"

"Skip it—I guess it was my turn to say something stupid."

"A hideous couple of months—but the end was peaceful."

"What's his name, Lyssy, promised me Carson never even knew what hit him."

"Thoughtful little bastard, ain't he?"

"That's the weirdest part," said Mama Rose. "How careful and gentle he tied us up, like he was a fucking nurse or something."

"Makes sense when you think about it," Pender told her. "The hospital is all he knows—who else does he have as role models?"

Time ticked by slowly—but not as slowly as it had before they were able to converse. "How long do you think it'll be before somebody finds us?" Pender asked eventually.

"Depends. Normally nobody would bother me and Car until late afternoon—they know we usually sleep in. But he would have missed an important meeting last night, so somebody might be by to check about that. Then there's L'il T., the guy who got shot on the patio? His wife Dennie is like twelve months pregnant; this'd probably be the first place she'd come looking for him."

While Pender was thinking that over, his stomach gave out with a long, loud grumble. "Quiet down there," he said.

"How long since you ate last?"

"Lunch yesterday—I had a chili dog," said Pender—then he chuckled.

"What's so funny?"

He told her Mick's story about the Jersey shore diner: EAT HERE AND GET GAS. "How about you?"

"I had dinner in town with Dennie, and a piece of mud pie at the coffee shop before you guys showed up." Then, after another minute or so: "Shit."

"What?"

"I wasn't hungry until we started talking about food—now it's all I can think about."

"Let's change the subject—what's your favorite song?"

"It's kind of obscure—you probably never heard of it," said Mama Rose.

Pender grinned. "Care to make a little wager about that?"

4

After driving hundreds of miles, when as far as he could remember he'd never driven a car before, navigating via the onboard GPS, and solving a zillion other quotidian mysteries along the way—the self-serve gas pump, the coin-operated vending machine, the hot-air restroom hand-dryer—Lyssy was not about to be deterred by the misgivings of one stubborn psychiatrist.

"Just fix her."

"And if I refuse?" she asked stiffly.

She was all but daring him to frighten her into cooperating. Same as Mama Rose. He remembered the knife on the bed, the terrifying flashback—and suddenly he realized something he must have known all along, deep down: to frighten somebody else, you first have to frighten yourself. You have to plumb the depth of your own fear and haul up the worst horror lurking down there. "Then you get what everybody gets when they cross me," he said, as harshly as he could manage.

"And what would that be, Lyssy?"

"Kinched. You get Kinched."

Lyssy was half-right, anyway. In the end, it wasn't his threat, but rather the fear she read in his eyes that persuaded Irene. He looked like a little kid who'd just dropped the F-bomb on his parents—proud and apprehensive in equal measure. Look what a big boy I am; please don't punish me.

Irene also knew enough about Maxwell et al., however much the system had evolved (or was it devolved?) over the last few years, to understand that it was to her advantage, and Lily's as well, to do all she could to reinforce Maxwell's relatively benign original personality.

Besides, the psychiatrist didn't really believe what she'd said about not doing Lily a favor by bringing her back to consciousness. Irene had seen this unnamed autistic alter only once before, when Lily was first brought to her for a consult by a pediatric psychiatrist who was sharp enough to recognize that autism didn't just pop up full-blown at the age of four, however textbook the symptoms.

It hadn't taken Irene long to diagnose dissociative identity disorder, especially as Lily's parents had recently been convicted of child abuse in its ugliest form—*the* standard marker for this particular dissociative disorder. And happily, the symptoms of autism had disappeared, along with the unnamed alter, as soon as Irene put the girl under hypnosis.

But now Lily was once again in her own little world. True, it was a world without fear or pain, but also without joy or understanding or volition, and Irene could no more have left her there than she could have lobotomized her.

Still, hypnotizing an autie was a tricky proposition. Irene turned to Lyssy. "Help me bring her downstairs to my office."

Gone like magic was the pasted-on scowl. "Great, great, thanks. C'mon there, honey, let's take another little walk." He wrested the coin sorter from the girl's grasp and lured her out of the bedroom as though she were a donkey, and the toy a carrot.

Irene preceded them into the office and quickly cleared her desktop, on which she placed a small wooden metronome from her drawer. "Pull that chair over to the desk," she told Lyssy. "Now sit her down . . . good, good."

"I just want to tell you, I'm sorry about, you know, threatening you before, I just—"

Irene cut him off. "Never mind that now—let's focus on the job at hand, shall we? I want you to take the coin sorter away from her now. . . . It's okay, dear, it's okay, look here, look what Dr. Irene has for you." She turned on the metronome, set it to the highest speed—*tick tick tick tick.* The girl ceased her squirming and mewling and leaned forward, focusing her attention, her very *being,* on this new and fascinating object. She wasn't just watching it, she was becoming it. Breathing rapidly, eyeballs following the rapid motion, pulse racing, *tick tick tick tick.*

Irene waited a full minute, then slowly began lowering the metronome's speed, one setting at a time, and with it the girl's breathing. And as her breath rate slowed, her heart rate slowed . . . and slowed . . . and slowed. . . .

"Lily?" whispered Irene. "It's all right, dear, everything's okay, you're safe now, it's safe to open your— There you go, that's my girl. Hello, Lily."

5

"Anybody home?" a female voice called from the living room. "Carson, Mama Rose?"

Lying on their backs, their hands cuffed through the headboard railing, Mama Rose and Pender exchanged complex, profoundly meaningful glances. *We made it!* was the primary message in both sets of eyes, but a sincere acknowledgement of the ordeal they'd gone through together was also in there someplace, along with a mutual recognition that their lives were about to get seriously complicated again. "Back here, Dennie!"

Footsteps; then a mahogany-skinned, pie-faced, burstingly pregnant woman, shirtless under faded overalls, appeared in the doorway, staring in horror from the denim-and-tie-dyed-clad body on the floor to the mummified couple on the bed. "Mama Rose? Mama Rose, what happened?"

She doesn't know, thought the older woman. Doesn't know L'il T.'s dead. Doesn't know she's a widow, doesn't know that kid inside her is never gonna see his father. "Cut us loose, then I'll tell you all about it," she croaked through dry, cracked lips.

It wasn't quite as simple as it sounded. Big-bellied and awkward, Dennie had to kneel and go through the corpse's pockets until she found the universal cuff-key in the watch pocket of his jeans, then climb onto the bed and lean across Pender to reach their handcuffs, her swollen, blue-veined breasts swinging free inside the overalls. Ever a gentleman, and unable to avert his glance, he closed his eyes until she had finished.

It took several minutes for sensation, in the form of a thousand agonizing pinpricks, to return to their unused limbs. In the meantime, it was Dennie who cut through their linen mummy wrappings with a pair of shears, and Dennie who held a glass of water to Mama Rose's parched lips, tenderly cradling the back of Rose's head on what remained of her lap while the older woman sipped noisily, greedily, water dribbling down her chin.

Then Dennie eased Mama Rose to a sitting position, propped her up with the bed pillows, rolled up Mama Rose's pant legs, and began massaging her calves with both hands to restore the circulation. "Now will *somebody* please tell me what's going on around here?" she asked. "Teddy never came home last night and he's not answering his cell phone."

Rose glanced imploringly at Pender, who was busily chafing his crossed wrists with his tingling hands. He refused to acknowledge her unspoken plea: You tell her. She turned back to Dennie. "Worse than that," she said.

"Is he . . . is he hurt?"

Tough-talking Mama Rose, who had always scorned euphemisms, found herself unable to get the d-word out. "Teddy's . . . he's gone, Dennie. Carson, too—they're both gone."

Dennie kept working, head down, rubbing the life back into Rose's legs. Mama Rose thought for a minute the pregnant girl hadn't heard her, or had misunderstood; then the tears began plopping down onto her bare shins, and she remembered something Dennie had told her once: that Eskimo babies were taught to cry silently.

She longed to take the younger woman into her arms, but they weren't working yet; she longed to cry for Carson—and for herself—but somehow the long night of horror had robbed her of tears. Which was just as well, because with a cry of surprise Dennie suddenly left off massaging Rose's legs, and pressed her hands to her own great belly.

"What? What is it, honey?"

"I think I felt a contraction," said the newly widowed mother-to-be.

"Well that fucking figures," said Mama Rose. "That goddamn fucking well figures."

6

Daylight crept reluctantly through the cracks in the blinds. Outside the darkened office, the small town stirred to life. A newspaper thudded onto a front porch; a neighbor's dog barked to be let out; a crow on the back fence angrily greeted the new day.

Inside, despair. "It's not fair," Lily moaned, rocking back and forth on the couch, her knees drawn up to her chin and her hands clasped around her shins. "*I* never did anything wrong, *I* never hurt anybody."

Lyssy sat next to her, his hand resting lightly on the nape of her neck. "We know, believe you me, we know," he murmured soothingly. His posture and manner, his facial expressions, even that *believe you me,* were so eerily reminiscent of Al Corder that if Irene hadn't known better, she'd have sworn there was a family resemblance.

The rocking slowed; Lily turned her tear-streaked face toward Irene, who was sitting in a side chair drawn up in front of the sofa. "What happens next, Dr. Irene? Where do we go from here?"

"*You* don't need to go anywhere, dear. If what Lyssy just told us is true—and if Lilith was telling *him* the truth—then you haven't committed any crime. Quite the opposite, in fact: Alison says you saved her life. So whatever Lyssy decides to do—keep running, turn himself in—there's no reason you couldn't stay on here with me."

"And you won't send me back to the Institute?"

Irene smiled ruefully. "I promise you, dear, that's one mistake your uncle Rollie and I won't be making again." She turned to Lyssy. "As for you, Lyssy, I strongly recommend you give yourself up before anybody else gets hurt—including yourself. But if you do decide to keep running—"

Lyssy cut her off in mid-sentence. "Dr. Cogan?"

"What is it, Lyssy?"

"Could I talk to you alone for a second?"

She glanced around the tiny office. "Yes, of course. Lily, will you be all right by yourself for a few minutes?"

"I guess."

Irene led Lyssy out into the hallway, leaving the office door open so she could keep an eye on Lily. "What is it?"

"What I told you before, about how Lilith said it was Max and Kinch who did all the killing back at the director's residence?"

"Yes?"

"What if it wasn't true? What if she told me she'd killed one of them herself? Like maybe the psych tech you found upstairs in the bathroom."

Irene felt her hopes sinking. "*Is* that what she told you?"

"Just say she did—do you think there's any way the police would be able to tell?"

"There's something called forensics, Lyssy. Fingerprints, fibers, transfer evidence—they've got it down to a real science. So I'd say yes, if Lilith committed one of the murders, there's a good chance they'd be able to figure it out."

"And if they did, what would happen to her? Would they still let her stay here with you?"

Irene recalled her brave speech to Pender in the airport yesterday morning: I don't care what she's done or how involved she was, I won't let them put her away again. "Probably not," she said, sick with longing for the good old days—say, five minutes ago, when her options had seemed so straightforward and uncomplicated.

7

What to do, what to do, what to do? Pender's initial instinct was to grab a phone and call 911—then he remembered what MacAlister had told him about Carson yesterday: dirty as can be, fingers in everything from meth to money laundering. And no doubt Mama Rose was up to both wrists in the same illicit pies. If he summoned help, the cops would be swarming all over the place in a matter of minutes—he pictured Mama Rose being led away in handcuffs.

But why, he asked himself, should that make a difference to him? So what if he'd grown fond of her? He'd been a lawman his entire adult life—he should have been jumping at the chance to help put her and what was left of her gang away. Besides, if he didn't make the call, he'd be helping Maxwell escape, or at least extend his head start, which was already close to twelve hours and counting.

So why was he feeling so goddamn *guilty,* as if he were about to do something dishonorable? Which instinct should he turn his back on, the professional or the personal? Was it once a cop, always a cop, or did being retired give him some wiggle room, ethically speaking?

The answer, he already knew, was no, it didn't. But having come to that conclusion, Pender found himself asking: Do I give a flying fuck? Then he realized he already knew the answer to that question as well.

Rather than use his own or one of the house phones, he knelt down next to MacAlister and went through his pockets—rigor mortis was just beginning to loosen its hold on the stiffened limbs—until he'd found Mick's cell phone, which he used to dial the FBI tipline from memory.

"Listen carefully," he said. "Ulysses Maxwell left Shasta County around eleven o'clock last night driving a red, late-model Cadillac convertible with white upholstery and California plates. The owner's name is MacAlister, first name Michael or Mick. He's not with Maxwell though. The DeVries girl *is* with him, but she's a hostage, *not* an accomplice—she seems to be in some sort of trance state."

"Sir?" said the tipline operator. "Sir, don't—" Pender pressed the End Call button.

"Good choice," said Mama Rose. "For a second there, you had me worried."

Pender looked up, saw her holding a handsome nine-millimeter Colt with a blue-steel barrel and a fine-grained hickory grip. His eyes went from the gun to the phone in his hand, then back. "Likewise," he said.

"Are you going after him?"

In the past, Pender's mind had always summoned up pictures of the victims to drive himself; now the first image that came to his mind was of himself, lying there helplessly while Maxwell trussed him up like a Thanksgiving turkey. "Oh, yes."

"Here, you'll probably need this." She turned the gun around and handed it to him butt-first. Their eyes met in ironic recognition of all they'd been through, and of the mutual, and extremely unlikely, bond of trust that had been formed; then Mama Rose looked away, embarrassed. "I'm going to drive Dennie to the hospital in her car. You can take the pickup in the driveway—the keys are on the bureau there. I have to warn you, though—when you're done with it, don't keep it or try to sell it. Just park it someplace and walk away."

"I understand," said Pender. "And thanks—for everything. But there's one more problem."

"What's that?"

He jerked a thumb in MacAlister's direction. "He had a wife, too."

8

The little office, scarcely large enough to contain Dr. Irene's desk at one end and the couch at the other, held a world of memories for Lily. Here, fifty minutes at a time, two or three times a week, she'd spilled out her hopes and fears, her childhood nightmares and adolescent insecurities—in a sense, she'd grown up in this room.

But as she sat waiting on the couch while Lyssy and Dr. Irene conferred in the hallway, Lily felt far from nostalgic. Just knowing that Dr. Irene was out there discussing *her* future with a man she scarcely knew (as far as Lily was concerned, their entire acquaintance consisted of a twenty-minute stroll through the funny little park in the middle of the Institute) made her stiffen with resentment. People were always making decisions for Lily, and yet things could hardly have turned out any worse if she'd decided for herself—or flipped coins or consulted a Ouija board.

Of course, at the heart of her resentment, as always, was a white-hot hatred for what her parents had done to her, and for this abominable disease of hers—but not, oddly enough, for Lilith. Instead she found herself admiring what little she had learned about the alter, who seemed to be everything she wasn't: fearless, remorseless, resourceful, and above all, capable of protecting herself.

"Lily? Lily, we need to talk."

She looked up. Lyssy was limping toward her, looking smaller than ever in the oversize white T-shirt and the button-fly jeans with the cuffs turned up. Dr. Irene had just sat down at her desk on the other side of the room and was putting on a pair of old-fashioned acoustic headphones the size of earmuffs.

"Pump up the volume," Lyssy told the doctor. "I

need to hear the squeaking from here." Then, to Lily, as he sat down next to her: "So she can't listen in on us."

"Why not just leave her out there and close the door?" They were both whispering; between whispers, they found themselves listening for the tiny, tinny music leaking out from the psychiatrist's headphones.

"Because we can't trust her not to turn us in." He leaned in closer. "Lily, you have to decide whether you want to come with me or stay behind with her." He saw her glance across the room. "Dr. Irene can't help you with this one—it's a decision only you can make."

"Why would I want to go someplace with you?" said Lily without thinking. "I hardly even know you."

He winced; there was a sadness in his gold-flecked eyes she regretted having put there. "I'm sorry," he said. "I keep forgetting you're not Lilith. You see, me and her, we were kind of . . . you know, we were kind of in love. We were going to go away together as soon as we got hold of those bikers' money. Only like I told you before, there was the accident with the radio in the hot tub, and you were like a zombie or something, so I brought you here instead so Dr. Cogan could fix you up."

"I know, I know—you *told* us all that." Except the part about Lyssy and Lilith being in love. Were they also *lovers,* in that other sense of the word? Lily wondered. Had that man had sex with *her* body? It was almost too weird, and definitely too uncomfortable, to contemplate.

"But there's one thing I didn't tell you the truth about," Lyssy continued. "That part about how Lilith said Max and Kinch killed all four people at the Corders'? That's what we want the cops to think. That way you could go free, while one victim more or less isn't going to make much difference to me as far as my sentence goes.

"But Dr. Cogan says the cops can probably tell from our fingerprints and stuff who killed which victim. So I figured that before you decided whether to come along with me or stay behind, you needed to know that it was Lilith who killed the woman in the bathroom—that's what she told me, anyway. She said she—"

"No, don't!" cried Lily, covering her ears with her hands. "I don't want to hear about the details." It wasn't guilt—she felt precious little of that. Some shock, maybe, and a mounting sense of panic as the full import of Lyssy's revelation began to sink in. Still, she couldn't help feeling it was like one of those mystery movies where the main character has an identical twin who does all this stuff the other twin gets blamed for.

Only an alter is closer than a twin, Dr. Irene was always saying—it's a part of *you,* a part of yourself that had broken off when your psyche was shattered. Lily glanced over at the psychiatrist, who was tapping her long, russet-brown fingernails on the desk in time to whatever music she was listening to, and suddenly it occurred to her how much easier it would be if she could just give up and let Lilith take over—and how much better for all concerned.

The thought was kind of scary (for Lily, not

being in consciousness was a little like what she imagined being dead would be like: the world goes on, but you're not there) but also tempting. She pictured herself waking up somewhere in the future, the way she'd awakened this morning, or in the airplane the other day, and looking around in confusion at palm trees and a white-sand beach, straw huts and turquoise reefs; on the patio table next to her there'd be a colorful drink with a tiny umbrella in it.

Where am I? she'd ask, and Lyssy would reply, *A safe place. We made it, Lily—it's all over but the happily ever after.*

Then Lyssy's voice yanked Lily back from her daydream. "Me, I'm already looking at life without parole, minimum," he was saying. "If I'm lucky. Lethal injection if I'm not. So basically, I've got nothing to lose. I don't know what they'd give *you* for just *one* murder, but if you want to take a chance on coming with me, I'm pretty sure it won't make any difference to your sentence."

"Do you think we really have a chance of getting away?" Lily asked him.

"More of a chance than we have if we don't do anything, if we just sit around here waiting for a knock on the door."

"What I still don't get is why you want me to come with you. You'd probably stand a better chance alone. And it's not like *we* were ever lovers—that was Lilith, not me."

"But I fell in love with *you* first," he blurted.

She thought she'd misunderstood him. "You what?"

"Fell in love with *you*—with *this* you—the second I laid eyes on you in the arboretum."

"But—but *why*?"

"I don't think love *has* any whys," Lyssy told her. "It just—" He broke off, cupped a hand to his ear. "Hear that?"

Footsteps on the front porch, then a clanking sound.

"It's all right," said Dr. Cogan, who had taken off her earphones when she saw they were listening for something. "It's just the mailman."

The footsteps receded. "We're almost done here," Lyssy told the doctor. "Would you mind . . . ?" He waited until she'd donned the headphones again, then turned back to Lily. "The sooner we get going, the better our chances."

"But we can't just drive away and leave Dr. Irene—she'll call the police the second we're gone."

"Does that mean you've decided to come with me?" Lyssy tried to keep his voice casual, though his heart was in his throat.

"You said it yourself—what do I have to lose? But what about Dr. Irene?"

"Oh, I can handle that," said Lyssy happily.

9

Driving south in the red GMC pickup, Pender didn't even try to pretend he hadn't crossed the line. Aiding and abetting, obstruction of justice, possession of a stolen vehicle—he'd broken enough state and federal laws to put him away for at least a couple years.

Of course, he could still put it all to rights with one call to the Shasta County sheriff. But in this new, topsy-turvy world Pender found himself in, he knew that if he did the right thing, dropped a dime on Mama Rose, he'd be ashamed of himself for the rest of his life. He knew his life had been in her hands back there. She could have killed him easily enough—*should* have killed him, from a strictly pragmatic point of view: it was the only option that would have guaranteed her safety. Instead, by trusting him, she had put her life in his hands—that had to count for *something*.

Meanwhile, he'd done all he could for Mick—or rather, Mick's wife, whom he'd never met. At least this way, *all* the widows would get to bury their husbands, was Pender's thinking. And he'd get another shot at rectifying the worst mistake of his career—not finishing off Maxwell when he had the chance.

The late morning sun glinted off the hood of the pickup. Pender flipped the sun visor down and found a pair of *Men in Black*-looking shades clipped behind it. The fit was a little tight around the ears. Carson must have had a much narrower head, thought Pender—but then, who didn't? He tilted the rearview mirror to catch a glimpse of his three-quarter profile. Pretty sharp for a fat old bald man, he told himself.

And there was no denying that it felt awfully exhilarating to be the Lone Ranger at long, long last. No Bureau-cracy to hem him in, no higher-ups to thwart him, and only one imperative to follow: find Ulysses Maxwell and take the sonofabitch *down.*

1∅

"Dr. Irene?"

Irene took off the headphones, paused Vivaldi's "Four Seasons" in the middle of the pizzicato winter ice storm. "Yes, dear?"

"I've made up my mind—I'm going with Lyssy."

"Are you absolutely sure that's what you want to do?"

"Um, *excuse* me? Isn't that what 'I made up my mind' usually means?" said Lily, her voice dripping with adolescent sarcasm. In other circumstances, thought Irene, that would have been a healthy sign—in our culture, it was one of the primary tools used by teenagers to effect the inevitable separation from the parent. "Only there's something you have to do for me first," Lily added.

"What's that?"

"I want you to put me under again and bring Lilith back instead."

"What?" Lyssy yelped. He looked as surprised as Irene felt—obviously this was something they hadn't discussed beforehand.

"It's the best thing," Lily explained to him. "She'll be a lot more use than I would—and I couldn't stand it if we got captured again. And maybe Dr. Irene could put in some kind of posthypnotic suggestion, so if we made it to someplace safe . . . " In her mind's eye she saw the beach again, the white sand and the palm trees. ". . . if you still wanted to, you could, you know, bring me back like?"

Lyssy tried to picture how that scenario might play itself out. It sounded like the rescue fantasy of all rescue fantasies, only for real. And of course he did miss Lilith: the memory of their lovemaking was never far from his thoughts. But when he looked over at Dr. Cogan, she was shaking her head.

"Absolutely not. Even if I thought it could work, which is far from likely, reinforcing an alter identity at the expense of the original personality could have far-reaching, potentially disastrous consequences for the system. And it's unnecessary besides—remember what I've been telling you all these years: Lilith is not a separate magical being, Lily—she's part of you. There's nothing Lilith is capable of that you're not: when you've finally internalized that, you'll have come a long way toward integrating."

Then Irene stood up—she was still wearing Frank's pajamas—came around from behind the desk, dragged the side chair over to the couch again. "Speaking of alters, there's one crucial point neither of you seem to have taken into consideration," she said, sitting opposite the two seated on the couch, her gaze traveling from one to the other, finally resting on Lyssy. "What if Max or Kinch comes back?"

It should have been the clincher; instead, Lyssy grinned.

"What's so funny?" asked Irene.

"Max already tried," said Lyssy. "I kicked his butt right back to the dark place." He put his hand on Lily's knee, gave it an encouraging squeeze. "What do you say, kiddo? You ready?"

"Ready as I'll ever be," she said. "C'mon, let's get this show on the road."

Part Three

La Guarida

CHAPTER NINE

1

A Ferris wheel turned slowly against the hazy Santa Cruz sky. An old-fashioned wooden roller coaster roared and rattled overhead, trailing shrieks and laughter. On the carousel, painted horses and other, more fantastical creatures bobbed to the cheerful piping of a calliope. The familiar scent of popcorn, cotton candy, and corn dogs packed a Proustian wallop, sending Pender back in time to the county fairs of his boyhood in upstate New York.

After wiping the cab clean of fingerprints, he abandoned the red pickup in a metered space in front of the Carousel Motel, across the street from the Boardwalk, then strolled casually back to the weedy lot behind the bowling alley where he'd left the Barracuda only—good Lord, was it only yesterday afternoon? It seemed like months had gone by—Pender had himself half-convinced that when he got there he'd find the car missing or up on blocks, stripped.

But the 'Cuda was intact, only a thin film of dust marring the gleam of the hand-polished black finish. With a turn of the key and a little babying of the accelerator, the engine rumbled to life, setting the dust motes on the hood vibrating aimlessly like the little plastic players in one of those old electrostatic football games.

From Santa Cruz, it was a relatively straight shot down Highway 1 to Pacific Grove. Driving at a sedate ten miles over the given speed limit, with the dashboard radio tuned to a Salinas oldies station, Pender made it in just under fifty minutes. Twice during the drive he tried to call Irene; twice he reached her voice mail. Detouring past her two-story cream and tan board-and-batten house, he saw that her driveway was empty. Since she rarely garaged her new beige Infiniti (central coast homes were built for the most part without basements or attics, so storage space was always at a premium), he assumed she was out and about.

Just as well, he told himself, driving another three blocks to his cottage—he and his clothes were decidedly gamy by now. He took a quick shower, ran an electric razor over his jowls, and changed into plaid Bermuda shorts and a chocolate-brown Hawaiian shirt patterned with green palm trees and a yellow sunburst, which actually caused certain aesthetically sensitive souls to wince when they first saw it. Black socks and logan green Hush Puppies completed the outfit. He tried Irene's phone again, got her voice mail again. Made himself a Pender-size sandwich of ham and Swiss on rye for supper. Redial; voice mail. Washed it down with a pony bottle of Rolling Rock. Redial; voice mail.

Man, I hope she hasn't left town, thought Pender. No doubt the BOLOs had been updated by now—cops in three states would Be On the Look-Out for the red Caddy. They'd have choppers out, dogs, the whole caboodle—and lord knows he wished them luck. But Maxwell had eluded the authorities successfully before. He had a talent for it that bordered on genius, and more than his share of luck. If he made it to ground with all that cash, there was no telling how long he could evade capture.

That's where Irene Cogan came in. She was Pender's ace in the hole. Between the two of them, they knew more about Maxwell and Lily than anyone else alive—their histories, habits, and psychological profiles, their likes and needs, their dislikes and aversions—so it stood to reason they had a better chance of predicting the direction and object of their flight.

Another twenty minutes went by, then thirty. The kitchen phone rang; Pender snatched it off the hook. But it was only Marti Reynolds from *The People's Posse* show. She was hoping that in light of recent developments Pender wouldn't mind doing a supplementary interview to discuss the latest murders. He told her he was kind of busy at the moment, asked her to call him back on Monday.

"Of course," she said. "By the way, do you have any other numbers for Dr. Cogan? I've been trying to reach her all afternoon, but I keep getting her voice mail."

That makes two of us, sister, thought Pender. "No, sorry. If I do see her, I'll tell her you called."

It's probably nothing, he told himself, pacing the tiny kitchen. Mountain out of a molehill. She's out shopping, or jogging down by the rec trail. Or maybe she's with a patient or taking a nap—you just assumed the car wasn't in the garage.

But *assumed* was a dirty word to a graduate of the FBI Academy, retired or not. He grabbed his madras sport coat and a powder-blue Pebble Beach golf cap on the way out the door, and walked the three blocks to Irene's place.

Cogan's garage jutted out from the corner of the house, leaving only fifteen feet of driveway between the garage door and the street—a common enough arrangement in space-starved Pacific Grove. Tall as he was, Pender still had to rise up on tiptoe to peek through one of the narrow, horizontal windows set high in the garage door. At first he saw only his reflection. Cupping his hand over his eyes to block the glare, he pressed his nose against the cold glass. The garage was dark, but not so dark he couldn't make out the outlines of the car inside.

Now, in his day, Pender had seen some truly awful sights. Mutilated corpses, severed heads stacked like cannonballs, that sort of thing. This was only a car in a garage. Nothing world-shattering about that—other than the fact that it wasn't Irene Cogan's new Infiniti, it was Mick MacAlister's Cadillac.

He tried the handle of the garage door: locked. He tried Irene's front door: ditto. Out of habit, he started to reach for his wallet—in the old days Pender had always kept a little jimmy in there for occasions such as this. But in those days, he'd also packed a badge—carrying one around without the other was a misdemeanor in all fifty states.

A narrow cement walk led around the side of the garage to Irene's office in back. The office door was locked, and the kitchen curtains drawn, but the horizontal sliding window that ventilated the downstairs half-bath was wide open. Irene often kept it open—not only was it six feet above ground, and scarcely large enough to admit a full grown adult, but if memory served, there had been a fixed screen there as well.

There was no screen now, though, and lying a few feet away, overturned in the flower bed bordering Irene's back fence, was a sturdy plastic recycling bin Maxwell could easily have used as a stepstool. *He came in through the bathroom window,* chimed in that irrepressible, and often annoying, little jukebox in Pender's head.

Okay, this is the part where the retired old FBI guy calls the cops, he thought. You tell the nice policemen everything there is to tell, then you go home, pop a cold one, put your feet up on the hassock, and watch the ball game.

Because this is no longer your business, old man. From here on in, all you can do is screw up somebody else's crime scene. Or if Maxwell's still inside, get somebody killed.

Then he remembered where he was: The Last Home Town. Crime rate slightly lower than Vatican City. This would be the most exciting thing that had happened in Pacific Grove since Princess Topaz's dragon boat had nearly sunk a few years ago during the annual Feast of Lanterns pageant. One call to 911 and the locals would be swarming the scene, sirens screaming and roof lights blazing. And if Maxwell *was* inside—whichever version of him was currently playing in the multiplex of his mind—and it *was* a hostage situation. . . .

Pender found himself picturing Irene wearing the filmy negligee she'd had on Monday night. Only now, in his mind's eye, he saw Maxwell standing behind her holding a knife to her throat. Her eyes were pleading for Pender to *do* something—anything.

Ah, fuck it, thought Pender, drawing the hickory-handled Colt from the flap pocket of his sport jacket. In for a dime, in for a dollar, he told himself, brushing off the muffin and Danish crumbs and jacking a round into the firing chamber before returning the gun to his pocket.

2

Perched on a wide flat boulder jutting out over the creek bank, bathed in the emerald light of the redwood forest, and serenaded by the babbling creek, Lyssy watched a dragonfly skimming lightly over the rippling water, its wings transparent and shimmering.

Lily joined him a few minutes later, wearing a Stanford sweatshirt—a red hoodie—over a dark-brown, V-neck T-shirt and a pair of Guess? jeans she'd borrowed from Dr. Irene's closet. Hours earlier, when they'd first arrived at her family's rustic retreat deep in the Lucia Mountains south of Big Sur, she'd hung a string bag bulging with items liberated from Dr. Irene's refrigerator—bottles of juice, sparkling Italian soda, a quart of 1 percent milk, and a pint of half-and-half—into the clear, cold running water from an eyebolt drilled into the underside of the rock. Now, kneeling and leaning out over the edge of the jutting boulder, she double-checked to be sure the bag was still there, still securely fastened. "Mother Nature's fridge, Grandma always used to call it."

"Cool," punned Lyssy, who was now wearing a faded orange S.F. Giants T-shirt over Dr. Al's button-fly 501s. The two had spent the first part of the afternoon unloading the car, sweeping out the cabin, putting fresh sheets on the bed, and hauling firewood from the shed—all the chores she and her grandmother used to take care of while Grandpa fished for their supper. ("Only the very rich or the very poor can afford to live this simply," he used to tell Lily.)

When the chores had been completed, Lily had selected a stout walking stick from her grandfather's collection for Lyssy to use, and they'd spent the rest of the afternoon exploring the five-hundred acre parcel known as La Guarida: the narrow canyon, the slow-running Little Bear Creek, the millennium-old redwoods.

"So what do you think of our little hideaway?" Lily asked him, leaning back on her elbows—*La Guarida* meant den or hideout in Spanish.

"I am *so* absolutely, I don't know, knocked out." Lyssy gazed about him in wonderment. "All these years, I never knew, I never dreamed— It's so rich and full and busy, it's like there's all these worlds, all these *realms.* There's a realm down there, with the fish and the insects"—the creek—"and another realm up there"—the redwood canopy—"with the birds. And we're in the middle realm with the deer and the bushes and the flowers, and it's all so full of, of life, it makes the arboretum look like a parking lot or something."

His eyes had all the colors of the forest in them, even the golden glint of the sun peeking through the redwood canopy. Suddenly Lily experienced a funny, melting feeling inside, and had to look away. Spotting a white-barked twig the size and shape of a slightly warped pencil on the boulder, she tossed it into the water, just to watch it float downstream.

"You want to know what really bugs me about all this, though?"

"Sure." She followed the twig with her eyes as it began its downstream journey.

"The timing." The twig narrowly dodged a mean eddy, took a ducking but bobbed up again. "The stupid darn timing. It's like, like— Did you ever see that movie *Time Bandits*?"

"The one with the English kid and the midgets?" Lily asked him.

"Right. And there's this scene, this lovey-dovey couple in old-timey clothes is standing on the deck of a big ocean liner holding hands. And you can tell how happy they are, how they're thinking about how much they love each other, and how they're going to spend the rest of their lives together. Then you see this life preserver hanging from the side of the ship, and then the camera gets closer so you can read the name of the ship on the life preserver: it says *HMS Titanic*—they're on the *Titanic.*"

Lily couldn't think of anything to say. The twig had gotten itself hung up on an exposed root sticking out from the stream bank. She held her breath, watching it fight its way clear of the root, then shoot downstream and disappear around the last bend, bound for the ocean.

"Made it!" Lyssy exulted.

Somewhat startled to realize that their thoughts had been running in harness, that without saying anything, they'd both been rooting for the little twig, Lily turned to Lyssy, her dark eyes searching for reassurance. "Did you ever think maybe they made it, too?" she said.

"Who?"

"Those two on the *Titanic.* Maybe they made it to a lifeboat and survived—the movie never said they didn't."

Their eyes met. Lyssy reached up to touch Lily's hair, his fingers sifting gently through its dark silky heaviness. Lily noticed that funny melting feeling again; she wondered if he'd touched Lilith's hair like that. "Pretend I'm her," she whispered, over the sound of the rushing water.

"Who?"

"Lilith—I want to pretend I'm Lilith."

"But I already told you, I loved you first."

"Yeah, but you *made* love to her. And she wasn't afraid, and she didn't freeze up, she didn't see . . ." *An impossibly swollen, purple-headed penis forcing itself into her mouth, choking her; a flashbulb exploding into white glare.* "Tell me about her. Tell me everything—what she was like, how she talked, how she moved, what she said, how she made love."

A fellow with some experience in these matters might have been more circumspect, but Lyssy took her at her word. He spoke uninterrupted for a good ten, fifteen minutes, for there was little about Lilith he hadn't hungrily memorized. When he was through, she leaned in close and whispered, "Kiss me. Kiss me like you kissed her."

His mouth was soft, softer than she'd imagined a man's mouth could be. And welcoming—instead of thrusting his tongue into her mouth, the sweet, gentle urgency of his kiss drew her tongue into his mouth. And here came that funny melting feeling, not so funny anymore. She felt herself tensing around it, her panic building. She broke off the kiss to whisper in his ear. "Talk to me," she said. "Talk to me like you were talking to her."

Her hair was disarranged; a strand had fallen damply across her eyes. "There was a little girl," Lyssy began, pushing it back gently, "who had a little curl, right in the middle of her forehead." He kissed her on the forehead, then again, softly, on each eye. "And when she was good, she was very, very good, and when she was bad, she was—"

"Lilith," she broke in. "When she was bad, she was Lilith." She kissed him again, more lasciviously, her mouth open, her lips soft and sloppy, her tongue expertly insistent, then broke it off. "Well," she said, panting for breath.

"Well, what?" He was breathing pretty hard himself.

"Who am I? Lily or Lilith?"

"Does . . . does it really matter?"

"Hell no," she replied, grabbing his head in both her hands and pulling it down to her breast.

3

You're not breaking and entering, Pender reminded himself as he circled Irene Cogan's house, looking for a way in. You're just—what was it they used to say when they needed a warrant?—effectuating a surreptitious entry.

He discovered an old wooden ladder lying on its side, next to a tarpaulin-covered stack of firewood by the side of the garage. It was in dubious condition, the mildew-splotched wood of the rails soft enough to dig his thumbnail into, but the rungs were dowels an inch in diameter, and appeared to be sturdy enough for the job at hand.

Pender carried the ladder around the side of the house and leaned it against the overhang of the flat, tar-papered roof above the office extension in back. He already knew the trick to hauling two hundred and eighty pounds up an old ladder: distribute your weight among all four limbs so that no single rung has to bear even half the load. Fortunately, the preponderance of Pender's avoirdupois had always been concentrated above the waist. His belly was the tipping point—once he dragged that over the eaves, the rest followed easily enough.

From the flat roof above the office, Pender boosted himself another four feet to the roof below Irene's rear bedroom window, which was closed. Balanced with difficulty on the slanting roof apron, he managed to get the merest fingertip purchase on the crossbar of the window sash, then let loose a prayer and leveraged upward with all the strength in his fingertips.

The window flew open, causing Pender to lose his hold on the sash, and with it his balance. Toppling backward, arms flailing, he managed to grab the windowsill; behind him, his Pebble Beach golf cap fluttered to the ground like a powder-blue autumn leaf.

Pender now found himself stretched out full-length on the sloping roof, hanging on to the windowsill with both hands, his Hush Puppied feet dangling in space. Kicking, grunting, he finally got his feet under him again, then duckwalked up the slope until he was at eye level with the windowsill, breathing hard and sweating harder. As he squatted there, trying to catch his breath, he felt an unaccustomed breeze from behind, and realized that with his shorts dragged down and his jacket rucked up, he was showing more crack than an inner-city coke dealer.

After a hasty sartorial adjustment, and a quick peek to make sure the bedroom was empty, Pender climbed through the window feet first, then took the Colt out of his pocket again and flicked off the safety—no way Maxwell would be getting the drop on him again.

Irene's queen-size bed appeared slept in and unmade, but there were no bloodstains, no sign of a struggle. Pender flattened himself against the door jamb with the Colt held sideways against his chest, then peered into the hallway. Empty. With the gun in two-handed firing position he made his way down the hallway to the guest bedroom at the top of the stairs. Aside from a rumpled bedspread with a few coins strewn around it, the little room was in apple-pie order.

He started down the stairs, keeping to the wall side of the carpeted treads to avoid any potential creaking. The paintings lining the staircase—landscapes, still lifes, and a portrait of Irene Cogan in her midtwenties, looking a little like the young Greta Garbo—all bore the signature of Irene's late husband, Frank.

The stairway opened out onto the white-carpeted living room. No sign of trouble there, but in the tiny downstairs bathroom, the rectangular screen lay on the tiled floor beneath the open window, and the state of the kitchen suggested either a break-in or a hasty departure—the cabinet doors were ajar, the counters littered with cans and cartons, and the usually tidy pantry appeared to have been ransacked.

As he looked around, Pender caught a glimpse of himself in the glass front of Irene's china cabinet. Hatless, dark circles under his eyes after his nearly sleepless night, his shoulders slumped and his once-snappy madras jacket practically in rags, Lily's Uncle Pen was now a ringer for Uncle Fester from the Addams Family.

Satisfied? Pender asked the poor dejected SOB, as he dropped the gun back into his pocket. Are you good and satisfied now? Maxwell's gone, he's taken Lily and

Irene with him, and however much of a head start he had, it's now half an hour longer thanks to you.

Pender turned away, hitched up his shorts, and crossed the kitchen. His intention—to call the police from Irene's wall phone—was a measure of his turmoil: he had the phone to his ear and his finger poised to call 911 before he caught himself on the verge of a classic rookie cop error. Not even rookie—trainee: calling in the crime on the crime scene phone, thereby destroying not just potential fingerprints or saliva for DNA (not all that relevant in the current case, which wasn't exactly a whodunnit), but also the ability to call *69 and instantly recover the last number accessed.

He patted through his pockets, took out his cell phone, realized he'd left it with the ringtone on. Another worse-than-rookie mistake: you're sneaking around looking for a perp who's sneaking around looking for you, somebody gives you a friendly ring-a-ding-ding on the old cell, next thing you know you're so full of holes they could read a newspaper through you.

He pulled the cell phone's antenna out as far as it would go, then pressed the green Call button. But as he raised the phone to his ear to make sure he had a dial tone, he became aware of another sound, faint, sputtery, and intermittent, that he must have been picking up on subconsciously for at least a few seconds.

It was the sound of somebody snoring, and it seemed to be coming from Irene's office—the only room he *hadn't* searched, Pender reminded himself.

Swapping the phone for the Colt, and borrowing a clean drinking glass from the cabinet, he hustled out of the kitchen and down the hallway, and pressed the rim of the glass to the office door, listening between snores until he was reasonably sure there was nobody in there but the snorer.

Pender set the glass down carefully on the hallway carpet, then turned the doorknob slowly with his left hand, while holding the unfamiliar Colt in his right with the safety off and a round up the spout. Probably should have dry-fired the thing earlier to accustom himself to the pull, thought Pender—but it was too late now. Just one more fuckup to add to the list, he told himself as he inched the door open.

4

The sated lovers lay entwined atop a patchwork quilt worn silky with age, their naked bodies rosy in the soft glow of twilight. Everything in the one-room cabin was invested with a reddish glow from the setting sun, even Lily's dark, shoulder-length hair reflected auburn highlights.

"The first thing I remember noticing about you was your hair," Lyssy murmured sleepily, burying his face against her neck—he hadn't had a full night's sleep since Tuesday. "Like moonlight on a midnight lake, I told myself—I don't know whether that's from a poem or a song, or if I just made it up, but that *is* what I was thinking."

The gentle, insistent pressure and the ticklish warmth of his breath reminded Lily of the way her pony used to nuzzle her with its velvety soft nose, searching for treats she'd hidden on her person. "I always hated it," she said. "I wanted to be blond, like Sunny Lemontina."

The name sounded familiar, but Lyssy couldn't quite place it. "Who's that?"

Lily rolled onto her side, facing him, and sang "Frere Jacques." When she got to *sonnez les matines* he grinned sleepily. "Right, right."

"She was my imaginary playmate," she told him. "In the beginning, anyway."

"Tell me about it."

"It was a week or two after I moved in with my grandparents." Lily rolled over onto her other side and snuggled backward against Lyssy. "At first she was like this imaginary friend—only I don't know if other kids actually *see* their imaginary friends. I could, though—I can see her to this day. Physically, she was almost the opposite of me. Short blond hair instead of long dark hair, blue eyes instead of brown, and instead of my sort of round face, a sharp witchy one with a pointy little chin.

"So this one morning we're sitting next to each other on the parquet floor of my grandparents' parlor, playing with my new Barbie my grandma gave me. The sunlight's pouring in like melted butter, making a warm yellow spotlight on the shiny-waxed floorboards, only it keeps moving, shrinking and moving, so every few minutes we have to slide over a few inches, me and Sunny Lemontina, to keep both of us in that warm puddle of sunshine. And the more it shrinks, the closer we get to each other, until pretty soon there's only gonna be room for one of us.

"Then Sunny Lemontina looks at me with those blue, blue eyes, and she laughs this evil laugh and says, '*I* know *your* secret.'

"I don't even have to ask which secret, because at this point in my life there's only one, and it's so big and so dark that I know if anybody ever finds out about it, *I'll* be the one who gets taken away and locked up forever and ever instead of my mommy and daddy.

"The next thing I know, I'm sort of floating outside my body, looking down at the little blond girl sitting alone in the puddle of sunshine, playing with my new Barbie.

"And the *next* next thing I know, I wake up in bed, it's night time, I can't remember anything that's happened since that morning in the parlor, and when I try to open the bedroom door, it's locked. I freak out, pounding on the door and screaming. Then the door opens, my grandmother's standing there looking down at me with this weird expression on her face, almost like she's afraid of me. She asks me if I'm ready to come out of my room yet.

"I say, 'Boy, am I!' Only now my grandfather's standing in the doorway behind her, he's like, 'I've already told you more times than I care to count: if you want to come out of your room, all you have to do is promise to stop the nonsense.'

"Now I have no idea what he's talking about, but by this point I'll promise anything. 'No more nonsense, cross my heart an' hope to die.'

"Grandma looks relieved, but Grandpa doesn't budge. 'What's your name? I want to hear you say it.'

"I'm still clueless—and getting scareder by the second. Doesn't he *know*? I'm thinking. 'Lily,' I say. 'It's Lily, Grandpa.' Then it's group hug time. Grandma's crying with relief and Grandpa's reaching around her patting my shoulder.

"All of a sudden I notice my head feels kind of strange—on the outside, I mean. Because it turns out I had spent the day chopping off most of my hair with the pinking shears, and Barbie's hair too, and trimming the fringes off all the furniture in the house that had fringes, and when the maid caught me, I told her my name wasn't Lily, it was Sunny Lemontina, and when she went to fetch my grandmother, I told her, 'You're not *my* grandma, you can't tell *me* what to do.'

"Oh, and the cat wouldn't come near me for a month," she added. "I never did find out what *that* was all about."

Lyssy turned over onto his stomach, his chin resting on the windowsill just above mattress level. The window, like the other windows in the cabin, was unglazed, with the wooden shutters opening outward; the redwood walls were unadorned save for an enormous USGS topographical map mounted next to the fieldstone chimney. "One thing I don't understand," he said. "I thought everybody already knew about the abuse by then—wasn't that why they moved you in with your grandparents in the first place?"

"Mmm-hmm." A tight-lipped affirmative.

"Then what was the big dark secret nobody was supposed to know?"

Lily stretched out next to him; together they watched the tumbling, quicksilver water of the creek turning coppery in the failing light. "That it was all my fault that my parents were taken away. That I was a dirty, wicked, ungrateful little snitch who deserved everything bad that happened to her."

Lyssy felt his heart breaking for her—for both of them, really. "Oh, jeez," he said. "Didn't anybody ever tell you that all abused kids feel that way sometimes?" He rolled over onto his back and shifted into his Dr. Al imitation: "Let me, ah, tell you something you may find difficult to believe, my young friend. Of all the cruel things your parents did to you, the, ah, cruelest of all was making you feel you deserved it."

"Of course I know that *now,* silly. Dr. Irene said it was because we couldn't blame our parents—that would have meant they never loved us, and to a kid, that's even *worse* than . . . you know."

"I surely do." A humongous yawn took Lyssy by surprise; he wasn't sure how much longer he'd be able to stay awake. "But you and me, we don't have to worry about that now."

"Why not?"

"Because we have each other," he murmured sleepily. "To love each other, I mean—we don' need no steenkin' parents." His head lolled to the side and he was *out,* snoring lightly, a drop of clear saliva trickling down the corner of his mouth.

Lily, who'd never seen *Treasure of the Sierra Madre,* had no idea why he'd switched over to an exaggerated Mexican accent. Maybe he was embarrassed about having used the L-word, however indirectly.

And maybe he was just pretending to have fallen asleep so suddenly—but she didn't think so. Somebody might fake snoring, nobody'd fake drooling.

"Okay, well, I love you, too," she whispered experimentally; she'd never said it to a man before, not counting her grandfather. It felt a little funny—but good. As she smiled down at him, noticing how much younger he looked when he was sleeping, she gradually became aware of a distant noise, a popping, Little Engine That Could *pocketapocketapocketa,* slowly rising in volume over the human-sounding babble of the creek.

Fano's mule, she thought—crap oh crap oh crap, how could I *possibly* have forgotten!

5

Irene swam upward from a deep dreamless sleep, saw Pender's face floating above her like one of those giant balloons in the Thanksgiving Day parade. It took her eyes forever to bring him into focus. He looked so *concerned,* hovering there. "S'matter, Pen?" she mumbled.

"Are you all right? Where are they? Did they hurt you? Do they have your car?"

"Too many questions. Just lemme . . . a couple more minutes, lemme sleep a couple more minutes." She rolled over onto her side, facing the back of the couch, and drew her legs up.

"Irene! Wake up, Irene, I need you to wake up now."

His hand was on her shoulder, shaking her. How rude, she thought, covering her ears with her palms and resuming the fetal position. But it was no use—her head was starting to throb, her back and knees ached, and her neck felt like she'd spent twenty minutes in the ring with Hulk Hogan.

"Did they drug you?" Pender was saying. "Slip you a mickey, something like that? Should I call an ambulance?"

"No!" For some reason, the suggestion alarmed her. "No ambulance." She rolled over onto her back, swung her legs off the couch, and tried to sit up. The blood rushed from her head; the room swam.

"Take it easy, I've got you." Pender helped her lie back down, positioned a throw pillow under her head. "How about a doctor—is there a doctor I can call?"

"I *am* a doctor," said Irene, almost pouting.

"Okay, *doctor.*" Pender pulled the side chair over to the couch to sit on. "Would you *please* tell me what the hell happened here?"

Irene sat up again—slowly, this time—and was surprised to find she was still wearing Frank's pajamas. "They must have slipped something into my orange juice," she told Pender. Nor would finding that something have been very difficult. They'd only have had to go as far as the medicine cabinet in the upstairs bathroom—in the last six years, Irene had self-prescribed, with varying degrees of success, every sleeping medication known to God, man, and GlaxoSmithKline. "I thought it tasted kind of bitter."

"When was that? Do you know when they left here?"

"One quesh'n at a time," said Irene, slurring like a ham actor playing a drunk.

"Sorry. How long ago did they leave?"

"What time is it now?"

"A little after eight."

Leaning forward, massaging her pounding temples with her fingertips: "A.M. or P.M.?"

"P.M."

Come back to me, little brain, thought Irene, working at the math. "Eight, ten hours?"

"In your car?"

"If it's gone."

"Do you know your license plate number?" asked Pender, taking his cell phone out of his pocket.

"I think so. Who are you calling?"

"The police," Pender explained gently. "So they can update the BOLO."

"That won't be . . . necessary." Irene was proud of having come up with the word—for a few seconds there it had been touch and go.

"Why not?"

"Because . . . " Blank. Blank mind. Because what? What was the question? Oh, right. Yes, of course: "Because there's only one place they could have gone."

"Where's that?" asked Pender—but Irene appeared to have nodded off again. "I'd better go make you some coffee," he said.

"Good idea," Irene mumbled. "Make some for me, too."

6

Lily dressed hurriedly. On her way out of the cabin she saw Lyssy's snubnosed revolver lying atop his 501s, at the foot of the bed. She snatched it up almost as an afterthought and stuffed it into the waistband of her Guess?'s, then tiptoed barefoot across the clean-swept boards, opened the door, and closed it ever so quietly behind her.

The *pocketapocketapocketa* grew louder; Lily waved from the covered porch as the open-sided, open-roofed contraption her grandfather had always referred to as the mule came chugging up the dirt road leading in from the highway. A skeletal vehicle with small rubber tires lined up four on each side, a frame of welded pipes supporting a bench seat up front and a railed wooden flatbed mounted over a noisy, sputtering gasoline engine in back, the mule was one of the few motorized vehicles capable of traversing the steep-sided canyons and narrow, deeply rutted trails of La Guarida.

"Hola, Tío Fanol!"

"Mija!" The driver, a small brown man with a bowl haircut, parked the mule a few yards in from the edge of the fan-shaped clearing, next to the beige Infiniti. Wearing a denim shirt, once-white trousers, and open-toed sandals, he hopped down from the cab and approached Lily with both arms outstretched and his leathery features contorted into a mask of tragedy.

She hurried down the steps and across the clearing. The ground was bare save for a sparse, limp growth of thin-bladed grass. She held out her hand; he took it in his weathered, work-callused hands and squeezed gently, as if he were giving her a blessing. *"Pobrecita.* I'm so sorry—my heart is . . ." His vocabulary failed him (Spanish was his second language, English his third); he let go her hand and pressed his fist against his sternum.

"Mine, too," said Lily, her mind racing. Fano, an ageless, undocumented Guatamalan Indian who lived in a shack on the far side of the northern rim of the canyon, had been the caretaker here for as long as Lily could remember. Somehow she had forgotten all about him when she suggested using La Guarida as a temporary refuge.

And now he held her and Lyssy's future in his hand. Although there was nothing in Fano's greeting or demeanor to indicate that he knew she was a fugitive, Lily couldn't discount the possibility entirely. But if he did know, would she have the courage, the wherewithal, to do what Lilith had once done? Could she kill someone in cold blood? Someone who'd never done her a lick of harm—someone she *liked*?

The answer was no, of course not. But the fact that she was even able to *consider* the possibility told Lily how much she had changed since this morning. It wasn't just that she'd finally made love—no one knew better than Lily DeVries that there was nothing illuminative or magically transformative about the sex act in and of itself; if there had been, she'd have been enlightened by the age of four.

But overcoming such a monumental blockage after a lifetime of suffering flashbacks, panic attacks, and alter switches at the mere thought of sex—now *that* was empowering, as Dr. Irene might have said. And never mind that she'd only been able to accomplish it by pretending to be Lilith—after all she'd been through, Lily was finally beginning, if not to accept completely, then at least to consider, what Dr. Irene had been telling her for years, and had reiterated only that morning: that the alters were *not* others. That Sunny Lemontina's anger was *her* anger, the unnamed little girl's flight into autism was *her* flight, Lilah's sexual desires were *her* desires, and most important, that Lilith's capabilities were her capabilities as well.

"The place is looking pretty good," she heard herself saying—one of her grandfather's stock greetings for Fano.

"Gracias. Señor Rollie came down last week, he told me whatever . . . how you say, *acuerdo?"*

"Agreement, arrangement."

"Sí, agrangement—whatever agrangement I have with your *abuelo,* now I got with him." He started to tell her something else, then caught himself.

Lily thought she had a reasonably good idea what it was. "Did—did my uncle happen to mention anything about me?"

"About *you*?"

Lily couldn't remember ever having felt so *present* as she did at the moment. She was intently aware of her surroundings: the sunset stillness in the clearing; the pale green, failing light through the towering redwoods, their feathery tops disappearing into the gloaming like so many Jack's beanstalks; the feel of the dirt beneath her bare feet and the cold metal of the revolver pressing against her bare belly; the sound of the creek off to her right; and the sweet, loamy smell of the surrounding forest.

But even with her senses fully engaged, Lily's mind was running as clear and cold as the creek, focused in laser sharp on Fano, noting the sideways shift of his eyes, the uneasy shuffle of sandals in the dirt. "Please, Fano, what did he tell you?"

"Just you ran away from home, and if you show up down here, I suppose to call him."

Okay, could have been worse, thought Lily. "Is that really all he said, Fano? He didn't mention I'd had a nervous breakdown or anything?"

"Que?"

"Loco—that I was *loco en la cabeza?"* She twirled a forefinger at her temple.

Fano was shuffling his sandals again, looking like the man in the TV commercial whose wife had just asked him, *Does this make me look fat?* "He just say you very . . . disturb? . . . about what happen, and everybody very worry about you."

"What if I asked you not to tell him I was down here?"

"Por que?"

"If I tell you, you have to *promise* you won't tell Uncle Rollie."

The shoulders of Fano's denim workshirt rose in what might have been either a shrug of agreement, or a *let's hear what you have to say first.*

Lily took a deep breath. "Okay, here's the thing—I didn't come down here alone. I'm here with my boyfriend. Uncle Rollie doesn't like him—he'll do anything to keep us apart. And if he finds out we're here, there's no telling what he might do. He might have him arrested, or put me away in a mental hospital, or both."

She leaned closer, locked eyes with him. "Please, Tío Fano—haven't *you* ever been in love?"

The clearing was nearly dark by now, the redwoods outlined black against the greenish glow of the sky. *"Sí,"* he said softly. "Very much."

"Tell me."

He was staring directly at Lily, but no longer seeing her. "One day they came to our village," he said, his voice steady, a distant look in his eyes. "Men with guns, men with big . . ." He shoved the air with both hands palm forward, bent upward at the wrist. "How you say, *empujatierra*?"

"Earth movers—bulldozers."

"*Sí,* bulldozers. To knock down our village. I say you cannot do this. Their head man, he say who are you, the *jefe,* the big chief? I say I am *alcalde* of this village. *Bueno,* he say, an' strike me"—he mimed a diagonal blow with a rifle butt—"here." He pushed his hair back from his temple to show Lily the scar. "I wake up under a pile of dead bodies with the smell of *gasolina* in my nose. Lucky for me, after they light the fire, they leave for the next village. Only I am left alive. I crawl from under the pile, but there is no water to put out the fire, because when they knock down a village, they also destroy the village wells, so nobody can build a village there again.

"So I start to pull the bodies off the pile. Then I find *mi esposa,* my wife. She was very much *embarazada—*" Lily was confused for a second; then he traced the curve of a swollen belly in front of his own flat stomach, and she remembered that in Spanish, they used the same word for embarrassed and pregnant. "I said my last prayer that day—that *mi querida,* she was already dead when those men, they cut the baby out from her stomach and throw it on the pile."

Darkness had crept over the canyon. High in the redwoods, an owl hooted, deep-toned and trembly; a throaty roar in the distance reminded Lily that there were still plenty of mountain lions left in the barranca. She didn't realize she was crying until Fano reached out and wiped a tear from her cheek. "Señor Rollie, he coming down Monday to meet with the man from PG&E to see how much money it cost to run the *electricidad* in from the highway. So a gift of two days, three nights, that is all that is in my power to give to you and your *querido.* Accept it with my love, *por favor."* Fano bowed formally from the waist, then turned and started back across the clearing to the waiting mule.

"Gracias," called Lily.

"De nada, mija," he said over his shoulder, and at that instant, four things happened in such quick succession that afterward Lily would remember them as occurring simultaneously:

She heard a loud popping sound behind her; something invisible *zzzz'd* past, disturbing the air; a cloud of birds rose up startled from the trees; Fano threw up his arms as though overcome by a sudden urge to shout hallelujah.

Then, as Lily screamed and the cloud of birds wheeled off angrily into the dusk, Fano dropped to his knees, swayed there for a moment, and pitched face forward onto the bare ground.

7

"Irene, I'm *not* taking you with me," said Pender. The two were seated across from each other at the round maple-topped kitchen table, under the rose-pink glow of a stained-glass chandelier shaped like a tulip. "It's much too dangerous."

After her shower, Irene had changed into a pair of roomy black cargo pants with plenty of loops and snaps and pockets, a navy pullover, and a pair of black-on-black Chuck Taylor high-tops; her damp hair was wrapped in a high towel turban. "Wrong, wrong," she said, making two check marks in the air; she had just finished her second cup of high octane dark roast. "One: you *have* to take me with you—otherwise I won't tell you where they are, not that you could find it by yourself even if I did. And two: you're exaggerating the threat level. Lyssy's frightened and confused, but he's not dangerous."

"Oh really?" Pender's big bald head, rosy in the glow of the chandelier, wagged stubbornly from side to side. "Try telling that to Mick MacAlister."

"That was self-defense. If MacAlister hadn't gone for his gun he'd still be alive—you told me that. But as far as shooting someone in cold blood? If Lyssy were capable of that, we'd both be . . . " Her voice trailed off as a new possibility occurred to her. "Oh, no! Please say it ain't so, Pen."

"Okay, I'm lost." He spread his hands helplessly. "What am I supposed to say ain't so?"

"That you were planning to just . . . gun him down. Sneak up on him and gun him down. That that's why you don't want me there this time around—you don't want any witnesses."

Pender had to force himself to keep his eyes trained on hers. "I'm not saying that's not an option—I mean, if the opportunity presents itself. But if that looks to be the safest way to get Lily out of that cabin unharmed, your being there or not is not going to make a difference one way or the other."

"But it will!" Irene exclaimed. "I can *talk* to them—they'll listen to—" Then, with a sinking feeling: "Hold on, Pen—I never said anything about a cabin."

"Not until now. But don't feel bad—I was about seventy-five percent sure when you said I couldn't find it on my own anyway. I'm thinking, that's got to be out in the wilderness someplace—which would account for why they ransacked your kitchen. Then I remembered about . . . what did Lyman and Dotty call that place? El Guard-o, something like that?"

Irene's fingernails dug painfully into her palms. Don't be too hard on yourself, she thought—he's a cop, this is his métier. "Please, Pen—I owe it to Lily to be there. If I'd fought for her a little harder in the first place, she wouldn't be in the situation she's in. I let that child down once—I won't do it a second time."

On the off chance she was bluffing, Pender countered with a bluff of his own. "You're not leaving me much of a choice," he said, slowly removing his cell phone from his pocket. "I have to call in the cops—*they'll* be able to figure out where the cabin is."

"No!" Irene raised her voice for the first time. "If you bring in the police, it's going to be Bonnie and Clyde all over again."

"We don't know that." Even more slowly, Pender's sausage-thick fingers drew out the antenna. "There are plenty of nonlethal alternatives—tear gas, flash-bang grenades, Tasers, rubber rounds. Deadly force is always supposed to be a last resort in these situations."

Irene sneaked a peek at Pender over the rim of her half-empty cup. Between the cold shower and the hot coffee, she was starting to feel more like herself again. And more critically, to *think* like herself again. "Okay, well, you're the expert," she said. "If you think calling the police is the best thing to do, who am I to question you?"

"All right, then." He pretended to press the green Call button, then stared down at the phone in his palm, waiting for her to fold.

"That's a nine followed by two ones," Irene prompted.

"Ah, shit." Pender jammed the antenna closed

against his palm and dropped the phone back into his pocket. "Remind me never to play poker with you."

8

Lily stared in horrified disbelief as Fano's lower limbs twitched feebly for a few seconds, like a frog in a biology experiment; then he was still. Behind her, she heard hollow, uneven footfalls crossing the porch, descending the plank steps. The clearing spun dizzily around her; she felt the strength draining from her legs, and had to squat on her hams to keep from toppling over.

"Why?" she moaned as Lyssy approached her, holding Mick MacAlister's stealth-black nine-millimeter pistol at his side. "He wasn't going to say anything—he gave me his word."

"Better safe than sorry," he replied, his voice high-pitched and almost cheerful as he stuffed the pistol into the waistband of his jeans, then reached down and helped her to her feet.

"But—but he was my *friend.*"

"News flash, baby: we don't *have* any friends anymore, except each other." He glanced from the body lying facedown in the dirt, to the cabin window from which he'd fired, and back again, estimating the distance. "You have to admit, that was one *hell* of a shot." Then, offhandedly: "He didn't have any family, did he? Or a girlfriend, somebody who's going to notice he's among the missing?"

Momentarily stunned by a sudden, heart-sinking realization, Lily could only shake her head no. It wasn't his voice that had clued her in—the voice was perfect, the voice was Lyssy—but rather the casualness of the afterthought, the utter lack of compassion, even humanity, that told her what she'd rather not have known.

"Great. Let's get him out of the open before somebody else comes bopping a— What're you looking at me like that for? I only did what had to be done, what you were too chicken to . . . Hey, what the . . . ?"

She had tried to keep the fear from showing in her eyes; it was her feet that betrayed her, taking a backward baby step, then another.

"It's only me, Lyssy. Just Lyssy—no reason to be scared."

Still shaking her head—no, no, no—she retreated across the clearing, her eyes wide and her heart pounding. He limped after her, swinging his artificial leg out wide for more speed. She fumbled for the pistol sticking out of the waistband of her jeans—and dropped it onto the carpet of fallen needles at the edge of the firebreak.

9

Pender tried to avoid gunning the Barracuda's engine while they were still in town—the low-pitched rumbling had a tendency to set off car alarms. But the 'Cuda was in her element once they hit the highway, and so was Pender, leaning back like a low-rider, one hand on the wheel and the other on the stick, his Hush Puppies tap-dancing gracefully on the pedals.

Soon sheer cliffs rose to the left, and fell away so sharply to the right that driving down Highway 1 was like driving along the edge of the world. The only distinction between the dense blackness of the Pacific Ocean below and the velvety blackness of the sky above was that there weren't any stars in the ocean.

"I once came down here with a friend who was a CalTrans engineer," Irene shouted to Pender, over the shriek of the engine and the rush of the wind. "When I asked him why they hadn't installed guardrails on some of these curves, he said it would only make the drivers overconfident."

Pender cranked up his window and signaled for Irene to do the same. With the windows closed, the ambient noise inside the car dropped so suddenly and profoundly that it felt to Irene as if they had driven into the eye of a hurricane—the 'Cuda was that tight. "Speaking of overconfidence," he said, "we ought to get some ground rules established."

"What sort of ground rules?"

"To begin with, once we get there, if I look things over and decide it's too risky to go ahead, that's it, we're out of there."

"Mmm-hmm?" said Irene, noncommittally.

"And if I do decide this thing has a chance, you have to let me call the shots. If I say stay behind me, you stay behind me. If I say wait here, you wait there. And above all, once we're in earshot, you can't say *anything* unless I give you the green light. If this goes south, having Maxwell believe I'm alone could be—" Your best shot at getting out of there alive, he was about to say, but changed his mind for fear she'd dismiss it as too melodramatic. "Could be the only advantage we have."

"That sounds reasonable enough," Irene said, and if technically her reply fell short of a promise, it was only because she understood, as a highly trained mental health professional (don't try this at home, kids), that in the absence of power, passive-aggressiveness could be a viable life strategy. "But I still think you're exaggerating the danger. Which could be dangerous in itself—we already know Lyssy's only a threat when he feels threatened."

And Max is only a threat when he's breathing, thought Pender, downshifting into a reverse-banked curve. Better to be overcautious with Lyssy than undercautious with Max. Or, since they share the same brain, why not put a couple rounds through it and let God sort them out?

When they reached the bridge over Little Bear Creek, the smooth hum of tires on concrete changed to a noisy, metallic chattering on the steel-reinforced grid. "Okay, start slowing down," said Irene; from the urgency in her voice she might have been talking Pender through landing a crippled jetliner on a too-short runway. "Better put on your left turn signal . . . slower, slower . . . get ready to turn at the other end . . . now! Here!"

"Hang on, Sloopy!" said Pender, downshifting and cutting the steering wheel to the left, then accelerating hard, sending the Barracuda darting across the northbound lane of the highway. He jammed on the brakes as a three-railed wooden gate suddenly materialized in the headlights; the 'Cuda came to a shuddering stop with its front bumper only inches from a PRIVATE ROAD, NO ADMITTANCE sign nailed to the top rail of the gate and dotted with reflective disks.

A bicycle lock secured the gate to the gatepost. Irene got out and felt around between the sign and the rail for the key that was usually wedged there. But not tonight; she spread her hands wide, squinting into the glare of the headlights. "They must have taken it with them," she called to Pender.

"Either that, or you were dead wrong about them coming here." Pender yanked the emergency brake and left the car juddering in neutral while he climbed out and examined the lock, then rocked the gate back and forth, testing its strength. "We might be able to force it."

"I'm not sure it would worth the trouble," Irene told him. "It's only a mile from here to the cabin, maybe a mile and a half. If we don't want them to hear us coming, we'd be better off leaving the car here and hiking in anyway."

Pender thought it over, shrugged. "I'm game if you are," he said. "Of course, you might have to carry me the last half-mile or so."

When he returned from jockeying the 'Cuda to the side of the driveway and locking it up, Irene had pulled her black knit watchcap over her damp, fair hair and was tucking in the stray ends. In her dark clothes and high-tops, she reminded Pender of a kid dressed up as a night commando for Halloween—all she lacked was eye-black and a toy Uzi.

Pender too had dressed for a night march before leaving Pacific Grove, trading in his plaid shorts for a pair of big-ass corduroys, his logan green Hush Puppies for the black pair he wore on formal occasions, and donning a black Members Only windbreaker he'd bought in 1985 over his gaudy Hawaiian shirt and calfskin shoulder holster; a stiff new baseball cap, black with a Green Iguana logo, covered his expansive scalp.

Before leaving, he ducked under the fence and walked down the dirt road a few yards, then ejected the clip from the Colt Mama Rose had given him, and made sure the chamber was clear before dry-firing to test the trigger pull. He held the gun two-handed, arms extended, elbows slightly bent. The hickory grip was smooth against his palms, but not slippery. He squeezed the trigger—*pyeww!* went his lips. He squeezed it twice more—*pyeww! pyeww!*

The pull was far too light—in the old days Pender had used a thirteen-pound trigger in lieu of a safety. So he'd have to keep his finger *off* the trigger until he was ready to fire, he reminded himself, as he reinserted the clip and slipped the Colt back into the too-snug holster, which had been custom-fitted both for his old SIG-Sauer *and* his old figure. When he looked up, Irene was watching him over the fence and shaking her head with tolerant affection.

"Pow, pow?" she said.

"Think of it as a visualization," he told her—

Pender had only been in California a few months, but he was already starting to learn the lingo.

10

Most people think of patience as a virtue. He has the patience of Job, they say, the patience of a saint. But then, most people were fools. It never occurred to them that Hitler was patient, too. Or Ted Bundy—no one was more patient than Ted Bundy stalking a coed.

Except possibly for himself, thought Max. After his failed coup in the attic yesterday, he had retreated into co-consciousness, waiting for Lyssy to fall asleep. It had taken a little longer than Max had planned—nearly thirty hours—but what were thirty hours to a man who'd sat out nearly three years of double incarceration, self-imprisoned in an imprisoned body?

The first thing he'd realized upon opening his eyes was that he was alone in bed—the girl was gone. Then, scrambling around for his leg and clothes, he realized that she'd taken the .38 with her. Quickly he'd retrieved the other gun, the longer-barreled black automatic, which turned out to be a blessing in disguise when he peered through the shutters next to the front door and saw Lily talking to a little Mexican-looking guy.

Because when the man turned to leave, Max had to take his shot from where he stood, some twenty, twenty-five yards away—a difficult enough shot with the longer-barreled nine millimeter, and probably impossible with the snubnosed revolver.

Now he stooped to snatch up the .38 she had dropped. "Naughty, naughty," he said in his own voice, stuffing the gun into his back pocket with a piratical grin. "Like the man said, either we hang together, or . . ."

He raised his hand over his head and a few inches to the side, holding on to the rope of an imaginary noose, then cocked his head and made a terrible gurgling sound deep in his throat. "Well, you get the idea."

But his cleverness was wasted on the girl. Quivering, she backed away, fists clenched at her sides, tears welling in her big doe eyes. Suddenly, instinctually, he loathed her for her weakness and uncertainty, for the aura of victimhood she had gathered around her like a cloak.

Even worse, from a strictly practical standpoint, she was all but useless to him in this particular incarnation. He didn't need another victim—there were plenty of victims out there—but rather an ally. Lilith, he thought, I need Lilith.

He decided to take a try at it, arranging his features in a deadly scowl and advancing on the retreating girl. "Where is she?" he demanded.

"I—I don't know what you mean." Still backing away, her hands spread helplessly.

"Then you'd better figure it out pretty goddamn quick, before I reach down your fucking throat and pull your lungs out through that lying mouth. Now where is she?"

"Who—where is who?" Her back fetched up against a giant, uncaring redwood.

"Lilith. I want Lilith. Come on dowwwn, *Lilith*!" Chanting now as he closed the ground between them, dragging his right leg behind him like the original Mummy, until his face was only inches from hers. "Get me Lilith or I will fucking kill you," he said evenly, his voice coldly menacing, not at all heated. "Get me Lilith or you will fucking die."

CHAPTER TEN

1

The road to La Guarida curved downward to the canyon floor, then turned due east, narrowing to a rutted dirt track that ran alongside and a few yards above the south bank of Little Bear Creek. The going was easy enough at first, but when the redwood canopy closed in overhead, Irene rediscovered two things she'd forgotten about the wilderness at night: how bright and numerous were the stars, and how utterly dark it was in their absence.

For the next three-quarters of a mile or so, she and Pender allowed themselves the luxury of flashlights. Walking single file between the ruts, shielding the beams with their palms, they could hear the creek chuckling and murmuring below them to their left; to their right loomed the south wall of the canyon.

"Pen?"

"Hmm?"

"Do you think we're doing the right thing?"

Pender was in the lead; he moved to his right and let Irene catch up. "You're probably too young to remember the Davy Crockett craze." With Irene walking the hump and Pender in the rut, their heads were almost level.

"Before my time. I've heard about it, though."

"It was huge. When I was around ten, myself and every kid I knew, we'd have *killed* for a coonskin cap." Pender dropped into line behind her and unzipped his windbreaker.

"Anyway, this one time, I remember I'm lying on the living room rug watching Walt Disney on our old Sylvania Halo Light, it's the episode where Davy tells his friend Georgie that his motto has always been *Be sure you're right, then go ahead.* And my father, he's an ex-jarhead, Semper Fi to the max, he's sitting behind me in the armchair we always called Daddy's chair, smoking his Camels and drinking his Genny—that's Genesee beer—and I hear him grumbling, 'Nobody was ever surer he was right than Ol' One-Ball'—which was the only way he ever referred to Hitler."

"Smart man, your father," said Irene, smiling to herself—she was trying to envision Pender as a ten-year-old, but the only picture that came up for her was a fat bald kid in a coonskin cap.

As the canyon widened, the creek curved away to the northeast, while the road continued to hug the canyon wall for another quarter of a mile before branching off. Irene stopped when they reached the fork, holding up her hand like a scout on point. They switched off their flashlights.

"The cabin's that way," Irene whispered, pointing toward the wide, grassy lane sloping downward to their left, descending through the trees toward the faintly audible murmur of the creek.

"How far?" Pender whispered breathlessly, bent over like a winded football player with his hands resting on his knees; little points of colored light, the kind you see when you rub your closed eyes, were swimming in the blackness.

"Maybe a hundred yards to the clearing, then another, I don't know, fifty, sixty feet to the house?"

Pender gestured toward the other, narrower fork. "Where does that lead?"

"All the way up to the ridge—on a clear day, you can practically see Japan."

"But is there a way to get back out to the highway?"

"From the ridge? Only by jumping off the cliff—it's several hundred feet straight down. Other than that, this road is the only way in or out."

Excellent, thought Pender—not having a back door to cover greatly simplified the mission and improved their prospects. And more good news: he was starting to get his second wind. "Wait for me here," he told Irene. "I want to scope out the cabin—I'll be back in a couple of minutes."

"Forget it, I'm coming with you."

"Laak fuck!" That was a little Caribbean-ism Pender had picked up on St. Luke. "Remember, you agreed to let me call the shots."

"Actually, I believe all I said was that it sounded reasonable—that's not the same as agreeing."

Pender glared down at her. "Of all the goddamn childish stunts," he whispered fiercely. "This is not a *game* here, Irene—I'm not going to debate with you."

"Good choice," said Irene. "Come on, let's get going before the moon comes up."

2

Lily covered her face. Clawlike hands closed around her wrists, tugging them down to her sides. Her mind flashed back to earlier, in bed, she and Lyssy getting to know each other's bodies, Lyssy showing her how tightly his scarred hands could grip, how weak they were when it came to letting go.

But worse than the welling fear, worse than the pain in her wrists, was the sickening realization that *that* Lyssy was gone. This dry husk of a voice trying to bully her into switching alters (as if it were something over which she had any control, something she wouldn't have done in a heartbeat, if only she had the power) was not *her* Lyssy's voice, any more than these soulless eyes glinting with false merriment were those of the man with whom she'd made love earlier. They reminded her more of her father's eyes, dead and glassy as he *whisk-whisk-whisked* his closed fist up and down his penis, getting hard, getting ready to hurt her.

Thinking of her father triggered that old familiar sadness that usually presaged an alter switch—perhaps if Max had had the sense to back away and let her drift, it might have happened. Instead he tightened his grip on her wrists, brought his face up to hers.

"This is your last chance," he hissed. She felt his breath warm and damp against her skin, and knew what she had to do: whatever Lilith would have done. Fearless Lilith. Fearless, foulmouthed, hot-tempered, biker-tough Lilith. She loosed a quick inward-directed prayer—Lilith, if you're there, for God's sake help me out here—then squared her shoulders, raised her chin, and forced herself to meet his eyes.

"Actually," she said, "it's *your* last chance."

A startled laugh. "For what?"

"To get your fucking hands off me before I knee your balls up into your throat." The words came with surprising ease; their effect astonished them both.

"Well, I'll be blowed," said Max, releasing her wrists, leaning even closer, peering into her eyes. "Lilith?"

"No, it's Princess fucking Di," she snapped. "Now would you mind backing off a tad, amigo?—your breath smells like you've been gargling raw sewage."

Any doubts Max may have had concerning Lilith's identity had been largely put to rest by the time they'd finished dragging the corpse into the under-brush. She hadn't winced when Max ordered her to take one of Fano's legs while he took the other, nor flinched at the way the lolling head went bumping over the rough ground—timid Lily could never have managed all that without breaking character.

Lily, meanwhile, had been steadily growing in confidence. If I can get through this, she told herself as she helped him cover her murdered friend with fallen redwood boughs, I can get through anything. Indeed, by the time the grisly task had been completed, there was no remaining effort, and very little volition, in her adoption of Lilith's personna—the longer she played the role, the more it felt like a channeling rather than an impersonation.

And afterward, sitting on the bottom step of the porch brushing damp earth and redwood needles from her bare feet, she made sure that he noticed her glancing around the clearing as though she'd never been here before—which she wouldn't have, not as Lilith, because in their system there'd never been any co-consciousness or memory-sharing among alters. "Who was that, anyway?" she asked him casually, nodding toward the edge of the clearing where they'd left the body.

"Just some Mexican in the wrong place at the wrong time."

"Sure looks that way." She forced a shrug. "Whose place is this—yours?"

"No, it's yours. The DeVries family retreat. Come on, let's go inside."

She felt his eyes boring into her from behind as she preceded him into the dark cabin. You've never been here before, she reminded herself, and made a point of feeling around the wall next to the door. "Where's the light switch?"

"There isn't one—there's no electricity."

"Oh, swell—fucking great. You got a flashlight?"

"Here you go."

The beam from a 12-volt lantern darted around the square, cluttered cabin like an obese Tinkerbell, coming to rest on a shelf with oil lamps, a Coleman lantern, and dozens of candles. In a nearby drawer she "discovered" a box of Strike Anywhere matches sealed in a baggie. They lit everything with a wick; when the cabin was ablaze with light, they closed the shutters while Lily made peanut butter and jelly sandwiches.

While Max rested his leg, Lily came within a whisker of blowing the masquerade. Having realized that all she needed to do to save herself was get a good running start on the one-legged man, then hike out of the canyon and flag down a car, she was just about to tell him she was going back outside to fetch the drinks cooling in the creek, it dawned on her that Lilith wouldn't have known anything about Mother Nature's fridge.

"Goddamn it, didn't we bring anything to drink?" she blustered, feeling cold sweat dampening the back of her T-shirt. "No fucking way I'm choking down a pb&j dry."

"Lily stashed everything that needed to be refrigerated in the creek."

"I'll get 'em," said Lily, quickly slipping on her sneakers. "Just tell me where."

"No, I'll do it—I know where they are."

"Fine by me," said Lily. It might even be better this way, she told herself—she could be long gone by the time he returned.

"I'll be right back." Max limped over to the door, opened it—and immediately slammed it shut.

"What? What is it?"

"Either I just saw Bigfoot out there," said Max, leaning his back against the door, "or we have company."

3

"Down!" Pender whispered fiercely, dropping into a crouch. He and Irene had just emerged from the road into the clearing when the cabin door had opened suddenly, revealing Maxwell standing in the doorway. He had peered briefly into the darkness, then retreated into the cabin, shutting the door behind him. "Of all the freak luck!"

They took cover behind the skeletal frame of the strange-looking vehicle parked at the edge of the clearing. From here, the cabin looked dark and solid as a blockhouse, with thin cracks of light outlining the shutters, which weren't quite flush with the window frames.

"Do you think he saw us?" whispered Irene.

Pender grimly unholstered the Colt. "Unless he's gone blind recently."

"What do we do now?"

"I'm not sure." He racked the slide, jacking a round into the firing chamber. "It'd be helpful to know who we're dealing with," he added, in what was possibly the understatement of the decade.

* * *

"I *knew* it," Max declared triumphantly, when a few more minutes had gone by without any bullhorns bellowing that they were surrounded. "I knew he'd come after me on his own."

"It could be a trap," said Lily, holding a lantern to the huge USGS map on the wall, examining the pale green swirls and spirals the way Lilith would have, if she were trying to find a back way out. There was none, of course, but Lilith wouldn't have known that. Neither would Max—Lily was counting on that.

He turned away from the window. "You just don't get it, do you? This is *personal* with him—he can't *stand* that I beat him."

"Don't tell me you're planning to go out there and take him on?"

"It's personal for me, too," replied Max. "Remember what I told you when we were planning Lyssy's birthday party? Revenge *is* the priority. First Corder, now Pender and Cogan, it's like they're lining up for me. I really would be an ungrateful bastard if I didn't at least *try* to take advantage." He double-checked both guns—the reloaded revolver had a bullet in each of the six chambers, while the black pistol had one round up the spout and another thirteen in the clip—then turned back to Lily.

"From here on in, job one for you is keeping your body between his gun and my body. Meanwhile, anything you can do to convince him that you're Lily and I'm Lyssy would be extremely helpful."

"Anything else, oh lord and master?"

He gave her a sharp glance, decided to let it pass. "Just follow my lead."

After several long minutes, during which they'd discovered that their cell phones were useless this deep in the woods, Pender and Irene abandoned the partial protection provided by the mule for the solid cover of Irene's Infiniti. From here, they watched the lopsided moon, a few days short of full, rising above the hills behind the cabin, turning the sky to the east a shimmering gray and casting a pallid silvery light over the canyon. Below them to their left, a ghostly mist drifted lazily behind the willows lining the south bank of the creek; above them to their right they could just make out the pale scar of a dirt road zigzagging up the canyon wall.

The cabin door opened again, throwing an elongated trapezoid of yellow light across the covered wooden porch. "Here we go," whispered Pender. He rose from a squat to a high crouch, holding the gun two-handed, fingers interlaced, using the roof of the Infiniti as a platform to steady his aim. A short, spidery figure appeared in the doorway, silhouetted dramatically in the streaming light like the alien emerging from the mother ship at the end of *Close Encounters*—if the alien had had two heads and eight limbs.

Pender eased his finger off the trigger. So much for the quick and dirty solution—he had never been much of a sharpshooter. FBI agents had to be range-qualified, of course, but even when he was young,

Aim for the middle and hope for the best had always been Pender's motto.

"Who's out there?" Max shouted from the porch.

Lily winced. "Not in my ear, bro," she said out of the corner of her mouth.

"It's Agent Pender."

"And Dr. Cogan," called the psychiatrist—from where Max stood, he couldn't see Pender glaring at her.

"Oh, good, Dr. Cogan, it's Lyssy. Lyssy and Lily. We want to come down and talk things over, but I'm scared your friend there is just going to shoot me the first chance he gets—could you get him to maybe just point his gun away a little?"

Max's eyes were beginning to adjust to the moonlight; looking over the girl's shoulder, he could see Pender bracing the gun against the roof of the car, twenty yards away.

"Lyssy!" he called. "I give you my word I won't fire first."

"You bet he won't," Max whispered to Lily. "Not while I have you for a shield."

"Well that cheers the shit outta me," Lily murmured as she started down the steps.

"Okay, that's far enough," Pender called, when the other two had crossed the clearing to within ten feet of the Infiniti, Lily trudging along in the lead with the hood of her sweatshirt pulled up, Maxwell limping behind her, wearing an old canvas knapsack containing their money and a few supplies. They were standing not far from where Fano had died; behind them, his blood was a dark stain in the moonlight.

"Hi, Dr. Cogan," said Max, in Lyssy's ever-hopeful voice. "We're sorry we put those sleeping pills in your juice, but we couldn't think of any other way to get a head start."

The voice, the timid stance, what she could see of his expression as he half-crouched behind Lily, all seemed to Irene to support his claim to be Lyssy. "No harm done," she told him, then turned to Lily. "Are you all right, dear?"

The girl nodded curtly, but it was Pender she was staring at, as though she were trying to telepath him a message. He thought he knew what it was, too. "Lyssy, I need to see both your hands. You can stay there if you'd like—just show me your hands."

"If you want to know do I have a gun, the answer is yes. But I'll ditch mine if you'll ditch yours."

"You first."

Half obscured by his human shield, Maxwell shrugged. "Dr. Al always said I was a trusting soul," he said, holding up the .38 with which he'd killed MacAlister, then clicking on the safety before tossing it away. "Your turn."

"Sorry, I can't do that," said Pender. That was a lesson every cop was taught in the cradle: No matter how bad it is, there's no situation that can't be made worse by surrendering your weapon.

"But—but you *lied*!"

The childish disappointment and disbelief in Maxwell's voice, the air of naiveté, went a long way toward convincing Pender that this might be Lyssy after all. He did not, however, lower his own gun or let down his guard. "Sorry I had to mislead you, son. Now put your hands in the air for me. Lily honey, you come on over here."

But before she could move, Maxwell snaked his left arm around her throat, drew MacAlister's automatic from the waistband of his jeans with his right hand, and pressed the muzzle against her right temple. "Drop your gun, or I blow her head off."

"Go ahead," Pender told him calmly. "You'll be dead before she hits the ground."

4

Being in the dark place is like being deaf, dumb, blind, paralyzed, and buried alive. Nothing here. Nothing but yourself and your thoughts. Crazy-making. Unbearable to contemplate. To think too closely about it is to risk becoming an endless scream resounding through the void.

Far easier to give yourself up to the darkness . . .

(but what about Lily?)

To surrender rather than risk the flames . . .

(but what about Lily?)

Because Max is so much stronger . . .

(but is he?)

And if you only let go . . .

(don't let go!)

If you give yourself to the darkness . . .
(again)
You'll never even hear her screaming . . .

"I do believe we've reached another stalemate, Agent Pender." Max had dropped Lyssy's simper; it was a relief to him to think that he'd never have to employ it again.

"Let the girl go and we can settle it the way we did the last time," said Pender, referring to the shoot-out in the barn at Scorned Ridge three years ago.

"I don't think so." When he was amused, Max's eyebrows tended to peak devilishly, like Jack Nicholson's. "I seem to be running out of legs."

"Then leave the girl behind—I give you my word I'll let you walk."

"I believe we've already established what your word is worth, Agent Pender. Oh, wait—I see where the problem lies! You think I'm abducting the young lady." He eased his crook-armed hold on the girl's neck, chucked her cheek affectionately, and swung the muzzle of his gun from her to Pender. "Tell them who you are, darlin'."

She coughed a few times, pulled down the hood of her sweatshirt and tugged the neck away from her throat, working her jaw and rolling her head like Rodney Dangerfield on speed. "They're so fucking smart, let them figure it out."

"Ohmigod—Lilith?" Irene said, rising from her crouched position.

"Fuckin' A," replied Lily, executing a mock curtsy

and momentarily leaving Maxwell's head exposed. But Pender was like an old prizefighter: he could see the openings, but his reflexes were no longer fast enough to take advantage of them. C'mon baby, he thought—one more curtsy for Uncle Pen.

Instead she turned her head and whispered over her shoulder to Maxwell.

"Sorry I had to mislead you, son."

Never before had Lyssy struggled so hard against surrendering himself to the darkness. But it was worth it to realize he was no longer alone. "I'm the one who misled you, Dr. Al. I should have been honest, I should have told you about the voice and the dark place."

They were in Dr. Al's office—sort of. No walls, no floor, just an archetypal psychiatrist's couch and chair suspended in featureless space, surrounded by darkness. Lyssy was lying on his back on the couch; Dr. Al was behind him to his right, just out of his line of sight. "It's not your fault—you were in an untenable situation."

"At least that's better than an un-eleven-able situation."

Dr. Al chuckled. "What I mean is, we, ah, put you in a situation where you would be punished for telling the truth, but rewarded for hiding it. But that's all water over the dam. Would you like to tell me why we're here today, and what you're hoping to accomplish in today's session?"

Lyssy felt a twinge of panic—for a moment he couldn't even remember where here *was, much less what he wanted to accomplish. Then it came back to him. "I'm worried about Lily—I'm worried something's going to happen to her."*

"Something like this?" said Dr. Al, leaning forward in

his chair until Lyssy was able to see his face. Or what was left of his face—it had been cut literally to shreds, raked from hairline to jawline with dozens of savage strokes. One eye was gone entirely; the lid of the other had been sliced raggedly away to reveal the eyeball, round as a marble, red-veined around the edges, pulsing in its dark socket.

Lyssy wanted desperately to look away, but he knew somehow that if he did, he would be lost. "Help us, Dr. Al," he said. "Tell me how to stop him."

The torn lips parted in a bloody smile, revealing slashed gums and shattered teeth. "If I knew the answer to that," said the phantom, "would I look like this?"

5

Pender took advantage of the whispered conference between Max and Lilith long enough to shake out his left arm, which had gone all pins and needles. The conference ended with Max nodding his head. Pender resumed his position, half-crouched, with his forearms resting on the roof of the car.

"Much as I hate to break up the party," said Max, "my partner here has suggested it may be time for us to make a strategic withdrawal. But keep in mind, you two—this is a postponement of our final reckoning, not a cancellation. Someday there will come a knock on your door or a tap on your window—"

"Can the Snidely Whiplash act," Pender broke in. "No point acting tough when you're hiding behind a woman."

But Max and Lily had already begun sidling to their left, toward the mule, which was parked facing the cabin. They circled around to the passenger's side. Lily climbed up to the raised bench seat ahead of Maxwell, then slid over behind the wheel, keeping her body between Max and Pender.

"Lilith," called Irene. "Lilith, stop—take a moment to think this over."

Lily who'd been driving the mule since she was twelve, was busily pretending to study the rudimentary dashboard. (She'd told Max earlier that she'd seen another route out of the canyon on the USGS map; when he'd asked her if she could figure out how to operate the mule, she'd told him if she could drive a Harley, she could drive anything.)

"I *have* thought it over," she called down from the cab, then pressed the starter button with her thumb and opened the choke wide. "And this is the best way for everybody." Then, with her back turned to Max, she mouthed the words *I love you* to Irene.

The engine back-farted bluish smoke, then sputtered to life as she gingerly fed it gas. The mule shuddered and puffed until she'd turned down the choke, then waited, trembling—*pocketapocketapocketa*—while she released the floor-mounted hand brake.

Expertly, she depressed the clutch and shifted into reverse, leaning out of the cab and glancing over her shoulder as she steered the mule backward. She cut the steering hard, guided the narrow, ten-foot-long vehicle through a tight backward turn, then shifted out of reverse and gunned the mule up the dirt track and into the cover of the trees before Maxwell could get off a clear shot.

"That was Lily," said Irene. "Dear God, that was Lily."

"It's getting so you can't tell the players without a scorecard," Pender muttered under his breath as he slid behind the wheel of the Infiniti. He turned to Irene as she climbed into the passenger seat. "Keys?" he said, extending his hand toward her, palm up.

6

"Doesn't this thing go any faster?" said Max. He'd tossed his knapsack into the back of the mule, and was facing rearward, with the barrel of the pistol braced on the railing behind the bench seat. But the way the mule was bucking along up the rutted track, he'd have been lucky to hit the taillight—if the mule had *had* a taillight, that is; it possessed only a single, center-mounted front spotlight.

"Yeah, right, I'll switch on the fuckin' afterburners," said Lily. Being Lilith was second nature to her by now—she hardly even had to think about it. "Look, don't sweat it—where we're going, they ain't gonna be able to follow in that fancy-ass Infiniti."

Max's head whipped around sharply. "How would you know?"

Whoops, thought Lily, almost jocularly—somehow, the longer she impersonated Lilith, the more of Lilith's qualities she began to take on. "Dotted line on the topo map," she improvised confidently. "Should be coming up right . . . about . . . Yeah, here it is. Hold on tight."

She jerked the wheel hard to the left and steered the vehicle through a steep, uphill, J-turn onto a rutted track only a little less narrow than the mule itself—one side of the vehicle almost scraped the rocky cliff as the mule jolted up the side of the canyon, while the other nearly overhung the steep drop-off.

"Where does this come out?" Max asked her.

"According to the topo map, it swings north back up toward Big Sur," said Lily, improvising hurriedly as she guided the mule through the first of a series of hairy-looking switchbacks.

"It goddamn well better," said Max.

Pender slumped forward with his head resting against the top of the steering wheel.

"I'm sorry," Irene said. In a way it would have been less painful if she'd simply forgotten to bring along her key ring. (Lyssy and Lily had thoughtfully taken only her spare car key.) But she *had* brought it along: it was in her Coach bag, which she'd left in the Barracuda. "I don't suppose there's any way you could . . . what do you call it, hot-wire it?"

By way of answer, Pender banged his head lightly against the padded wheel—*thud, thud, thud.*

"No, I suppose not," said Irene.

"Oh well." Pender sighed. He sat up again and reached for the door handle. "You know what the Chinese say about a journey of a thousand miles, don't you."

Irene: "It begins with a single step?"

Pender: "Bingo!"

But they hadn't gone much farther than that first step when Pender pointed to the lonely light winding its way up the side of the cliff, a hundred feet or so above the canyon floor. "I thought you said that way doesn't lead anywhere but the top of the ridge?"

"It doesn't," said Irene, taking off her watch cap.

"Does Lily know that?"

"Of course." She ran her fingers through her damp, flattened hair. "What could she be *thinking*, Pen?"

"You're the shrink, you tell me."

"I don't *know*!" Despairingly. "Sometimes I think I don't know *anything* anymore."

"Knowing one knows nothing is the beginning of wisdom, Grasshopper," said Pender.

Irene smacked him across the arm with her sweaty watch cap. They started off again, and again hadn't gotten far when Irene tripped over something small and hard. When she saw what it was—the snubnosed revolver Max had tossed away earlier—she knelt down and, under the pretext of tying her sneaker, slipped it into the roomy front pocket of her cargo pants before Pender could decide to pull rank again and take it away from her.

Dr. Al is as gone as the day before yesterday. In his place, a dreamlike sense of motion—bucketing along, rising and falling, swaying, a roller-coaster ride through sheer undifferentiated blackness. Then a vision coalesces out of the blackness, a soundless, slightly skewed, camera's-eye vision, which Lyssy can neither control nor direct, of a narrow dirt road winding dead ahead through the darkness along the side of a cliff.

Suddenly the camera's-eye view rotates to the left. Lyssy catches a glimpse of Lily in profile, the hood of her sweatshirt thrown back, her eyes narrowed in concentration and her lips pressed resolutely together as she wrestles with the steering wheel. Lily, *he wants to shout*—Lily, I'm here.

But before he can figure out whether it's a dream, or his first experience of co-consciousness, the view rotates around to the right again, then shifts downward, and instead of Lily, Lyssy finds himself looking down at a black pistol gripped tightly in a clawlike, fire-scarred hand.

7

They left the clearing at a fast walk, then by mutual and unspoken agreement broke into a trot as the trees began to close in overhead until they could no longer see the tiny light clinging doughtily to the side of the canyon.

Irene, a veteran jogger, started to pull ahead, shining her flashlight in front of her. Pender called to her to wait; he was breathing hard when he caught up. "What is it?" she said.

"It could be . . . a trick. . . . Max could have . . . bailed out, he could be . . . hiding in the bushes waiting to . . . pick us off."

She extinguished her flashlight and they started off again, Pender walking ahead of her, gun in hand.

When they reached the fork in the road Pender turned to Irene. "Guess what?" he whispered, his big hand resting on her shoulder.

"Forget it," said Irene.

"One of us *has* to go for help." The top half of his face was in deep shadow; against the dark background, the green iguana logo on his baseball cap seemed to be floating an inch or two over his head. "You're a faster hiker, I'm better with this." Indicating the Colt in his other hand.

"But—"

"You know I'm right, don't you?" he whispered, almost tenderly.

Seconds ticked by while she tried to think of a reason to say no, but all she could come up with was an atavistic need to *not* be alone, and an unreasonable fear that if she left now, she'd never see Pender or Lily again. "Is this one of those Davy Crockett moments?" she said, looking up at him, feeling dwarfed by his height and bulk in the dark as she never had in the light.

"Yes, ma'am," said Pender, in his best frontier drawl. "Yes ma'am, Ah reckon it is."

"I reckon we'd better go ahead, then," said Irene.

The last switchback was the tightest, the steepest, and the most severely banked. As it jolted upward the mule tilted precariously to the right, sending Max sliding sideways across the cracked vinyl padding of the bench. At the last second he managed to hook his elbow over the railing behind him, and found himself leaning out over empty space, staring down into the abyss.

"Jesus *fuck,*" he said, hauling himself back to safety as the mule righted itself. "You trying to get us both killed?"

No, just you, thought Lily. "Looks like we're over the worst of it," she told him, as the track began to level off. They traveled briefly northward along the ridge at the top of the canyon, then turned due west, the mule bumping across the gentle rise of a broad, grassy, humpbacked meadow dotted with widely spaced live oak and madrone.

The road itself, though, seemed to have petered out. Behind them were two shiny tracks made by moonlight refracted off the blades of grass flattened under the mule's tires; ahead there was only virgin grass. Then the mule topped the rise and Max saw that the grass ended abruptly at the edge of the continent. Far below, beyond the meadow, there was only the flat black expanse of the Pacific, stretching onward beneath a dome of stars toward a nearly indiscernable horizon.

Pender walked ten, jogged ten, walked ten, jogged ten, while his internal Rock-Ola played an appropriate medley of oldies: I'm walkin', yes indeed: walkin' in the rain, walkin' to New Orleans, walkin' back to happiness, these boots are made for walkin', and you'll never walk alone.

Pick 'em up, lay 'em down, pick 'em up, lay 'em down. The footing was treacherous, the incline pitiless, the ache in his thighs relentless. Whether he walked in or out of the ruts, his ankles, unsupported by the Hush Puppies loafers, threatened to turn at every step. Cursing himself for all the miles of exercise he'd blown off riding in golf carts, Pender soon abandoned even the pretense of jogging.

The first time he went down (what looked like shaley rock in moon-shadow turned out to be a shelf of dirt that crumbled underfoot), he landed hard on his left side and lay there in suspense, waiting to see how badly he'd fucked up his ankle.

Not at all, as it turned out—the shooting pain he'd been anticipating never materialized. So he picked up his gun, picked himself up off the ground, and resumed the upward trudge, his infernal jukebox kicking in with "Twenty-five Miles."

But it soon felt like he'd already gone fifty miles. His breath coming harder now, his stride degenerating to an oldster's shuffle, at first Pender attributed the pain in his left arm to his earlier tumble. He flexed his shoulder, worked the arm around in a circle. The pain sharpened, grew jagged, turned a screaming crimson. A steel band tightened around his chest. He saw the fireflies again, points of dancing, colored light, then the world tilted crazily onto its side.

8

Lily had toyed with the idea of driving the mule over the edge of the cliff and jumping out at the last second, but every time she took her foot off the accelerator, the mule slowed, with the obvious intention of rolling to a complaisant halt. And even if it didn't, what was to stop Max from bailing out as well?

So she shifted into neutral and engaged the hand brake. The vehicle shuddered and trembled, *pocketa-pocketapocketa,* until Max leaned over and switched off the engine by closing off the choke. The mule backfired and fell silent. The vista, even at night, was magnificent: the domed, starry sky; the endless ocean; the faint glow marking the vast arc of the horizon.

"I thought this was supposed to be the back way to Big Sur," said Max, turning toward Lily and placing the muzzle of his gun against her right temple.

"I musta misread the map," said Lily evenly. The Lilith persona was coming to her effortlessly now—she no longer needed to ask herself what Lilith would do or say, how Lilith might react—but something in Max's eyes told her the distinction was rapidly becoming irrelevant to him. "Think about it. Why the fuck would I bring you up here? What do *I* have to gain?"

"I don't know yet," said Max. "But I'm going to find out." His left hand shot out, grabbed the bunched hood of her zippered sweatshirt, rammed her head against the steering wheel, yanked her upright, jammed the pistol against the side of her head again. "Now, what are you trying to pull?"

It was all so *like a dream—a sense of gliding movement, of a perpetual nightscape, of darkness around the edges, and of helplessness. Heartbreaking helplessness when his (no,*

Max's, he reminds himself) hand slams Lily's head against the steering wheel. But Lyssy knows better. It's not a dream, it's co-consciousness. He's seeing through Max's eyes. And hearing now—distantly but clearly, although there's a hint of disconnect between what he sees and what he hears. It's not as severe as a streaming video: more like watching singers trying to lip-synch on TV.

"Put the fucking gun down," Lily is saying. . . .

Dazed and angry, with a trickle of blood descending from her hairline, Lily said, "Put the fucking gun down, Max, before I take it away and shove it up your ass—assuming there's room for it with your head up there."

Max twisted the bunched hood, choking her with her own sweatshirt. "Don't try to out-badass me, girl."

"I wouldn't . . . think of it."

"Think anything you like—just *do* exactly what I tell you to do." It felt so good, so right, to have a live body wriggling in his grasp again. A warm, intensely familiar feeling washed over Max. It was the closeness, a sense of connection, a feeling almost of oneness, of love turned inside out, that the sadist develops for the masochist, the torturer for the subject, the psychopath for his victim, which supersedes all other considerations. Suddenly he *had* to have her.

"Get out—no, this way." He climbed backward out of the mule, good leg first, hauling her with him by the hood of her sweatshirt. Still holding the gun to her head, he shuffled to his left, dragging his right leg, and

Lily, all the way around to the back of the mule. He ordered her to unsnap the plastic webbing that served as a tailgate. When she'd done so, he pressed himself tightly against her from behind, gently pushing the hair back from her ear with the barrel of his gun.

"Drop your drawers and bend over," he whispered. He wasn't hard yet—like many psychopaths, Max had trouble achieving erection. Still, there were always alternatives to an erect penis: he was holding one of them in his right hand, it had a nice long barrel, and when it came, it came with a bang.

Circling around the wagon, or whatever it was, dragging/shoving Lily by her sweatshirt, Lyssy watching from a Max's-eye view, thinking stop, thinking don't, thinking let her go, goddamn you, let her go.

Then he hears Max say, "Drop your drawers and bend over."

No, thinks Lyssy, you can't, I won't let you. But he's powerless . . . or is he? If he could hear Max talking to him when he *was conscious and* Max *was in co-con, then maybe there's a way to make* Max *hear* him. *He fills his mind the way you fill your lungs, then: no, stop, let her go! Screaming the thought, thinking the scream. Stop, let her go, leave her alone. . . .*

It had seemed so *simple* at the time, Lily remembered: lead Max away from Uncle Pen and Dr. Irene, give him the slip, then outrun him—he's a cripple, after all.

But somehow the right moment had never presented itself. Or if it had, she had missed it—one minute she was driving the mule, the next he had her by the hood of her sweatshirt and was holding a gun to her head—slip *this,* smart girl—and now here she was, bent over the back of Fano's mule and apparently out of options.

Except of course for the old reliable: give in. They're big, you're little, they have all the power, you have none. And if you cry or struggle, they'll only hurt you worse.

Only this time it wasn't working. She'd been tasting what it was like *not* to feel helpless all the time, *not* to feel an emptiness at your very core, *not* to define yourself by what had been done *to* you, or lose yourself in the delicious, unabashed self-pity of childhood—in short, what it was like to be Lilith—long enough to realize that *that* avenue of retreat had been closed to her forever. She could no longer lose herself in the old familiar sadness—nor did she really want to.

So up *your* ass with a piece of glass, Max, she thought to herself as he shoved her head down toward the oily-smelling boards. And twice as far with a Hershey bar. If you want to actually *do* anything to me, sooner or later you're gonna have to let go my hood or put down the gun. And then you'll find out what it means to fuck with me and Lilith.

Me and Lilith—she kind of liked the way that sounded. Like she wasn't alone, like she had an ally.

Then suddenly she sensed Max growing distracted. He muttered something under his breath . . .

she felt the absence of the constant pressure of the gun muzzle against her temple . . . but he still had that death grip on her hoodie.

Next time, she promised herself—once again he had shoved the muzzle against the side of her head—next time she'd be ready. Slowly, she began unzipping the sweatshirt, her mind running faster and clearer than ever, thinking up and dealing with contingency after contingency: if he says anything, tell him you thought he told you to get undressed. Be ready to go when he moves the gun again. Whatever you do, don't let him get your pants down. If he does, get them all the way down, step out of them. He won't stop you. Because he can't fuck you if—

But the moment had arrived: Max was talking to himself again, and the gun was no longer pressed against her temple. No more hesitating: Lily threw herself violently to her left, her arms stretched straight out behind her like a high-diver, wriggled free, and ran for her life, leaving Max holding her empty sweatshirt by the hood.

9

For some reason—or maybe for no reason: he didn't seem to be thinking all that clearly—sitting up had become of immense importance to Pender. It felt as though lying there in the dirt was the same as giving up—and he already knew that giving up was the same as dying.

So he dragged himself over to the side of the road and pulled himself to a seated position with his legs outstretched and his back against the cliff wall, feeling like a beached whale. What with all the pain, he couldn't even get the ol' jukebox working right, though there were so many songs about hearts breaking it would take days to get through them all. Instead he found himself listening to that old Beatles song, the one about turning off your mind, relaxing, and floating downstream.

Tempting—oh so very tempting. Except for this friggin' tyrannosaur crushing his chest between its jaws.

It wasn't until she was over the rise of the hump-backed meadow that Lily stopped feeling the tingling in her spine, dead center between her shoulder blades, and was finally able to banish the image of Fano throwing his arms into the air and pitching forward, dead.

She even allowed herself a triumphant, Rocky Balboa double fist pump. We did it, she thought, trotting steadily downhill, sneakers pounding the dirt as she followed the beige ribbon of the mule path in the pale moonlight. Nobody got shot, nobody got raped, and surely Uncle Pen and Dr. Irene would have contacted the authorities by now—soon the cops will be here with their dogs and helicopters, and sweep up Max like yesterday's garbage.

And as for Lyssy, it only took a little clear, Lilith-like thinking to understand that if he couldn't maintain control over Max, their sketchy plans to escape to the villa in Mexico were only so many pipe dreams. Like what's-her-name says in *Casablanca,* we'll always have fucking Paris. Or in their case, La Guarida.

Slowing as she reached the first switchback, Lily listened for pursuing footsteps and heard none. Leaning back, brushing her hand against the ground for balance, she half-skidded down the slope, regained her feet, and broke into her steady, downhill trot again, until she reached the next switchback. Then it was ease up, lean back, skid down, stand up, jog on to the next switchback, and the next, achieving an easy, comfortable rhythm, stopping only when she rounded the fourth or fifth turn and spotted a bulky, shadowy figure, like a bear in a baseball cap, sitting up with its back to the cliff wall.

"Uncle Pen?" She stooped by his side.

He turned his head slowly. "Lily?"

"What happened? Are you all right?"

"Ticker. Turns out the . . . doctors were . . . right. Imagine my . . . surprise."

"Where's Dr. Irene?"

"Gone for help. On foot." The corners of his mouth twitched; if it was a grin, it was a ghastly one. "She forgot . . . her keys."

"Can you walk?"

"Where's Maxwell?"

"Up—" Up there, Lily started to say. Then she heard footsteps above her, and falling pebbles. "Please get up, Uncle Pen—here, I'll help."

But before he could get his feet underneath him,

she saw a small figure limping down the road toward them. "Where's the gun?" she whispered frantically. "Do you still have your gun?"

He glanced around, dopey and confused by the pain; she followed his eyes and saw the wooden-handled pistol lying in the road only a few yards away, its blue-steel barrel glinting in the moonlight. She darted over to it, snatched it up, brought it back to Pender. "The safety," he said. "Right there . . . on red . . . dead red. Two hands for . . . beginners. Aim for his chest. When he gets closer. Then squeeze . . . the trigger and . . . hold on."

The gun felt surprisingly comfortable in Lily's hands, considering she'd never held one before. But Lilith had, she reminded herself. With this same hand.

Maxwell was twenty yards away, hunched under the weight of the canvas knapsack and dragging his right leg; the black object in his hand was probably his gun. Fifteen yards.

"Any . . . time," whispered Pender.

Ten yards—and he saw them. But instead of raising his pistol, he stuffed it into his waistband, then staggered forward with both hands out in front of him like the return of the Prodigal Son. "Lily!" he said in a high, piping voice. "Lily, you're okay! I was so scared he'd done something to you."

"Lyssy?"

"Shoot him," said Pender, slumping sideways, feeling the darkness stealing over him again. "For God's sake, shoot him now!"

10

Lily tucked Pender's gun into her waistband and ran to meet Lyssy; their hardware clanked together as they embraced. "I beat him," piped the voice Lily thought she'd never hear again. "I was in co-con, and I stopped him from hurting you, and we had like a mind war, and—" In a tone of astonished wonder: *"I won!"* Then, as if he'd just noticed the slumping figure propped up against the side of the cliff: "Holy cow, isn't that the guy I tied up last night? What happened to him?"

"I think he's having a heart attack—we have to get him some help."

"Are you kidding? What we have to do is get *out* of here before— What? You're looking at me all funny."

"I'm not going with you, Lyssy."

"But I thought . . . you and me, I thought. . . ."

Lily put her hand on his cheek. She felt as if she were the older and more experienced of the two, and was enjoying, on a barely conscious level, the drama and adolescent romanticism of the moment. "I'm glad we had . . . before," she said. "But even if I thought we had a chance of getting away, how could I ever go to sleep at night, knowing that when I wake up, you might have turned into that . . . that monster?"

"But I can *handle* Max now."

"That's what you said before."

"Okay, what about the woman Lilith killed in Oregon?"

"Me and Lilith, we'll just have to cross that bridge when we come to it—us and a shitload of expensive lawyers."

"But this morning you said—"

"This morning was a million years ago." Lily drew back from him. "I'm sorry, Lyssy, I don't have time to stand here arguing with you. I'm going to go back up to the ridge and get the mule. I'd really appreciate it if you'd stick around to help me get *him*"—she jerked her head in Pender's direction—"loaded onto it, but if you want to book it on out of here, I'll understand, no hard feelings."

"I'm here for as long as you need me," he replied, tears welling, lower lip quivering.

Pender opened his eyes, turned his head, saw Maxwell sitting next to him, leaning back against the cliff wall. "God *damn*!" said Pender. "I *told* her to . . . shoot you."

"Shoot me? Lily loves me—why should she shoot me?" The other man turned his head toward Pender. "How're you feeling?"

Pender ignored the question. "Where is she?"

"She went to get the mule." Then, earnestly: "Don't worry, it's not a real mule. It's more like a wagon with an engine—they just call it that."

Pender felt the tyrannosaur tightening its jaws again. Maxwell's face swam in and out of focus. Pender heard his pulse pounding jaggedly in his ears.

When that stops, he thought, I'm dead. Then, over the ragged drumbeat, as Pender's head slumped forward onto his chest, knocking his baseball cap onto his lap, he heard a faint, hopeful-sounding *pocketapocketapocketa.*

"Here she comes," called Maxwell, picking up the cap, examining it as though he were trying to decide how it would look on him. Then he lifted the now-unconscious Pender's head by the chin, put the cap back on him, and spun it around backward. "Whazzzzup?" he said, grinning, his eyebrows peaking devilishly.

Lily drove the mule past Pender, backed up until the tailgate was only a few feet from him, shifted into neutral, tugged the hand brake upright until it locked, then hopped down. "How is he?"

"Hanging in there. He's in a lot of pain, though."

"Thanks for sticking around. Here, help me get him into the back." Lily squatted next to Pender and draped his left arm around her shoulders. Lyssy—or at any rate, the man she assumed was Lyssy—took Pender's other arm. Lily counted, "One, two, three, *lift*!" and they hauled him up onto his feet, the one-legged man grunting as he rose with all his weight on his real leg, his artificial leg stretched out in front of him like a Cossack dancer.

Together they walked Pender over to the mule, *Weekend at Bernie's* style, gently toppled him forward onto the platform, then lifted his legs up after him.

"Thanks," said Lily.

"For what?"

"For staying—for helping."

"Well, actually, I've been kind of thinking it over, and I decided you were right. I can't take the chance on Max killing who knows how many more people, just to buy myself a few more days—'specially if you're not coming with me."

"Are you going to turn yourself in?"

"Unh-hunh," he said, climbing into the back of the mule and snapping the plastic webbing into place. "And I'm also going to tell them that *I* killed Patty, so you don't have to worry about that anymore." He crawled up to the front of the flatbed, facing rearward, and cushioned the semiconscious Pender's big head on his lap.

"And I'll tell everybody how you stayed behind to help me save Uncle Pen, instead of trying to get away," Lily reassured him, as she climbed up to the driver's seat.

Yeah, that'll help, he thought as she released the hand brake. They'll probably give me an extra Jell-O with my last meal.

11

Irene figured the return hike would be a piece of cake. Didn't she jog the rec trail from Lovers Point to Fisherman's Wharf and back, a round-trip of four miles, three times a week? Well, okay, once or twice a week—still, she wasn't expecting any problems.

Then her flashlight gave out. But the moon was well up by now, the earlier, impenetrable blackness under the trees replaced by a shimmering latticework shadow. After the creek had curved southward to rejoin the road, she could see the rushing water shining silver through the slender riparian willows. She tried her cell phone again—no bars, no signal—then jogged on, the soles of her Chuck Taylors *pat, pat, pat*ting the ground, the endorphins kicking in, the dirt road stretching on before her, pale tan in the moonlight. But endorphins sometimes make treacherous allies—she didn't feel the blisters on the pad of her right foot (at the base of the piggy that had none and the piggy that went wee-wee-wee all the way home) until it was too late.

And now she was paying the price. Wincing at every step, hobbling, then limping as the blisters broke and the steady *pat pat pat* turned into *pat squish pat squish.* She tried varying her gait—walking on her heel, half-skipping, half-hopping to minimize the pain. She ran through a series of visualizations—what color is the pain? What shape? If it were a container, how much water would it hold?

But nothing seemed to be working, so to distract her mind, Irene fell back on her old standby: composing haiku. Three lines of five, then seven, then five syllables. And against all odds, she even managed to come up with a keeper: *Pain is sharp and red / And my shoe is full of blood / Stupid old blister!*

But to her credit, she never seriously thought about stopping, not even to bathe her blisters in the creek . . . which seemed to be running closer to the road than she had remembered . . . and come to think of it, the road, which should have been curving and climbing, was instead running flat . . . and straight . . . and narrowing . . . until it was only a rocky footpath running by the side of the creek.

And looming dead ahead, Irene saw when she raised her eyes, was the graceful, towering, monumentally enormous concrete arch of the bridge the Barracuda had rattled over only a few hours earlier. Under its shadow, where the creek widened before merging into the Pacific, the damp, dauntless fog known as the marine layer had begun to drift in from the ocean, swallowing up the rocky beach where Lyman DeVries used to fly-cast.

Irene trained her flashlight straight ahead, under the bridge, then shined it back the way she had come, and realized that the road she'd meant to follow had curved off to the left and begun the long climb to the highway several hundred yards back. She sighed and began retracing her steps.

The mule jounced downhill, picking up speed. With the wheel clenched tightly in both hands, Lily carefully chose the line for the upcoming curve, then stood hard on the brake pedal; the mule skidded down the harrowing switchback, sending dirt and pebbles tumbling down the slope.

"You okay back there?" she called, when they'd rounded the curve.

"No problem."

"Good—'cause here comes another one!"

And another, and another, until the mule had shot the last of the downhill rapids, and they'd rejoined the comparatively unexciting, if rough and rutted, road out to the highway. With only one forward gear, Lily kept the gas pedal to the sheet-metal flooring, maintaining a steady eight to ten miles per hour. "Hey, Lyss?"

"Still here."

"I think you're doing the right thing. And I promise, wherever they send you, I'll come visit as often as they'll let me."

"Don't forget the cake with the file in it." He twisted around to face front, leaning his arm over the railing. "You *sure* this thing doesn't go any faster?"

Lily chanced a curious backward glance. "Don't sweat it—really. Even on foot, Dr. Irene is bound to have made it out by now—the cops'll probably get here before we even reach the highway."

"Oh, right," he said. "For a second there, I forgot I was giving myself up."

Using a springy willow branch as a makeshift walking stick, Irene had just finished retracing her steps, and had begun the long trudge up the hill to the gate when she heard the distant chugging of the mule. She turned and saw the headlight emerging from the trees. At first she couldn't tell which of the three was behind the wheel. Didn't matter—even if she could have run, there was no place to hide on the grassy hillside.

"Dr. Irene, Dr. Irene!" Lily had spotted her and

was half-standing behind the wheel, waving. Irene limped back down the hill, leaning on her stick, and met the mule at the bottom of the slope. Lily shifted into neutral, drew the creaking hand brake. "Uncle Pen had a heart attack," she called. "And Lyssy's back—he's been helping me."

Irene threw down the willow branch and hurried around to the back of the mule. Oh, Pen, she thought. He lay supine, his windbreaker unzipped to the waist, his head pillowed on a wadded-up sweatshirt, and his face a shiny, unhealthy blue in the moonlight.

"Hi, Dr. Cogan," Maxwell said brightly, clambering down from the flatbed, which was scarcely wide enough for two. "I took real good care of him on the way down, honest."

It *was* Lyssy's voice—but then, Lyssy's voice had come out of Max's mouth before, Irene reminded herself as she swapped places with him, climbing up onto the railed-in platform and kneeling beside Pender. Best not to make assumptions, she thought, pressing two fingers against the side of Pender's throat—cross that bridge when you come to it.

The constant, uneven vibration of the engine rumbling under the boards prevented Irene from getting a pulse, but she could see Pender's chest rising and falling in shuddering increments. She took out her flashlight, trained the beam up and down his body, then around it, looking for blood or bullet holes, finding only a scraped elbow and a skinned knee. "Can you hear me, Pen?"

His eyelids fluttered, but did not open. She

pulled them up one at a time, shined her flashlight into them, watched the pupils contract. Equal and reactive, she thought, the phrase coming back to her through the mists of time—except for a little first aid, Irene hadn't treated anybody for a physical illness since her residency, almost twenty years ago. She slipped her hand into Pender's big meathook, told him to squeeze. His fingers tightened around hers—it was an excellent sign, if Irene remembered correctly, an indication that oxygen was still getting to his brain.

"How is he? Is he going to be all right?" asked Lily, turning around in the driver's seat; Lyssy had climbed in beside her.

"He will be if we get him to a hospital soon," said Irene. She took her cell phone out of her pocket, snapped it open—still no dial tone. "Drive us up to the top of the hill—it'll probably work there."

"Okay—hang on, everybody!" Lily turned back, patted the dashboard. "Just a little farther, amigo," she said, talking to the mule, thinking about Fano. At least it was almost over, she told herself, depressing the clutch and reaching for the gearshift. Almost over, and thanks to her, no one else had gotten killed.

Then a claw-like hand clamped over hers; once again she felt the cold steel of a gun barrel pressing against the side of her head. "Change of plans," announced a dry-as-dust, unbearably intimate voice, and for Lily the words *almost over* took on a terrible new meaning.

12

"I'll take that." Max's left hand shot out, snatched Pender's gun from Lily's waist, and slipped it into his own waistband. It was a glorious moment for him—until a few minutes ago, when Lily had spotted Dr. Cogan trudging up the hillside, he'd been convinced the cops were already on their way, and that even if he managed to avoid being shot down, he'd have to settle for a hasty closing of accounts and a quick getaway.

But now he had all the time in the world, he realized. Not since he'd taken his revenge on the deputy sheriff who'd arrested him in Monterey three years ago—the late deputy *and* her late lover—had Max had two women so completely under his thumb. Oh, the games they could play back at the cabin! And this time he wouldn't have to worry about someone hearing their screams.

Nor would he have to share them with the other alters. There were no *others* anymore, except for Kinch, who was helpless without a knife in his hand, and Lyssy, whose earlier attempt at a palace coup had ultimately proved a failure. True, he had managed to distract Max long enough for the girl to get away—but that had been due largely to the element of surprise. As soon as Max had realized what was going on—that the shouting in his head emanated from Lyssy in co-con—he was able to ignore it, treat it as so much white noise.

Even so, it was with a crushing and unfamiliar sense of failure that after trying unsuccessfully to get the mule started up again, he'd left the ridge alone, on foot, his shoulders hunched against the sky, expecting with every step to hear the *whap-whap-whap* of the police choppers and find himself bathed in the glare of their searchlights.

Limping down the dirt track, scrambling down the switchbacks on his ass, Max had come closer to despair than he cared to remember. He'd even begun thinking about putting an end to the farce, and had gone so far as to draw the gun from his waistband, when he'd spotted Pender and the girl by the side of the road.

And when he discovered that it was Pender's heart attack that had saved him, Max, who was a big fan of irony (like many psychopaths, it was what he had in place of a sense of humor), was almost giddy with delight. Once again the Creator had demonstrated his utter disinterest in the battle between good and evil.

Tough shit for them, thought Max, tender shit for me. Then he'd learned that Dr. Cogan had gone off alone to contact the police and was herself on foot, and a situation that had seemed at first hopeless, then barely survivable, had turned rosy as a whore's cheek: all Max had to do was pretend to be Lyssy, and hang on for the ride.

From that point on, things couldn't have gone more smoothly if he'd planned them out months in advance. "What we're going to do now," he said over the chugging of the engine, tracing the curve of

Lily's ear with the end of the gun barrel, "as long as we have a little more time to spare than I thought we had, we're all going back to the cabin to get to know each other a little better." He glanced over his shoulder. "How's that sound to you, Dr. Cogan?"

"Whatever you say, Max," Irene said evenly, her hand stealing into the front pocket of her jeans. She felt almost relieved, now that he'd unmasked himself. No more uncertainty, no more paralysis by analysis. All complexities, moral or otherwise, pared down to the stark geometric simplicity of the spatial relationship between a cylinder and an arc, between the muzzle of Max's gun and the side of Lily's head.

Lily too experienced a moment of frozen clarity, during which she was, briefly, neither Lily, nor Lilith, nor Lily pretending to be Lilith, but only herself, all tangled up with conflicting emotions, feeling heartsick over losing Lyssy again, foolish for allowing herself to be tricked, righteously angry at having been betrayed, afraid for all the obvious reasons, and at the same time determined to think of *something,* to do *something.*

But for Lily too the possibilities began and ended with the gun muzzle pressing against the side of her head. So when Max turned back to her after his brief exchange with Dr. Irene, and said, "You heard her—get this thing turned around and let's get going," it seemed pure common sense to refuse him at least that much.

"Not until you point that thing someplace else," she told him.

It must have made sense to Max, too; it was the

last thing that ever would. He tilted the barrel upward, pointing toward the sky. "You satisfied now? Okay, let's get—"

Crack!Crack!Crack!Crack! Jagged muzzle flashes lit the night. Lily threw herself backward as Max toppled sideways off the bench. Irene, who'd fired the .38 from a seated position, holding it in both hands in emulation of Pender, now scrambled to her feet, aiming the gun straight downward at Max, who lay head-down, crumpled into the narrow, V-shaped space between the dashboard and the front seat with his neck twisted at a grotesque angle, his cheek jammed against the floorboard, and his artificial leg sticking out sideways.

And yet he lived. Shot three times at close range, his neck broken in the fall (or to be precise, the sideways landing on his head), Max stared hungrily toward the pistol, lying only a few inches away from his left hand, and was still trying to *will* the hand into motion when a red haze washed over his vision.

Standing over him, holding the revolver in both hands and pointing it straight down at Maxwell, Irene glanced to her left and saw Lily lying on her back a few feet from the mule. "Are you okay?"

"Yeah, I just got the wind knocked out of me," the girl replied, sitting up gingerly. "Is he . . . dead?"

"Not yet," said Irene grimly. "Get his guns."

Lily rose, brushing dirt and damply clinging spears of grass from her jeans, walked over to the mule, picked up the black pistol, then boldly plucked Pender's wooden-handled Colt from the waistband of Max's jeans. It was impossible to be afraid of him any longer—with his neck bent and his leg sticking out like that, he looked to her like a broken doll some spiteful little girl had tossed into the trash.

She cut the mule's engine. "Give me your cell phone," she told Irene. "I'll go get help."

Irene hadn't realized how badly the constant chugging and shuddering had been getting on her nerves until it was gone and relative quiet had descended over the hillside. "Tell them we have two critically injured people that need to be evacuated by helicopter," she said. "You can tell them one of them is Ulysses Maxwell, but try not to say too much else until we know how things stand with you, legally speaking, if you get my drift."

She tossed the phone down to Lily, who caught it deftly. "I'll be right back," she said. "Take good care of Uncle Pen."

"I will," Irene called after her, then turned to Pender again, kneeling beside him and pressing two fingers against the side of his neck again. She felt his pulse, weak but steady, and watched his great chest rising and falling, rising and falling. "Don't die on me," she told him. "Don't you dare die on me."

Pender opened his eyes. "I'll drink to that," he said with a wink, then closed his eyes again, and let the darkness wash over him.

EPILOGUE

EIGHT MONTHS LATER

1

The People's Posse ended tonight, as it did every week, with host Sandy Wells alone in the spotlight, seated on a three-legged stool on an otherwise darkened soundstage, with a stark, textured black drop cloth for a background. He was wearing his trademark leather jacket and his silver hair was razor-trimmed to perfection; as the theme music faded, he turned to face the camera in three-quarter profile—his best angle, all his media mavens assured him.

"And so ends the bloody saga of Ulysses Christopher Maxwell," Wells declared, his gunslinger eyes narrowed and his bulldog jaw outthrust. "There are, as always, many questions that remain unanswered. Forensics and ballistics can only tell us so much—we may never know, for instance, exactly why or where veteran private investigator Mick MacAlister met his fate, or how his tarpaulin-covered corpse wound up in the back of a pickup truck parked only a few blocks from his office, riddled with bullets fired from the same revolver that eventually terminated Maxwell's monstrous reign of terror.

"But this much we *do* know. . . . " As he did every week when it came time to deliver his closing homily, Wells turned to his left to face camera three. The sudden move had the effect of a theatrical aside, adding an inclusive intimacy, as if he had been addressing a wider audience, but was now speaking directly to the individual viewer. *"Ulysses Maxwell was not born a monster.* It was the extreme abuse he suffered as a child, from parents who had no doubt been abused themselves as children, that turned him into one. Ultimately, of course, each of us is responsible for his or her own actions—still, it's incumbent upon each of us to do what we can to *break the chain."*

As he spoke, camera three had been tightening in on him; by now he was in extreme close-up, his exquisitely barbered face filling the screen. "If you were abused as a child, I urge you to get professional help—*break the chain.* And if you know someone who was abused, a spouse, a friend, a relative, encourage them to do the same and *break the chain*—you'll find plenty of links to mental health organizations on our website, www dot peoplesposse dot com. And most crucially, if you suspect someone of child abuse, but want to protect your anonymity, we've set up a brand-new dedicated tipline at 1-800-NOCHAIN—it's a free call, guaranteed confidential—drop a dime and stop a crime. *Break the chain."*

Wells turned back to camera one. "So until next week, I'm Sandy Wells, and you *are* The People's Posse. Take care and be safe."

"You too, Sandy," Irene Cogan muttered from her living room sofa. It had been a slightly disconcerting experience, watching herself being interviewed by a man she'd never met or even spoken with. But at least they'd withheld Lily's name, and the unknown actress who'd played Lily during the "re-creations" had been a buxom blond in her early twenties. The unknown actress who'd played Irene looked more like Matt Damon in drag, and wore a shiny reddish-blond wig that kept threatening to fall off during the chase scene at Scorned Ridge.

It had also felt kind of weird to see Scorned Ridge again. The dilapidated cabin, the domed Plexiglas drying shed where Maxwell and his foster mother used to keep the strawberry blonds—reexperiencing it all through the filter of the boob tube, with actors and actresses playing herself and Maxwell, had an oddly distancing effect. Irene found herself wondering which version she'd be seeing in her next nightmare.

As soon as Wells had signed off, the screen split vertically in two, silently rolling the TPP credits on the right half, while the left half ran a visually elongated promo for the show coming up next on The Crime Channel. It was a two-year-old documentary about a DID patient up in Washington whose alter had attacked his therapist.

Irene, who'd seen it before, turned the volume down and began channel surfing idly, her mind a thousand miles away again. She was thinking about her upcoming trip to Salem, the Oregon capital, to testify before a committee looking into the alleged abuses of electroshock therapy protocol at the Reed-Chase Institute. Irene had at first been reluctant to participate in what looked like a very public flogging of a very dead horse, but eventually she'd decided that *someone* had to speak up for poor Al Corder, if only to point out that however misguided his methods, he might very well have been on to something.

Exhibit One, of course, was the astonishing improvement in Lily DeVries's condition. As soon as the legal hassles were behind her (in light of Alison Corder's testimony that Lily had saved her life, the Portland DA had decided to go the slam dunk route and charge Maxwell with all four Oregon murders), she'd enrolled full-time at CSUMB—California State University Monterey Bay, also known jocularly as UFO, the University of Fort Ord, because it was situated on the vast, decommissioned military base.

The university was currently on spring break, Irene was reminded, when she looked up and discovered she had channel surfed her way from The Crime Channel to MTV's *Spring Break Party—Cancún.* Lily had been frantic for permission to attend the event with a few of her college girlfriends, but after conferring with Irene, now counseling Lily on an as-needed basis, Uncle Rollie had made a counteroffer of an all-expense-paid trip to Washington, D.C., for Lily and a friend.

And judging by the goings-on currently being aired, thought Irene, they'd made the right decision. The overheated atmosphere, the girls in their skimpy tops and butt-floss thongs, the bare-chested, sweating boys, the orgiastic dancing, the overt sexuality, the whole suds-and-Ecstasy subculture, would surely have been—

Ohmigod! thought Irene, doing a full Wile E. Coyote double take, jaw dropped, neck outstretched, eyeballs all but popping out on springs. "Pen!" she shouted. "Pen, get down here quick!"

Pender had never much enjoyed watching himself on television. He'd been up in his study, formerly the spare room, playing poker on the Internet when he heard Irene shouting. He tore off his computer glasses like Clark Kent turning into Superman, grabbed a 3-iron from the golf bag leaning against the wall, and was out the door and down the stairs in seconds, hauling ass faster than he'd hauled it in years.

But then, there was a lot less ass to be hauled. The Grim Reaper is a hell of a motivator—Pender had lost fifty pounds since his heart attack, given up cigars, and cut way down on the Jim Beam. He'd also kept his promise never to use a golf cart again, and coincidentally or not, had lowered his handicap two whole strokes—it was now under the drinking, if not the driving, age.

"What is it?" he called, racing into the living room.

"Take a look at this." Without turning around, Irene nodded toward the television

Pender circled around behind the sofa, sheepishly dropping the 3-iron behind it, and sat down next to her. The two had been living together for almost seven months—Irene had insisted on Pender moving in with her while he was recuperating from his heart attack, and once they'd become lovers, it hadn't seemed to make sense for him to pay rent elsewhere when they were sleeping together every night anyway.

"What is this, some kind of a test?" he asked her incredulously. In Pender's experience, women Irene's age—or any age—did not customarily insist upon their boyfriends watching nubile, half-naked college girls shaking their hooters.

"Wait, she just moved out of the picture . . . watch the right side of the screen . . . there! There she is—red top."

He had already spotted the well-developed girl in the red top—he just hadn't looked up at her face. "Oh shit, oh dear," he said, feeling like a dirty old man. "I thought she was supposed to be in D.C., taking in all the fine educational sights."

"So did I," said Irene.

"She does seem to be enjoying herself," said Pender after another few seconds.

"She does, doesn't she?" Neither of them had taken their eyes from the screen.

"Are you going to tell Rollie?"

The show cut to commercial. Irene hit the Mute button on the remote. Her heart (to use a nonpsychiatric term) was so full she couldn't find words to express what it meant to her to see Lily dancing, happy, surrounded by kids her own age. Pride was in there somewhere, parental and professional. Also awe, and a little understandable trepidation. She turned to Pender with tears in her eyes. "Sweetheart," she said softly, "if I'd had boobs like that when I was her age, I'd have been shaking them, too."

2

"Good evening, Mr. Maxwell—and how's my strong silent type this evening?" Swingshift nurse, fat, cheerful, sloppy in white. Max, paralyzed from the neck down, followed her with his eyes, mentally gagging and hog-tying her.

"Ooo—if looks could kill," she said forbearingly. "Look here, I've brought your dinner. Let me see now, we have . . . sirloin steak, medium rare, peas, mashed potatoes, garlic bread, Caesar salad, hold the anchovies. . . . "

All nonsense, of course. Max received his nutrition through a nasogastric feeding tube. He tried to stop her from talking by the sheer force of his loathing, but all she had to do was move out of his direct line of sight and she would disappear. Max could no more have turned his head than he could have tap-danced his way out of the state-run shit hole to which he'd been confined since his extradition to Oregon, pending a dozen trials that were now unlikely to ever take place.

For one thing, Max's lawyers could now legitimately argue that he was unable to aid in his own defense—the doctors were split on whether his continued mutism, even when the feeding tube was removed, was physical, voluntary, or psychosomatic. For another, not many prosecutors were all that keen on trying a man who'd have to be wheeled into the courtroom tied to his wheelchair, with urine dripping into a baggie at his side and his respirator, plugged into a permanent tracheostomy hole, going hiss-*suck!,* hiss-*suck!* every five and a half seconds.

So the view from the antique, horizontally rotating Stryker frame never really changed. It only shifted between the discolored, water-stained, off-white ceiling tiles and the one-foot-square, black-and-white floor tiles whenever the staff got around to clamping a canvas stretcher on top of him and spinning him around like a pig on a spit. There was a window somewhere off to one side, but all he could see of it was the waxing and waning of daylight.

As if being sentenced to life without parole in his own body weren't punishment enough (only the State was debarred from cruel and unusual punishment: nature practiced it on a regular basis), every so often Max would be stricken by a headache. For the able-bodied, even the able-bodied migraine sufferer, it's hard to fathom the effects of a headache on someone who only has sensation from the neck up—let's just say that old cliche about being in a world of pain had never been more applicable.

And there was another factor that exacerbated his suffering: Max had skated through most of his existence without having to endure even prolonged discomfort—that, after all, had always been Lyssy's job. From youthful boredom to third-degree burns, from gas pains to gunshot wounds, from aches to amputations, the system had always had Lyssy as its scapegoat.

But Max could no longer summon Lyssy at will. He'd tried, those first few months, fucking Jesus how he'd tried. Raging, cajoling, threatening, promising—nothing worked. Even worse (dear God and all the angels in heaven and all the devils in hell, how many layers of "even worse" were there in this stinking onion of existence), Max himself had been unable to retreat to the dark place—it was as if Lyssy had somehow locked the door behind him. The door in the wall that didn't exist.

Sleep was the only refuge left to Max—but with sleep came dreams even less bearable than his waking hell. He could never fully recall them when awake, but they must have been pretty awful if he could wake up to all *this* with even a transitory sense of relief.

There were only two things that kept Max going, or rather, that kept him from letting go of his tenuous hold on sanity. One was that it couldn't last forever: when he'd first arrived, he'd overheard a doctor telling the nurse that on the life expectancy charts, a C-3 quadriplegic fell somewhere between a hamster and a house cat.

The other thing standing between Max and the

Big Scream was that he still hadn't given up on Lyssy. The little bastard was in there, all right, and Max remained convinced that sooner or later he'd come up with a way to get him out, to swap places. A few minutes ago, in fact, he'd come up with what felt like a very promising approach, but one that would require his complete concentration.

So he waited for the nurse to leave before closing his eyes. *Lyssy!* he called. *Lyssy, it's Lily. I'm in trouble—I need your help.*

And again: *Lyssy, it's Lily. I'm in trouble—I need your help.*

And again and again and again, without a hint of a response. Unable even to sigh unless he timed it to the hiss-*suck!* of the respirator, Max opened his eyes again and settled in for another long night in hell.

3

Lyssy, it's Lily. I'm in trouble—I need your help.

Utter darkness. Lyssy was afraid for a moment—then he heard the creek burbling and remembered where he was. He opened his eyes. It must have been around sunset—the inside of the cabin was all lit up with a rosy, comforting glow.

"Lyssy, it's Lil." He couldn't see her—her voice was coming from the porch.

"So who else vould it be?" A credible imitation of the querulous old man played by Billy Crystal in *The Princess Bride.*

She laughed. "I need your help."

He hopped out of bed, crossed the room without a trace of a limp, on an artifical leg so natural he could hardly even remember which leg it was, and opened the door. Lil (that's what she wanted to be called, to signify the consolidation of her two identities) was standing there with both arms so full of kindling she couldn't manage the door latch.

Lyssy stepped back, ushered her in with a gallant sweep of his arm, then stepped out onto the porch. The clearing too was bathed in a roseate light. "You feel like going down to the rock?"

She joined him, brushing leaves and twigs from the front of her sweater. She was wearing that soft brown cashmere number—without a bra, Lyssy couldn't help but notice as they negotiated the rocky path around the side of the cabin and down to the flat rock overhanging the creek.

But he wasn't in a sexy mood—just mellow. Mellow as the sunset as he followed Lil onto the rock. She took off her sandals and dangled her legs over the side, her bare toes idly stirring the silvery clear, slow-moving current. Lyssy stood over her, looking down into the water. "See those waterbugs there, right on the surface?" she said, pointing to a few tiny, nearly transparent insects with two wide round paddles, larger than their bodies, for feet. "You know why they have those big feet? It's so when fish look up, they think, 'Duh-uh, those must belong to some really humongous bug, no way I could swallow that.' "

Lyssy laughed. "Maybe that's what Bigfoot is—

some monkey three or four feet high, with *really big feet.*" He lowered himself easily, even gracefully—his new leg was *amazing,* it felt like it was becoming *part* of him—and stretched out athwart the sun-warmed rock with his head in her lap. You couldn't actually see the sun from here, but the sky was a melting rainbow of colors and the creek a fiery red-gold ribbon. "I probably asked you this before, but I can't remember. How long did you say we get to stay here?"

"Forever," she said without hesitation.

"And is it . . . real?"

She smiled down at him, her face in shadow, curtained by her dark brown hair. "You can have forever, or you can have real," she told him, "but honey, you can't have 'em both."

Lyssy smiled back at her. "Forever," he said dreamily. "I'll take forever."

POCKET BOOKS
A Division of Simon & Schuster
A CBS COMPANY

POCKET
STAR BOOKS
A Division of Simon & Schuster
A CBS COMPANY